5

"What's this legend you were talking about?" Kate asked warily.

"It's an old story from your grandfather's side of the family," her grandmother replied. "Rubbing that onyx ring you found is supposed to bring some old love back from the West."

"Some old love?" Kate echoed. "I don't have an old love from the West."

"Oh, not yours," Granny said with a mischievous smile. "Caitlin O'Malley's. Your great-great-grandmother."

This was getting stranger and stranger. "Why would my rubbing a ring bring back an old love of my great-great-grandmother?"

"I never actually said it would," Granny mused. "But don't you wonder why Jake MacNeill, a Montana cowboy, arrived on your doorstep only a few days after you found the ring?"

Kate shivered. And the thing she wondered about was, what was happening to her sanity?

Dear Reader,

Welcome to Silhouette Special Edition...welcome to romance. Our New Year's resolution is to continue bringing you romantic, emotional stories you'll be sure to love!

And this month we're sure fulfilling that promise as Marie Ferrarella returns with our THAT SPECIAL WOMAN! title for January, *Husband: Some Assembly Required*. Dr. Shawna Saunders has trouble resisting the irresistible charms of Murphy Pendleton!

THIS TIME, FOREVER, a wonderful new series by Andrea Edwards, begins this month with *A Ring and a Promise*. Jake O'Neill and Kate O'Malley don't believe in destiny, until a legend of ancestral passion pledged with a ring and an unfulfilled promise show them the way.

Also in January, Susan Mallery introduces the first of her two HOMETOWN HEARTBREAKERS. Was sexy Sheriff Travis Haynes the town lady-killer—or a knight in shining armor? Elizabeth Abbott finds out in *The Best Bride*. Diana Whitney brings you *The Adventurer*—the first book in THE BLACKTHORN BROTHERHOOD. Don't miss Devon Monroe's story—and his secret.

The wonders of love in 1995 continue as opposites attract in Elizabeth Lane's *Wild Wings, Wild Heart*, and Beth Henderson's *New Year's Eve* keeps the holiday spirit going.

Hope this New Year shapes up to be the best ever! Enjoy this book and all the books to come!

Sincerely,

Tara Gavin
Senior Editor

Please address questions and book requests to:
Silhouette Reader Service
U.S.: 3010 Walden Ave., P.O. Box 1325, Buffalo, NY 14269
Canadian: P.O. Box 609, Fort Erie, Ont. L2A 5X3

ANDREA EDWARDS

A RING AND A PROMISE

Published by Silhouette Books
America's Publisher of Contemporary Romance

To those who take time to listen to the past,
may the voices always be true

 **SILHOUETTE BOOKS**

ISBN 0-373-09932-0

A RING AND A PROMISE

Books by Andrea Edwards

Silhouette Special Edition

Rose in Bloom #363
Say It with Flowers #428
Ghost of a Chance #490
Violets Are Blue #550
Places in the Heart #591
Make Room for Daddy #618
Home Court Advantage #706
Sweet Knight Times #740
Father: Unknown #770
Man of the Family #809
The Magic of Christmas #856
Just Hold On Tight! #883
*A Ring and a Promise #932

*This Time, Forever

Silhouette Intimate Moments

Above Suspicion #291

Silhouette Desire

Starting Over #645

ANDREA EDWARDS

Anne and Ed Kolaczyk have been writing together for more than fifteen years. Their four kids are pretty much grown, but their cats and dogs are still around to occasionally wander through their stories.

Anne and Ed have always believed that our present is the result of our past, be it hair color, temperament or emotions. Living in northern Indiana, where the past has not been entirely obliterated by "progress," they have the time and space to listen to the voices from yesterday. It is in these voices that their characters learn to listen, and in doing so, find truth and happiness.

FAMILY TREE

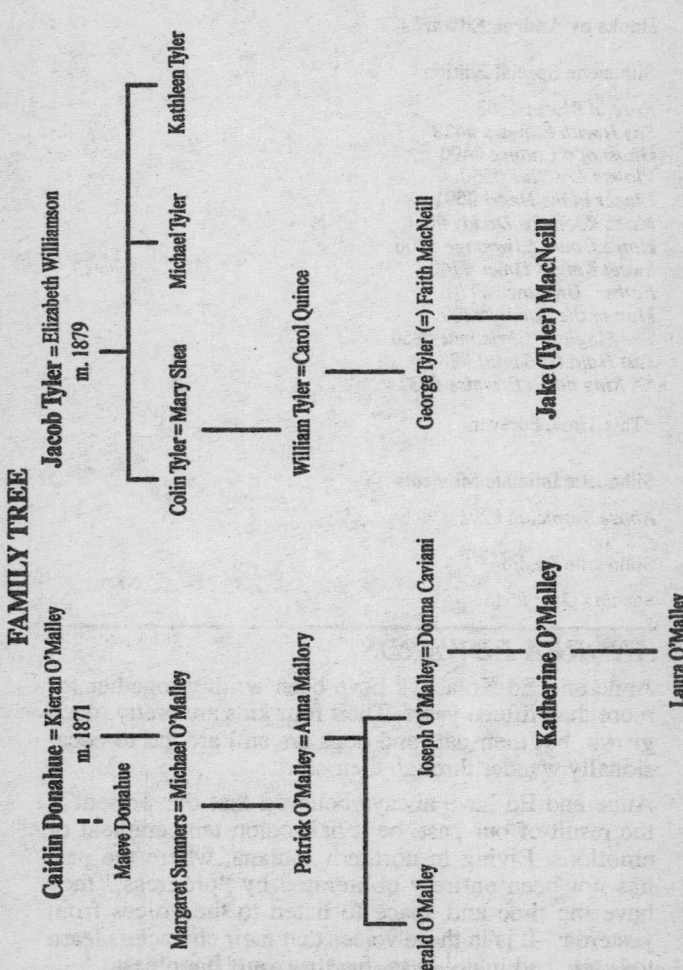

Jacob Tyler = Elizabeth Williamson
m. 1879

Colin Tyler = Mary Shea   Michael Tyler   Kathleen Tyler

William Tyler = Carol Quince

George Tyler (=) Faith MacNeill

Jake (Tyler) MacNeill

Caitlin Donahue = Kieran O'Malley
m. 1871

Maeve Donahue

Margaret Summers = Michael O'Malley

Patrick O'Malley = Anna Mallory

Joseph O'Malley = Donna Caviani

Gerald O'Malley   **Katherine O'Malley**

Laura O'Malley

Prologue

Caitlin Donahue knotted the thread and bit it off close, then added the shirt to the pile of others. She was done for the day, her shoulders hurting and her eyes weary. She sat back for a moment, letting her weariness flow over her as she watched the flickering candle send shadows dancing across the tiny room. The candle's wee light had no chance against the coming night, just as she felt the pennies she earned with her sewing would never be enough.

It was silly, she knew. Simply her aching limbs weighing down her heart. Or more likely, Mrs. O'Leary's words coming back to taunt her. It wasn't as if the old woman had the sight. Caitlin shouldn't have let the words into her soul, to lie there and fester.

"I see such distrust in your heart, child. It's like a weed in the garden—growing and crowding until there's room for naught else. Loneliness and grief will be your lovers until you open wide your heart."

Better loneliness and grief than some smooth talker who'd steal your innocence as well as the few coins Papa had hidden away, Caitlin told herself. The shame came back as did the fear of being weak, and she got to her feet. Sitting here fretting was doing no one any good. She blew out the candle, then eased the door open just enough for her to slip outside.

"Caitlin?"

"Yes, Mother." Caitlin whispered the words. It was bad enough that her mother was awake, but she didn't want to waken little Maeve. The poor babe had had a bad day, with the terrible heat that had been scorching the city.

"Where are you going, lass?"

"I'm just stepping out to catch a breath of air," Caitlin replied.

"'Tis no better out than here, dear."

Her mother's voice held a hint of disapproval, and Caitlin clamped her jaw tight. Her mother's ill humor had little to do with the sick headaches she was prone to and nothing to do with the heat.

"I'll be just a short while, Mum."

Caitlin hurried out before her mother could pull her back. Once outside, she paused for a moment to wipe beads of sweat off her forehead. This was a strange land. It was autumn already and yet as hot as the middle of summer. She sat down on the rain barrel leaning against a corner of their house. It hadn't rained for so long that the barrel was good for nothing but sitting on.

Sighing, Caitlin closed her eyes and leaned back, trying to shut out the night. The heat was like a thick blanket, trying to smother them all, and clinging to it was the heavy scent of smoke from the fires that had been plaguing the city. The crying of babies and the quarreling of couples filled the air, warring with the moaning of the O'Leary's cows. Poor beasties. They didn't like the heat any better than she did.

A terrible row erupted over toward the O'Leary's, and Caitlin opened her eyes. People were shouting and the cows grew even noisier. The heat made everyone so irritable. She closed her eyes again.

God willing, someday she and Jacob Tyler would be as well off as the O'Leary's. They weren't as wealthy as the butcher, Kieran Mallory, who had been calling on Mama recently, but they were certainly comfortable. Their big, two-story house on DeKoven Street, for just their family alone, had two rooms and a kitchen downstairs, with a big sleeping room upstairs for the children. And they had any number of chickens, pigs and cows.

"Fire! Fire!"

Caitlin's eyes flew open. A fearsome glow came from down the street, lighting the night as if the pits of hell had opened before her. Smoke danced up to the heavens and the evil crackling of flames filled the air. Grabbing the bucket from the back stoop, she raced out into the alley. It was the O'Leary's barn.

The alley was filled with piglets running and squealing, with dogs and chickens and a calf someone was carrying from the fire, as well as people running to help. But before Caitlin could join the others, filling buckets at the old pump, a huge ball of flame roared up toward the stars. It swallowed the O'Leary's barn in one single gulp, then turned toward the little cottages nearby.

"Mother of Mercy, save us." Caitlin dropped her bucket and ran for home. "Ma! Maeve!"

She was sure she was screaming loud enough to wake the saints in heaven, but her mother and the little girl were just sitting up when she burst in.

"Quick, get up!" she cried. "Everything's burning. We must get out."

"Saints preserve us," her mother gasped, while little Maeve started crying.

"Out!" Caitlin grabbed up Maeve and thrust her into her mother's arms, then pulled them toward the back door. Her mother paused, trying to reach for her robe, but Caitlin threw a coverlet around the woman's shoulders as she dragged her brutally along. There was no time for more.

Out on the tiny porch, it was as if they'd stepped into the center of the fire. Hungry flames whirled about, licking at the walls and roofs of their neighbors' homes, like the tongues of wolves licking at a deer carcass.

"The wind is blowing the flames toward the north and east," Caitlin shouted above the roar of the fire. "Get to DeKoven. You will be safe there."

"Where are you going?" her mother asked.

"Our money," Caitlin replied. "I must get our money."

"Caitlin!"

The screams rang in her ears, but she was already back inside their cottage. The flames were devouring their roof. Hot coals dropped from the rafters as she stumbled about in the smoky interior. She felt as if she were standing in an oven, the heat was so intense, baking her skin and drying all the moisture from her eyes.

She pulled at the pallet that her mother and Maeve slept on. She had to get to the far corner, to the knothole near the floor.

"Caitlin!" It was Jacob's voice.

"Jacob! Here. By the bed," she cried out.

A spray of embers showered down on her, singeing the skin on the back of her neck, but she just wiped at them. The smoke was so thick she couldn't see. Jacob must not have had that problem, though, for his strong hands grabbed her by the shoulders and pulled her back from the pallet.

"No, Jacob," she screamed. "The money!"

"No time," he shouted.

"Jacob! Without it, we're nothing!" She had to make him understand.

"And with it, we're dead."

"No!" She struggled against him, but he was too strong. "Jacob, please. Please help me move the bed."

But Jacob only wrapped his arms about her waist and carried her from the cottage. She kicked at him, struggled and twisted, but it was no use. He didn't let go. Through the door and into the yard he went, and three or four steps later the house collapsed in on itself in one last ball of fire.

Caitlin saw her world collapse with it and let out a terrible scream. Now they had nothing. It was worse than when Papa had died. Pain and fear wrapped around her heart and tried to squeeze the life from it.

Jacob put her down, but kept his arm around her as he led her through the smoke and flying ashes over to DeKoven Street. She wanted to cry, but her eyes were too dry to make tears. It didn't matter none. Her heart was crying enough for all.

"Our money," she sobbed. "Our money is all gone!"

"We've our lives," Jacob said. "And there's naught else we need."

Caitlin knew the words were true, but her heart refused to accept it. They'd almost had enough for Jacob to buy a horse and carriage. Then he could have gone into the livery business for himself. He would have been a man of property instead of just a poor day laborer.

Jacob stopped and looked back, his arm still around her shoulders. "The fire's moving toward the center of the city."

She looked to the north and east, her heart not able to accept the horror. The flames had grown like an unruly monster. Who would be able to stop them? The center of the city with all its fine stores and shops would be destroyed. Then people wouldn't be buying the shirts she sewed, and they'd have no need for a liveryman. Saving money would be almost impossible.

"This city is done for," Jacob said.

But she couldn't hear that. "London burned and they rebuilt."

"That was London." Jacob's voice was a sneer. "London is one of the great cities of the world. This is Chicago. A legion of shacks built on a swamp."

"Caitlin!" her mother cried.

Caitlin looked up to see her mother running toward her, and she pulled away from Jacob to fall into her embrace. They clung for a long moment, but Caitlin only felt her fear grow as she picked Maeve's cry out of the noise.

"Where is Maeve? Is she hurt?"

"Mrs. O'Leary has her. She's just frightened." Caitlin's mother stepped back and looked at her in the light from the nearby fires. "And you? Are you all right?"

"The money is all gone."

"'Tis said, Caitlin, that when God closes a door, he leaves a window open."

Caitlin shut her eyes, but felt her mother move nearer. In spite of the heat and ashes and raging smoke, she also felt a chill.

"The butcher, Kieran Mallory, has been talking to me," the older woman said in a low tone.

A spark of hope flickered against the dread in Caitlin's heart. The butcher and her mother had been seeing each other for a number of weeks now. He'd even had the three of them to his house for dinner the Sunday before last.

"Oh, mother." Caitlin threw her arms around her mother. "I'm so—"

"'Tis you he wants, lass."

Caitlin's arms dropped slowly, as if she could not bear the weight suddenly set on her shoulders. "No," she said, but her voice came out weak as a babe's. She reached behind her for Jacob's hand and clutched at it.

"He wants children, Caitlin," her mother said. "Without children, all his work will be for naught."

"But, Ma—" Caitlin broke off abruptly, closing her eyes to the misery around her. What of her dreams, her hopes, her love for Jacob? The butcher was a man of property, a voice inside her said. He would survive the fire, and so would those under his care.

"Mrs. Donahue?" Above the din of the fire a man called out.

Caitlin turned wearily to see a livery wagon on the edge of the crowd.

"Mrs. Donahue?"

"Why, it's Timothy," Caitlin's mother murmured. "Mr. Mallory must have sent him. Over here, lad," she shouted, then turned back to Caitlin. "Come, lass. Timothy'll take us to safety."

Without waiting to see if Caitlin was following, the older woman left. Caitlin watched for a long moment as her mother took Maeve from Mrs. O'Leary's arms and handed the child up into the wagon. Then Caitlin turned to Jacob, her eyes searching his.

"You cannot do it," he said, his voice ripe with anger. "She's got no right to ask it of you."

"How else are we to live?"

He took her hands in his, holding them tightly. "I've a mind to go west," he said. "It's a land of opportunity, Caitlin, where a man needs naught but a strong back and a willing heart. Come with me."

She shook her head. "And what of Ma and Maeve?"

"Your mother can find work sewing or cleaning. She will care for Maeve, as she should."

Caitlin looked away, the lie hanging heavy over her heart. She couldn't tell Jacob the truth about Maeve. She couldn't bear to see the love in his eyes die....

"I cannot leave them," Caitlin said. "It would not be right."

Jacob looked away for an eternity. "You must do what you must," he finally said. His voice cracked like timbers breaking when weakened by fire. "The butcher is a good man, Caitlin. He'll care for you and your family."

"It isn't fair, Jacob. I love you, not Mr. Mallory."

His arms came around her. He smelled of smoke and the toil of his day, but she only wanted to be held closer. Instead, she slipped from his arms and stood before him, knowing goodbyes had to be said, but not knowing how.

Jacob studied the ground for a long moment, then reached into his pocket and put an object in her hand, closing her fingers around it. "'Tis a ring, Caitlin. My father gave it to me. Keep it to remember me. Although we part, my soul will always be yours."

He pulled her into his arms and held her tightly, kissing her with a savage need that she'd never felt before, never even dared dream about. She was breathless when he pulled back, and she could do naught but lean against him.

"The same stars that look down on you will look down on me," he told her. "And did you know…each star is but an angel with a lantern."

"Oh, Jacob." The tears came again, her pain too great to hold them in. Tell him, her heart cried out. Maybe he could understand and even forgive. Maybe there was a way.

But the words would not come. She could live apart from him, but not if she knew his love for her was dead.

"I've just now spoken with my angel," Jacob said. "I told him that I'm a man and can care for myself. I asked that he watch over you, instead." He pushed her away to arm's length. "I'll keep you in my heart forever, Caitlin, my love. Until the rivers run dry, until the mountains fade away and until all the saints have gone to their eternal reward."

"You'll find another, Jacob. You must. That is as it must be."

His eyes glistened, too. "If you ever need me—no matter where, no matter when—I'll come to you. Just put your breath to the ring and I'll come, I promise."

Then, turning on his heel, he strode rapidly away into the shadows. He never paused, never looked back.

Caitlin clutched the ring and walked slowly over to Mr. Mallory's wagon.

Chapter One

"Kate?"

The sweet, childish bellow echoed down the stairs, but Kate Mallory's only response was to turn the wet-dry vacuum on again. Chicago had had a torrential downpour over the last twenty-four hours and she now had an indoor swimming pool in the basement of her new, three-flat apartment building. Granted, it was only a wading pool, but still not the chosen decor for the place.

Hopefully, though, Laura would react like any normal ten-year-old when faced with a flooded basement and run in the opposite direction. Kate was in the midst of her usual early October blues and wanted to be alone. Granny Nan, her paternal grandmother, always said nothing chased away the blues like hard work, and Kate's funk was dark enough that she wanted all the benefits of cleaning this mess for herself.

"Kate?" Laura's voice had risen from a normal bellow to a mega-bellow. "I know you're down here." The words were followed by the stomping of little bare feet.

"Ah, ha!" The door went flying open and Laura stormed into the room, dark eyes blazing and finger pointing. Yesterday had been the kid's birthday, the day she'd traded in a cocky nine for an obnoxious ten. "I'm going to tell Mom on you."

"Why?" Kate asked, turning the vacuum off. "Does she want to keep this water?"

Laura stood still, hands on her hips and a frown ruling her face. "She said we'd all clean this up after dinner. She said she didn't want you down here by yourself after you were sick yesterday."

"Mom shouldn't be cleaning up down here. She just got her cast off," Kate said. "Besides, I'm better."

Laura didn't give up her frown. "You're always sick on my birthday," she said.

"I am?" Kate was startled, as if the past were suddenly open to view through her actions. She swallowed her rush of fear and tried to smile. "Must be an allergy. You know, like the beginning of fall makes my nose run."

"I never heard of anything like that."

"'Cause you're still a kid."

Her real allergy was to memories, though. Of Dad. Of Miguel. Of loves and losses and lies. She felt again the sensation of being lost, of being a child alone in a crowd, calling out for those she loved but not finding them. The feeling swallowed her up for a moment, complete and whole with its utter misery, then let her go. But only partway. Like the traces of a cobweb, bits of the hurt clung to her soul. If only she could develop selective amnesia.

She tried to shake off her gloom as she reached for the vacuum switch again. Now that Laura was down here, she might as well make use of her. She hadn't the strength to send her away, anyway.

"Are you helping Mom with dinner?"

"Nope." Laura shook her head.

"Then how about if you help down here?"

Surprisingly, Laura dropped her little-sister act. "Okay. What you want me to do?"

"One of Granny Nan's boxes got all wet, so I emptied it out. See if you can find room for the stuff in those other boxes. If you can't, maybe you could find a new box upstairs."

Laura sloshed through the inch or so of water still on the floor and made her way to the card table stacked with cardboard boxes. "We shouldn't have moved," she told Kate. "Our old house never flooded."

"It might have this time."

During one hour this morning, five inches of rain had fallen; a total of ten inches had come down by midafternoon. They were actually fortunate that only the few things stored in the basement had been soaked.

"This place has so much more room than the old one," Kate pointed out. The three of them had moved just two weeks ago to this newly renovated triplex, though it wasn't that much of a move—just two blocks. But the new building gave them a lot more space. Kate, her mother and Laura lived in the apartment on the second floor. Kate's catering business occupied the first floor, while the basement contained more storage, plus a one-bedroom apartment.

The plan was to rent out the basement, but Kate hadn't gotten around to looking for a tenant yet. So, aside from some miscellaneous family junk, the only things down here were trays and metal folding chairs—nothing that was bothered by the few inches of water.

"Is all this stuff Granny Nan's?" Laura asked.

Kate looked up. "It's memorabilia she kept from Grampa Pat's side of the family, so be careful with it."

"Neato," Laura exclaimed as she began pawing through the boxes. "Maybe there'll be a buried treasure in here."

"Right. Except those boxes aren't exactly buried."

Laura's enthusiasm was contagious as always, and Kate left the vacuum. The girl had such a spirit of adventure about her. She did everything with a passion. Kate had been that way once. Before she learned that passion had a price.

Kate slammed the door on the memories that had leapt alive, and wandered over to the table. The stuff spread across it wasn't all that exciting—mostly old papers of one

sort or another, a box of old army patches and pins, a bag
of buttons. All things that Kate had seen before when
Granny Nan or Grampa Pat had been in a story mood.

Kate idly picked up the army pins. They'd been given to
her uncle, Granny Nan and Grampa Pat's oldest son, Gerald, who'd been killed in France during the war. Kate had
never met him, but felt the sadness of final partings as she
stared at the tarnished bronze pins.

"Wow. This stuff is cool," Laura cried. She had opened
another box and was gently taking out an old shawl, brightly
colored with a long black fringe. Beneath it was a leather
drawstring purse with beaded trim. "Think Granny used
it?"

"Either her or someone in Grampa's family." Kate fingered the fringe slowly. Had someone worn this on a special occasion? Was that why it had been saved, only to be
stuffed in a box in the basement?

These October blues were the pits, Kate scolded herself.
She might as well go sit out in the rain and sing country
songs about heartbreak and despair. She was finding melancholy everyplace she looked. Desperate for a diversion,
she glanced into the box and spotted something lacy under
several stacks of yellowed letters—from Grampa Pat's older
brother while he was fighting in World War I. She pulled it
out carefully, but was disappointed to find it was just a small
tablecloth yellowed with age. The sampler she found next,
embroidered by some childish hand, brought only a vague
smile, as did the chipped plate from the Columbian Expo-
sition. She pounced on a small booklet of black-and-white
photos with eagerness. Old pictures were always great.

Kate flipped slowly through them, certain she would find
smiles there. Grampa Pat as a little boy did start a few grins,
but Kate was puzzled by the adults. She had no clue as to
who they were. That smiling woman must be Grampa's
mom, Kate's great-grandmother Margaret, but Kate had
never seen a picture of the elderly woman with the distant
look in her eyes before. Somehow she felt drawn to her.

"Hey, neato!"

She glanced up as Laura uncovered a small wooden box at the very bottom of the carton. It was about the size of a cigar box, brown and tarnished with age, but the name carved into the lid could still be read. Caitlin Mallory. Kate put the photos down.

"That's a real rad name, ain't it?" Laura said. "I wish I had a name like that."

"What's wrong with Laura? It's a nice name."

"Get real," Laura muttered as she flipped through the letters, ribbons and thimbles filling the box. "Hey, there's a ring in here. I bet it's worth a lot of money."

"I doubt it," Kate replied. "Granny Nan wouldn't have left it in the box if it was."

But she felt a strange stirring in her soul, as if the ring might indeed have great value. It was clearly nothing special, though. Just a man's ring, with an onyx stone set in silver.

Laura continued turning the ring over in her fingers. "Who's JT?" she asked, looking at the inside of the band.

Kate shrugged, wanting to touch the ring yet almost fearing the very strength of that need. "I don't know. Probably some ancestor of ours."

"Mallory doesn't start with *T*," Laura pointed out.

"I know." Kate frowned, trying to remember some other family surnames, but drew a blank.

"I bet it's a magic ring."

"Girls!" Mom's voice came down the stairs. "It's dinnertime."

Kate sighed, freed from the pull of the ring by her mother's voice. She glanced around at the mess still awaiting them. "Guess we'll be cleaning this up tonight after all."

"Abracadabra," Laura said, waving her hand over the ring. "Hocus-pocus. Hubba hubba. Make all this water disappear." She set the ring on the edge of the table and jumped back, but nothing happened.

"So much for magic," Kate said. "Come on, we'd better get upstairs."

But Laura was still poking through the wooden box. "Hey, this looks like you." She held out an old photograph.

Kate took the picture from her hand. It was an old wedding portrait of a middle-aged man and a young-looking bride—the woman with the distant eyes, but younger this time. And she did indeed resemble Kate. It was a weird feeling, staring at this photo. Like looking down a deep well, expecting only darkness, but finding yourself looking back. A chill slid down her spine as she remembered her wish for selective amnesia.

Laura leaned over, still gazing at the picture. "Look, her hair's probably red like yours, and your eyes look just the same," she muttered.

No, this woman's eyes had a resignation to them, a weariness that said life was something to be endured, not enjoyed. What kind of sorrows had she seen? The eyes seemed to capture her. The ring was part of this woman's pain, Kate suddenly knew.

"This is really far out," Laura was saying. "What d'ya think it means? That you'll be getting married soon?"

Kate put the photo back into the box, trying to escape the strange sensations. "I think it means I share some genes with an ancestor."

Laura gave her a disgusted look. "You don't understand romance," she said. "That's probably why you don't have a boyfriend."

"Hey, I've had plenty of boyfriends."

"Right." Skepticism, mockery and just plain orneriness were rolled into the one word.

Kate stared at the girl as memories played against pride in a quick and deadly battle. She wasn't sure who won. "I had one special boyfriend when I was a freshman in college," she said. "And I guess I haven't looked much since."

Curiosity flooded Laura's face. "Oh, yeah? What happened to him?"

"He died. He was from Central America and went back there to fight the junta."

"Wow. He was a hero."

"I guess." Hero or accident victim, his death left her alone, all the same.

Laura frowned, doing other calculations. "That's the same year Dad died, isn't it?"

"Dad died in June. Miguel died in August." Though she hadn't learned of it until October.

"And I was born in October to cheer you all up."

Kate swallowed hard and looked away, fearing that the lid would somehow fall off and the secrets would come spilling out. Laura *had* cheered them up. Her birth had brought life and sunshine into their shadows, but it had taken Kate years to feel that joy. To escape the pain of her father's fatal illness, Kate had turned to Miguel. Then she had suddenly been left with nothing when Miguel had gone back home. Well, not with nothing. Six months later, Laura had been born, a month early because of Kate's recklessness behind the wheel, a recklessness that had almost cost both of them their lives. At that time Kate had been in no condition to nurture an infant, paralyzed as she'd been by her own pain and so afraid to love again. So her mother had stepped in— unwilling to lose another member of their family—as she'd put it and offered to help raise the baby.

They hadn't actually planned for Kate and Laura to be raised as sisters, but that was how it had happened. Kate had been unable to step forward and so had stepped aside. When Laura started talking, it seemed only natural that she call Mom Mom just as Kate did.

So Kate had gained a sister and time to heal. What she hadn't counted on was her growing feelings toward the girl over the years. The need to nurture and cherish, to care for and openly love, didn't dissipate because it wasn't her role. The needs twisted around her like a jungle vine, trying to choke off her breath at times, and always trying to conquer.

But Kate knew that she'd relinquished her chance to mother Laura because it had been best for the girl. And even though Mom occasionally pointed out that Laura had a right to know the truth, she still thought it was best for her.

Kate accepted all that, only slipping into a blue funk around Laura's birthday.

"Oh, you cheered us up all right," she teased. "Crying all the time. Spitting up on us."

Laura made a face and flicked water at Kate with her foot. But when Kate retaliated, the girl grabbed at the table, knocking the ring into the water in the process.

"Oh, no!" Laura cried.

Something clutched at Kate's heart, too, but she just bent and fished out the ring. "It's all right," she told Laura and her own silly nerves. "A little water won't hurt it."

The ring felt weary, though, as if it had been waiting a long time, and Kate found she couldn't put it down. It deserved better than to be stuck away in some box, she told herself as she first breathed on it, then polished it on her shirt.

"Make a wish on it," Laura demanded. "Wish for a boyfriend."

Kate frowned at the girl. "The only thing I wish I had is someone to help clean up this mess."

"You got me."

"I mean someone nice. Someone helpful." Kate made a face at Laura. "Someone who thinks I'm smart and pretty and fabulously fun to be around."

"Hah! A boyfriend!" Laura cried.

"Hah! A respectful little sister!"

"Girls!" Mom's voice came down the stairs again. "Dinner's getting cold."

Both Kate and Laura dissolved into laughter.

"Come on, let's get out of here before Mom feeds our dinner to the pigeons," Kate said.

She slipped the ring on her finger as she headed for the door. After holding it open for Laura, she followed her up the steps. A little niggling urge ate at her, though, as they reached their apartment door. She wanted Laura to admire her.

"And I'll have you know that I just might have a boyfriend. I met him on a job and we might go out Saturday."

"What's his name?"

"Lance Aikens. He's a financial adviser."

Laura looked like she'd swallowed a lemon. "Nobody has a boyfriend named Lance," she informed Kate. Then she smiled. "I know! We'll wish for a better one for you on the ring after dinner."

Kate glanced at her hand, almost surprised to find the ring still on her finger. "We'll clean up the basement after dinner."

And put the ring back where it belonged.

The flames devoured the old barn like a hungry child scarfing up chocolates. From the west came a bullying, blustering wind that incited the flames to ever greater heights until they reached the roof. Then the whole structure caved in on itself, sending sparks flying high, an offering to the ancient gods of the prairies and mountains.

Jake.

Jake MacNeill turned from the conflagration consuming his old barn and looked to the east. He thought someone had called him; rather, he'd felt someone calling him. But the Montana prairie flowed on endlessly with nothing and no one trying to catch his attention.

He turned back to the barn. At least the fire hadn't been without warning. Lightning had started the prairie aflame this morning, and they hadn't been able to turn it aside. The best place for the firebreak had been just beyond the old barn, so it'd had to be sacrificed. But at least they'd had time to get out everything of value.

Please come. I need you.

Jake turned again. The prairie fire faded. The sweat that beaded his brow was forgotten. The burns and blisters on his hands and arms became minor irritations. Something was drawing him to the east. Pulling at him, dragging his attention and his heart.

He turned to the short, stocky man at his side. "You hear something?"

Bo Werntz stared at him, forehead knotted so that his eyebrows were pushed into a single, thick black line. "I hear a whole hell of a lot of things." The ranch foreman spat out the words. "Prairie fires ain't known for tiptoeing."

That wasn't what Jake meant, but he didn't try to explain as he squinted at the scene before him. It had been one hell of a fire, blackening close to a hundred acres. Smoke still filled the sky above them. The air was thick, making breathing a chore.

But this new sensation was even stronger. It was like some giant hand pulling at him. He saw a city, felt the grit and noise and scent of ancient smoke in the air. Chicago? Something or someone was pulling him toward Chicago.

What the hell was going on? Had locoweed been planted out here, causing the smoke to be laced with some hallucinogenic drug?

"Fire made a hell of a mess," Bo said.

"It'll grow back." Jake was glad for the commonsense words that came out. Now he was back on comfortable ground again—back in his world of farming, soils, prairies and forests, and all the other ecological sciences. As Bo often said, Jake had enough degrees to damn near make him an expert. "In fact, periodic fires are good for the prairie. Kills off the shallow-rooted weeds. The indigenous plants come back even stronger."

"Didn't do much for the barn."

"Nothing's forever except the mountains," Jake said. "And there's some of us that ain't too damn sure about that."

He turned and let his eyes flick back over his shoulder, just a quick little glance. It wasn't as if he expected to see anything. He just needed a little movement to ease the strain in his neck.

"What in the hell are you looking at?"

"Nothing," Jake snapped. "Not a single dag-gone thing."

"You'd think there was fifty dancing wimmen back there. All young and pretty, with the sun shining off their legs."

They took a long moment to trade glares, bucking up against each other like two rams in the rutting season. Bo had been with the ranch for almost forty years, having hired on back when Jake's father had owned the spread. But Jake hadn't ever held that against him. His old man was dead, and so was the past.

Jake looked away first, letting his eyes go where they wanted. After all, it was his property, no matter which way he looked. Fifty thousand acres of prime Montana range land backed up here on the foothills to the Rockies.

But his glance roamed and stayed fixed on the east. That strange calling was still in the air, hanging there as if waiting for Jake to pluck it out and take it home. It was as if someone were crying out, needing his help. Jake looked and looked, but there wasn't a damn thing to see.

Actually, that wasn't true. There were the usual things. Miles and miles of rolling prairie interspersed with large stands of forest and covered by an endless stretch of blue sky. When Jake was a little tad, Bo had told him that Montana was just one of fifty states, but it had almost half the sky available to the lower forty-eight.

Bo had always fed him little gems like that. If it hadn't been for Bo, he would have spent his youth in reform school and graduated on into prison. If anyone deserved an explanation of what was going on, it was Bo. And Jake would be more than happy to give it to him.

If he had one.

"I know the prairie'll come back," Bo said. "But I 'spect we're gonna have to do something about the barn ourselves."

Jake nodded. A few of the boys were splashing water on the building's remains, while others were herding the horses into the lower forty. A few were straggling toward the bunkhouse. Darn convenient of the fire to finish up an hour or so before supper like this. Gave them a chance to wash up and all.

"We're gonna need it 'fore the snows come," Bo said.

Jake's eyes focused on that spot of woods across the lane, a little south of a line due east. No, there weren't any dancing girls there. Just trees, prairie grass and maybe a dust devil or two mixed with the ashes in the air. Nothing else.

So what was this strange compulsion he was feeling?

This wasn't like him. Poll one person or the whole population of Cold Spring and the vote would be the same: Jake MacNeill was good to his mother, would never forgive his father and never acted on impulse. He'd been a loner from day one and happy to be that way. He didn't need anybody.

The land was all that really mattered to him. All he wanted was to restore it to its natural glory, as it had been before pesticides, erosion and his father's bad management had brought it to near ruin. The land was what he put his trust in. The prairie wouldn't ever betray him or turn its back on him. The mountains wouldn't refuse to acknowledge him or act as if he didn't exist. The land would test and challenge him, but always stayed true to its nature. It held the answers to his questions, if only he looked close enough. It was all that could be counted on in the long run.

Those beliefs had been built over the past thirty-five years, yet the last ten minutes had reduced them to ashes just as surely as the fire had destroyed this old building.

"What the hell we gonna do about the barn?" Bo was asking.

Jake shook his head, but doing so didn't clear up any of the muddle he was in. He owed Bo Werntz, owed him big, but for the life of him, he couldn't come up with an explanation for what he was about to do. He had a deep-seated certainty that he had no choice, as if the decision had been made for him ages ago and he was just playing out a role.

He turned to Bo. "What are we going to do about the barn? Build a new one."

"Good." Bo's voice was soothingly sarcastic. "And what kind of a barn are we gonna build?"

"The old one lasted fifty or sixty years. Put up another like it."

Bo's old face creased with confusion. "Put up another like it? What the hell is this? Am I going to be in charge of building a new barn?"

"Yup."

"What are you going to be doing?"

"I'm going to Chicago."

"Chi-caw-go!" Bo was shouting. "What in the hell for?"

"Got to."

"Got to? You ain't never in your life done something because you 'got to.'"

"I have to shave and shower," Jake said.

"But—but how ya going? When? Are you going alone?"

"I'm driving," Jake replied. "Leaving as soon as I'm clean and packed. And I'm taking Boris and Nickolai with me."

"Boris and Nickolai?" Bo jerked his hat off and threw it on the ground. "Now I know you done lost all common sense. The sheriff won't even let you bring them dogs into Cold Spring. What the hell you think they gonna do in Chicago—welcome them monsters with open arms?"

"Bo, I surely do enjoy chatting with you, but I gotta go."

"What the hell for?"

Jake was turning to walk away. If it had been anyone but Bo asking, he would have just brushed him off like some pesky bug, but he owed Bo the best he could give. "I've a need that needs filling."

Bo stared at him openmouthed, and Jake took the chance to hurry on toward the house.

"Jake!"

He tried to force his feet along the path, but they froze up. He turned his head.

"We got wimmen in Montana, you know."

Jake just stared at him.

"Why don't you go to Missoula? Got a lotta pretty ones there. Young, too. I mean, with the university being there and all."

"That ain't the need that needs filling." Jake turned on his heel and strode off in high gear.

"Hellsfire," Bo called after him. "You're just as bull-headed as your old man, even if you ain't carrying his name."

It was a remark designed to make Jake stop and shift into reverse, and it might have worked some other time. But not today. There was no denying this calling.

* * *

"My, my, don't you look nice!"

Kate stopped applying her mascara and let her eyes flicker toward the bedroom door. Her mother was standing in the doorway. "Oh, hi, Mom."

The older woman came farther into the room, wiping her hands on a dish towel as she did. "I can't tell you how glad I am that you're going out tonight," she said. "It's about time you were dating."

Kate frowned at her mother's reflection in the mirror. What was this belief everyone had that she wasn't dating? "Mom, I date."

"I don't call stopping for a cup of coffee a date."

"I've had other dates. Real dates."

Her mother just snorted and sank onto Kate's bed. "And when was the last time you bought a new dress because you were going out?"

The strange note in her voice made Kate pause. Wistfulness was mixed up with sadness and regret. She had a sudden vision of everyone holding their collective breaths until Kate got her life back together. She wanted to view it all as an intrusion into her personal life, but couldn't. Her mother had given her too much to be resented for her concern.

The older woman leaned forward. "Have you given any more thought to telling Laura the truth?"

All the soft, cozy feelings disappeared as Kate felt her insides twist up. "We've been over this a million times, Mom."

"The lie should never have lasted this long."

Actually, it probably would have lasted longer if her mother hadn't fallen last month and broken her wrist. Her new bifocals had made her dizzy and she'd misjudged the steps in their old home. Since then, she'd decided she was in the grandmother range, not the mother one.

"It's not that I don't want her to know," Kate said. "Or that I don't want to be her mother. It's just that . . ."

"That you're afraid."

"Well, yeah." Afraid that Laura's reaction would not be one of pleasure.

"Better sooner than later, though. Anger at ten is a lot easier to get over than at sixteen."

"I guess."

Her mother got to her feet. "So what's this guy you're going out with like?"

Kate accepted the reprieve and went back to her makeup. "I think you'll like Lance," she said. "He's really nice."

"You sound like you like him and that's what's important."

Did she? Kate wondered as she finished her mascara. She couldn't decide if she was excited or just plain nervous about going out. She knew something was dancing in the pit of her stomach and getting more active with every flash of her digital clock.

In spite of Kate's constant protests, it had been awhile since she'd been on a real date. She was hoping it was like riding a bike and that she'd remember how to make small talk and flirt once she had to. But what if she couldn't? What if she couldn't think of a single thing to say?

When she was in high school and just starting to date, her father used to tease her about being tongue-tied. Then he'd tell her jokes, little odd news facts and all sorts of things she could fall back on if the silence got too bad. He was always taking care of her.

She got to her feet and smoothed down the skirt of her navy silk dress. Well, her father wasn't here to help her out, but she didn't need him. Lance was a gem, a real treasure. She'd never met a man as nice and considerate as he was.

The doorbell rang. "I'll get it," Laura called out.

Kate and her mother exchanged glances, then Kate hurried out into the hallway. "Laura, wait." But she was already starting down the stairs. Kate followed her, arriving at the door as the girl was looking through the one-way mirror panel beside the main door.

"It's a geek," she announced. "He's got combed-back hair, a funny little mustache and flowers."

"Oh, for heaven's sake." Kate unlocked the front door. "It's Lance."

"That's the kind of name a geek would have."

She wanted to give Laura a fierce glare that would stuff some respect into the child's soul, but was afraid the glare would linger and spill over onto Lance. She forced a smile to her lips and pulled the door open.

"Lance," she said. "Won't you come in?"

"In a moment, my dear." His rich baritone rolled around their small entryway, filling the corners like the deep, heavy scent of brandy. "Let me look at you first."

Sudden embarrassment flushed Kate's cheeks, but it wasn't an unpleasant sensation. Nor was that appreciative look in his eye hard to take, even if it did make her feel as if she were on stage. Thankfully Laura stayed quiet.

"*C'est magnifique.*" Lance put his fingertips to his lips and blew her a kiss. "That dress is *très, très* lovely. It makes your hair look afire and sets your beautiful eyes to glowing."

There were gagging noises behind her back that Kate was almost tempted to join in with, but she took herself in hand. She shouldn't be so self-conscious over a compliment. Just because Lance talked like something out of a soap opera didn't mean he wasn't sincere.

She smiled at him and took his hand. "Come on in, Lance. My mother is anxious to meet you." She led him up the stairs, then into the living room.

Lance bowed slightly and took her mother's hand. "Mrs. Mallory. It is indeed a pleasure to meet you." He handed her the flowers. "Lovely flowers for a lovely woman."

Kate's mother blinked once. "Thank you," she murmured. "And you've already met Laura?"

Laura grinned at him and waved.

"Ah, yes," Lance replied. "A lovely young lady."

Kate glared at Laura long enough to feel reasonably certain she was going to behave, then turned back to her mother. "Lance has his own business, too, Mom," she said. "He's a personal financial adviser."

"Oh, really?"

"Your daughter feeds people's stomachs," Lance said with a chuckle. "I feed their wallets."

"I guess both of them need care," her mother replied.

Kate felt a little tightness in her stomach. Was conversation always this tense on a first date? Maybe it would be better once they were away from the house. "Isn't our reservation for seven?" she asked.

"Yes, it is, my dear."

"We probably should be going then. You never know what traffic will be like on Lake Shore Drive."

"Whatever you say." Lance sprang forward, once again taking her mother's hand in his. "It was a pleasure meeting you, my lady." Then he turned to Laura. "And I look forward to meeting you again, my little one."

"I'm not really that little," Laura replied.

"Ah." Lance chuckled. "Children. They are so beautiful."

"See you guys later." Kate quickly grabbed his arm and pulled him toward the door. Laura was lenient and allowed them to leave without any more trouble.

Kate breathed enough on the way down the stairs to be able to make small talk. "You get flooded in the rain earlier this week?" she asked.

He shook his head. "My condo's on the sixteenth floor."

"Oh." So much for sharing flood stories. Well, she'd think of something else to say when they were in the car.

But once outside, she realized she wouldn't have to. Lance had brought his Mercedes Benz convertible. Conversation wouldn't be possible with the lake breeze rushing around them. She would be able to think, though. And she would. She'd spend the whole ride planning out their dinner conversation so she wouldn't be tongue-tied.

"Would you like the top up or down?" he asked.

"Leave it down," Kate said quickly. "It's too beautiful an evening to be cooped up."

"Ah, but what a joy to be cooped up with you."

She just smiled and let him help her into the car. A wonderful evening lay ahead of her, she assured herself, relaxing as they pulled away from the curb. Her mother probably thought she was still mourning for Miguel, and that's why she didn't date much, but Kate knew that was wrong. Miguel had been a refuge, not the great love of her life. He'd been a wild, passionate escape from the brutal reality of her father's cancer. Miguel had been so alive, so free, that in his arms anything had felt possible.

But not for long. That mirage of invincibility had been short-lived and all too fragile. She'd found that out when Miguel had had to go back to Central America that spring. In the course of a few short months, she'd learned that she was pregnant, she'd buried her father and had then gotten word that Miguel had been killed in a military ambush.

Losing Miguel had been the final blow, pushing her into an ocean of grief. She hadn't been able to think of anything but her losses and had almost created another one. She'd been driving too fast and had lost control on rain-slicked pavement.

"The wind's not too much for you, is it?" Lance shouted to her.

"It's great," she called back with a smile. A few more rides like this and maybe all those memories would be blown from her soul.

She was so lucky to find someone like Lance. Someone so open and caring, so solicitous of her wants and needs. They would have a good time and she would learn the fun of being a couple again.

They rounded the curve at Oak Street, and Kate breathed in the cool lake air. Off to her right, the surface of Lake Michigan looked so peaceful. She loved Chicago. Right in the middle of the hustle and bustle there were these islands of incredible calm.

Lance reached over and took her hand as they stopped for the light near St. Joseph's Hospital. "Hungry?" he asked.

"Starving," Kate said. "I haven't eaten all week, so I'd really appreciate going to—"

The squeal of tires on pavement interrupted her and she glanced over her shoulder to see a big blue pickup make a U-turn. It had been going south, but it suddenly crossed over the divider and started heading north in the empty lane next to them.

"What is that fool doing?" Kate muttered. "He's going to run the light."

No, she was wrong.

"Lance!" she screamed. But it was too late. The fool driver had swerved suddenly and clipped Lance's front fender before coming to a stop in front of them.

A tall, broad-shouldered man in a cowboy hat rushed out of the truck and over to her side as if he were the cavalry coming to the rescue.

"You're okay now," he said.

Chapter Two

"Okay? After you rammed into us?" the woman asked, looking at Jake as if he were on the near side of loco.

And that was pretty close to how he felt. His mouth wasn't working any better than his brain.

He'd been driving down this roadway, wondering what in the world he was doing in Chicago, when out of the blur of auto-exhaust fumes and the smell of the lake, this woman's face had smacked him square in the eyeballs. He'd wanted to lean out the window and call her name, but he didn't know what it was. He didn't know anything about her, except that she'd just reached out and filled the empty canyons of his heart.

The next thing he knew he was driving like a regular down-home Chicago motorist, slipping sidewise across a hundred lanes of traffic, jumping a big old grass-filled strip in the middle and running this bright, shiny, expensive-looking convertible to ground. He wasn't just acting out of character; he'd become certifiably insane.

And now this lady with the angel eyes definitely looked as if she needed help. It worried him, and he hoped he hadn't been the cause.

"You are okay, aren't you?" he asked, doffing his hat. "I didn't mean no harm. I just—"

"You didn't mean any harm?" she repeated, her voice edging up to a screech. "You mean you did this on purpose?"

She swung the car door open, and Jake took a step back. It seemed a bit safer to concentrate on the driver of the convertible, who was coming around toward him. The guy was tall and slick looking, like he earned his keep schmoozing with rich widows. His very appearance set Jake's blood to boiling. What was the angel doing with Slick?

"You ran into me," the man said.

"I surely did, sir," Jake replied. His first inclination was to flatten the guy, but being here in the big city, he had to act a bit more civilized. Especially until he found out what was going on. "And I expect to pay for my deed."

A few cars were getting backed up behind them, the drivers honking their horns and shouting obscenities as they maneuvered into the free lanes. The man glanced at the traffic uneasily, then turned back to Jake.

"You have insurance?"

"Ain't no reason to involve those folks." Jake put his hat back on as he pulled a roll of cash out of his jacket pocket. "Why don't I give you a few bills to start with?"

The man gaped at the money Jake had handed him. "Three hundred dollars?"

"That's just for the fuss and bother, sir. I'll pay whatever you need to fix your buggy as good as new." Jake extended his hand and raised his voice to counter the noise of the passersby. "I'm Jake MacNeill."

The man took his hand. "Lance Aikens."

"Lance," the angel protested loudly. "He hit us on purpose. We should call the police."

But old Lance wasn't giving back that money any more than a desert gives back rain, Jake knew. And he wasn't going to call in any arbitrators.

"We'll have this settled in a sec," Jake told her reassuringly. The light changed and a new set of impatient drivers drove by. Lordy, city folks were downright nasty. "Ain't nothing that can't be settled here between us men."

"Yeah, Kate, relax. We'll—"

But Kate didn't seem to want to relax. "You can't just buy us off," she snapped, advancing toward Jake. "Somebody could have been hurt. You shouldn't be allowed to drive like that."

He stepped back as a tiny smidgen of concern entered his stomach. First she looked like an angel, then a wounded doe. Now she was closer to a grizzly bear than anything else.

"Hey, don't start fretting," he said, keeping his voice smooth and calm. That was the way to handle an excitable filly—lace your voice with milk and honey. Of course, the honking and shouting around them wasn't exactly soothing. "Everything's fine."

"Don't get so excited, Kate," Lance said. "Jake's sorry."

The boy had the words right, but he sounded like he'd left all his sugar back home on the kitchen table.

"What?"

Lordy, but the angel could shriek. Outdid even the car horns. Jake moved slowly toward her. "Easy, Kate."

She turned to glare at Lance. "This stupid cowboy runs us off the road and it's all right because he's sorry? We could have been killed."

"Now, now, Kate." Jake kept his voice all gentle and smooth. Bo would have been proud of him. "Ain't nobody hurt, and the car can be fixed easy enough."

"Shut up!" Kate shouted as she slammed him in the head with her purse, knocking his hat off. Someone in a passing car shouted approval. "You have no idea what car accidents can do."

"Easy there, Katie."

"You irresponsible jerk!"

Kate hit him again, but Jake didn't say anything this time. He just ducked, wishing Bo were here. This gentle-handling thing wasn't getting him anywhere and he could have used a bit of advice.

"Kate, Kate." Lance moved between Jake and Kate. "Calm down. I have everything under control."

"Oh, you do, do you?"

She hit him in turn with her purse, and he quickly stepped behind Jake. But Jake wasn't ready to return to the line of fire, either, and tried to get behind Lance. They'd barely started their little tango when Kate turned away from them to kick Lance's car. She'd found his Achilles' heel.

"Kate!" Lance cried out as if cut to the quick. He raced over to check out the damage a lot faster than he'd raced over to check her out earlier.

Jake just sighed. Prairie fires were easier to figure out than a woman. He should've stayed home and built his new barn.

But all he had to do was look into Kate's eyes to forget about Montana.

What was happening to him? He'd always been immune to such weaknesses.

A whimpering sound was coming from Lance. "You sure hit him where it hurts," Jake told Kate. "Guess city folks are made different from us country boys."

Before he could blink an eye, Kate's face crumbled and she let loose about five-hundred gallons of humongous tears. Good Lord, the woman ran through emotions quicker than a set of newborn quints ran through diapers.

"I'm not criticizing," Jake said quickly. "I'm just stating a fact."

But Kate continued crying, and he felt real worry rising in his stomach. Emotions weren't his province at all. He looked toward Lance for help, but the man appeared to be checking his car for scratches. Jake turned back to Kate.

"Hey, there, Katie," he said quietly. "Ain't no cause to be so upset."

His words didn't seem to be inciting her to more violence, so he took a step closer, then another one. "Come on, now. It was just a little accident."

He reached around to pat her on the shoulder, but suddenly found himself holding her. She had crumpled into his arms and was sobbing on his chest. Even a mite wet, she sure felt good to hold.

"Where were you folks going?" Jake asked.

Lance finally looked up. "To Armand's. It's a restaurant about two miles north of here."

His voice was tinged more with annoyance than concern, and Jake fought the urge to teach him some manners. Kate needed him more than his stupid car did.

"It looks like the little lady here needs some tender loving care," he said. "Why don't you go on to the restaurant and I'll take her over to that hospital down the road?"

"I could take her," Lance said as he got to his feet. His eyes kept straying to the side of his car, and then to the traffic passing within a breath of it.

"No, no," Jake said quickly. His hidebound, ironclad, no-exceptions rule about staying uninvolved vanished like dew under a summer sun. "This is part of making it right. You get on to your restaurant and relax. I'll bring her along quicker'n you can say howdy."

Lance seemed to be vacillating, so Jake got busy leading Kate toward his truck. Boris and Nickolai stared at them from the back seat, unmoving, as he opened the door. "Those are my dogs," he told Kate.

"Oh."

He helped her up into the cab, then went around to the driver's side. He first fastened Kate's seat belt, then his own. He was just acting responsibly, he told himself. He'd caused a minor accident and was trying to make amends.

"We'll go to the emergency room and have you checked out," he told her.

"I'm all right." But she made no move to leave.

He took the portable red flasher that he had as a member of the Cold Spring sheriff's posse and volunteer fire department and put it on top of the roof. That would show her he was respectable, he decided. And prove that he was just carrying out his regular duties, even if he was a might out of his normal range.

"Hang on." He looked in his side rearview mirror and began to ease the truck into traffic. "We're gonna put the pedal to the metal."

Suddenly, she let out an ear-piercing shriek. Jake slammed on the brakes, practically standing the truck on its front end. "Now what?" he asked.

"Those beasts are chewing on my neck."

Nickolai was looking at Boris, and Boris was looking guilty. Sighing, Jake put the engine in neutral and pulled up the hand brake. This woman didn't have but two points on her volume knob: loud and louder. "Those aren't beasts, Kate. They're dogs."

"Dogs don't grow that big."

"Well, excuse me, ma'am. Maybe you should have told them that before they got all growed up." Clenching his teeth, he shifted into first gear. "And they were licking, not chewing. No way you'd still be sitting there frowning at me if they'd been using their teeth."

She turned her frown toward the side window, where she could see Slick as Jake pulled into the traffic. She turned further, keeping her eyes on him as they drove away.

Hellsfire, she couldn't be missing the guy! He was a toad, a lowlife who would be tossed out of any respectable town before he could get close to the womenfolk.

Why should he care? Jake asked himself.

Kate sighed and closed her eyes as she leaned her head against the headrest. Her lashes lay like an angel's breath against the pale softness of her cheek. He fought the urge to touch her, to tell her it would be all right, and concentrated on his driving.

Hellsfire, indeed. Jake felt like he was swimming in a waterhole full of snakes, all poisonous and all mad at him. He had to get back home and fast.

"Everything looks just fine," the doctor said, pulling open the curtain to Kate's cubicle. "You might feel a little stiffness tomorrow, but that's normal."

She didn't feel fine. What she felt was incredibly embarrassed. She had never fallen apart like she had. Never.

Jake came rushing over as if he'd been lurking in the next cubicle. "Is she all right?"

Kate bit back the scream that was fighting to surface. "I'm fine. Just like I said I was."

She'd hoped that he would have left while she was waiting for the doctor, but obviously her luck today wasn't of the good variety. She slid off the gurney and got her purse from the chair. When she turned around, the doctor was gone, but Jake wasn't. He had a worried frown between his eyebrows that made him look both like a refuge of safety and incredibly vulnerable. An uneasiness settled on her shoulders as she realized she owed him an explanation for her strange behavior.

They walked in silence through the emergency room, catching brief glimpses of life's little dramas behind other curtains. Quiet crying came from one cubicle, laughter from another. There were whispered conversations and breath-catching moans of pain. Weaving through it all was the antiseptic smell of a thousand disinfectants, the utilitarian practicality of tile everywhere and the constant murmur of doctors being paged and codes being called.

There was a strange sense of intimacy about it all, as well as familiarity. She remembered the whispered conversations from when they'd brought her father back to the hospital for the last time, the horrendous pain after her own automobile accident. That smell had seeped into her blood so that, like the memories, it seemed she could never be free of it.

She found herself wanting to reach over and take Jake's hand, to hold onto him as if he were the pilot that would steer her through these choppy waters and get her back to safety. But that was a stupid thought. An irrational one.

Just the thought of leaning—however briefly—on the idiot who'd deliberately run into them made her blood start to churn all over again. She'd keep her hands to herself, apologize politely, then send him on his way.

"Look, I really owe you an apology for the way I acted," she said as they passed through the swinging doors to the reception area. "I'm not usually so uncontrolled. It's just that—"

"Oh, Mr. MacNeill," one of the clerks from the reception desk called. "We forgot to have you sign this."

Kate stopped. "Sign what?" she asked him.

He just shrugged as he kept moving toward the desk. "Some paper, I suppose."

Kate followed. The urge to take his hand was growing more and more distant. "Why should you sign anything? I gave them my insurance card."

"I tore up the form," he said, then flashed her what she suspected was supposed to be a charming smile.

It fell short of its mark.

"Why should you have to pay for my mistake?" he went on. "I screw up, I pay the price."

But she didn't want anything from him. "That's crazy. I wasn't hurt in the accident."

"So there won't be much to pay then," he said, presenting her with that smile again. He turned to the clerk at the desk and scrawled his signature across some paper. "There. Let's go get some dinner."

"Some dinner?" It was a toss-up which item to fight first, but Kate leaned past him and caught the clerk's eye. "I want it billed to me."

"But, ma'am—"

"Whatever she says, Mandy," Jake said as he took Kate's arm.

His voice was so patronizing that she didn't need to see his wink at the clerk to know he had given her one. Damn Lance for leaving her with this guy. She'd been his date; he should have brought her here if she needed bringing, not this cowboy.

"Look, Mr. MacNeill," Kate said, pulling her arm away with force. "Thank you for your concern, but I am perfectly capable of taking care of myself."

"That why you're dating that jerk Lance?"

"Now just a minute." Her allegiance abruptly shifted. "He is not a jerk!"

"Prime dating material, huh?" He gave the outside doors a shove and cool evening air washed over them. "If he's the best Chicago has to offer, you ought to move."

She charged out into the courtyard along with him. "Maybe some women prefer the gentler type. A man who's quiet and considerate."

He stopped walking and pinned her with a glance. "The type that cares more about his car than his woman?"

"I'm not his woman," Kate protested, but it was a weak argument at best. "This was just our first date."

Jake started walking toward his truck again. "And your last, if you have any sense."

The nerve of him! Ordering her about like she was his kid sister. She resisted the urge to wallop him with her purse again, but it wasn't easy. Lance would never treat her this way. That's why she'd been attracted to him in the first place. He was kind and considerate. He'd just been overwrought this evening, and she'd behaved badly herself.

She wasn't looking for permanence, but if she was, Lance was the type she'd want. Not someone like this cowboy, who seemed to think she was just a silly sheep to be herded into his pasture. He was too loud. Too bossy.

Too big.

Next to him, she felt almost like a child. Like she could look up to him and know he would keep the storms away. Like she could depend on him completely.

Sure. Like she had depended on her father. Like she had depended on Miguel. Never again.

Kate hurried after Jake and caught up with him at his truck. "Look, I appreciate your help, but I'll just get a cab from here."

"Why? I told you dinner was going to be my treat." He opened the truck door and barked out some command. The two monsters tumbled out and ambled over to the fountain in the middle of the courtyard for a drink.

"You've paid for the damage to Lance's car and, I suspect, for my visit here. Dinner is unnecessary." Besides, she was anxious to see him on his way.

"I have to eat. You and Lance have to eat. We might as well eat together, don't you think?"

No. But she didn't say it. Why couldn't she stand up to him? She ran her own catering business, placated demanding customers and planned delicious menus while coping with disastrous dietary restrictions. Why couldn't she tell this cowboy where to get off?

"Besides, I'm a stranger here in town," he went on. His blue eyes took on a little-boy look. "If you turn me loose, I might get into trouble all by myself."

As opposed to her getting in trouble with him. Kate didn't know what was wrong with her, but she just sighed. "All right. But let's get going." Maybe she'd hit her head in the accident and didn't know it. There had to be a reason for this continuing insanity. "Or are you going to let your beasts drink all the water from that fountain?"

Jake whistled, and the monsters came charging back—really fast. Unless they had terrific brakes, they were going to trample her.

With a small squeal, Kate jumped behind Jake. The dogs screeched to a stop and sat down, staring around him at her as if she was going to be dinner.

"Boris and Nickolai, this is Kate," Jake said. "She's our new buddy, so treat her nice."

Nickolai's tail wagged. Boris just licked his lips. Not a good sign, Kate thought. Jake turned to her, as if waiting.

She forced a smile of sorts at the dogs and waved slightly. "Hi, guys."

Neither made a further response, so Jake opened the truck door. The dogs piled into the back seat. Kate, with Jake's help, climbed into the front. She could feel hot breath on the back of her neck as Jake went around to the driver's side, but she refused to turn her head. Show fear and lose the upper hand.

Assuming she'd ever had it.

Jake climbed in and started the truck. His arm brushed hers, causing a sudden panic to fill her heart. She liked things predictable, controlled, and there wasn't one damn thing controlled about Jake MacNeill. He was going to do what he wanted, when he wanted, and she was willing to bet he didn't carry a pocket agenda with a list of things to do as she did. She wanted to move away, to sit closer to the door, but stayed put. Show fear and lose the upper hand.

"Nice dogs you have," she said as they left the hospital parking lot. "Are they some Russian breed?"

"Nah."

He smiled at her, a smile so filled with life and energy and passion that it scared the hell out of her. She knew what Lance's smiles meant, and what they didn't mean. Jake's seemed determined to wake up a long-sleeping sweetness in her heart, something she was not about to let him do.

She forced her eyes straight ahead and watched the traffic. "I just thought with their names and all . . ."

"They're just mutts," he said. "But I found them in Moscow."

"Oh, really?" Travel. Now there was a safe topic. A civilized topic. "You've been to Russia?"

"Me? Nope. Never been out of the United States."

"Then how did you get to Moscow?"

Like magic, he had drawn her eyes to him. "Took I-90 west and then headed down 95. It's just east of the Washington-Idaho border on 8."

"Moscow, Idaho?"

"Yup."

Kate shut her eyes for a moment and suppressed the groan that wanted to escape from deep within her chest. Why did she think she could have a normal conversation with this man? Why was she even bothering to try?

"So anyway, where's this restaurant we're going to?"

Kate opened her eyes and got him back on to Lake Shore Drive. Once that was accomplished, the silence seemed to weigh on her. There were so many things hanging in the air between them. She'd like to tell him off for his irresponsibility. She ought to explain why she'd gotten so emotional. She'd like to know what Moscow, Idaho, looked like.

That was a danger sign that even she recognized. Time to put some distance between them. "Sorry I kind of lost it at the accident," she said quickly. "I was in one before and it felt like I was back in time for a moment."

His eyes swept over her—gentle, sympathetic, warmer than a fire in the middle of winter. "A bad one?"

She looked away. "I guess. No one died. I was in the hospital for three weeks."

"Anyone else hurt?"

She saw Laura, so tiny and helpless lying in the pediatric intensive-care unit, and closed her eyes. "Yes." But she gave him no more information.

His hand closed around hers, bringing a promise of comfort, a sense of permanence. And a strange and eerie feeling that this was somehow part of forever. She wanted to let go but couldn't. It was her heart that was holding on, not her hand. The whole thing scared her half to death.

"I really owe you then," Jake said.

She didn't want him to. She wanted them to be even. No debts, no IOU's, no anything. "That's not why I told you."

"But I do owe you," he said. "I acted like a jerk and made you suffer. I'm going to make it up to you."

Oh, great. She'd never be rid of him now. She leaned back with a hearty sigh to find that hot breath very close behind her. Friendly Nickolai or hungry Boris?

"Do I just park out on the street?" Jake asked.

"Yes." Kate felt as if she were doomed. There was no escaping. "Anyplace you can find a space."

Jake pulled into a spot down the block from the restaurant, then opened all the windows partway. He looked back at Armand's. "They serve buffalo meat here?" he asked.

"Why? Do you prefer buffalo?"

"I raise them on my ranch up in Montana."

So he wasn't just an ordinary cowboy. Probably just an extraordinary liar. "Shall we go in?" Kate asked.

"Sure thing."

Kate kept her smile up as she got out of the truck, but she considered clubbing him. She wasn't stupid, though; she'd wait until they were away from his little pals and his back was turned. He shut her door for her, then took her arm.

"Aren't you going to lock the truck?" she asked.

"Nope," Jake replied. "They get mad if I do."

The two dogs appeared to be grinning at her. Would she read about some would-be car thief slaughtered by monsters in tomorrow's paper?

"Come on, little lady." He pulled gently at her arm. "Time to do some high steppin'."

She let him lead her into the restaurant. This date was not going as planned. She'd wanted to add a dash of social life to her calendar; she thought she needed to get out more. But this was not what she'd had in mind.

"Kate!" A maître d' in a tuxedo rushed toward her. "What a wonderful surprise. Are you here to beg more mushrooms or to rescue Maurice's soufflé?"

"Neither." Kate knew most of the chefs around the city from the early morning produce markets or the informal classes some gave. "I'm meeting someone here. A Lance Aikens."

"Ah, Mr. Aikens. He said to expect you." The man's pointed glance at Jake said the table was set for two, not three.

"We have someone else joining us," she said with a smile that hopefully meant Jake was an unexpected pleasure. "I trust that won't be a problem."

"Of course not," the man hurried to assure her. "We're delighted to welcome your friends here."

She turned slightly toward Jake. "You'll like it here. Everyone feels like family."

"And you are like a favorite niece," the maître d' said.

Kate smiled her thanks. She had to stop worrying. The evening would go well. She and Lance would have a lovely time, Jake would have some company, then she could go back to her quiet, pleasant life.

"So when do the fights start?" Jake asked.

She and the maître d' stared at him. "Fights?"

"Yeah," Jake replied. "You know how families are. They start out all lovey-dovey, then they exchange a few words. And before you know it, you got yourself a brawl."

The maître d' looked bewildered, and for a moment Kate was at a loss for words. Finally she asked, "Is Mr. Aikens here yet?"

"*Oui*. He just stepped away for a moment."

Kate saw Lance walking from the direction of the restrooms. He glanced their way—or was it a glare?—before continuing on to a table in the center of the small dining room.

As they followed the maître d' to the table, a little pinch of annoyance tried to surface. Lance was her date, yet so far she'd spent more time with Jake. Lance wasn't even coming over to meet her.

Or help her with her chair. "Thank you, Henri," Kate said as she sat down in the chair he pulled out for her.

Jake sat down and put his big hat on the floor. "Say, Hank," he said. "How about you draw us each a tall one?"

"A tall one?"

Henri's obvious bewilderment was a signal for Kate to rush to the rescue. "This establishment doesn't serve beer," she said.

"No beer?"

"No, sir," Henri replied.

Poor man, Kate thought. It was also obvious that the cowboy spent too much time with his buffalo. "Why don't you bring us a carafe of your house white, please?" she said.

"Very good."

Jake stared at Henri's back for a long moment before finally shaking his head. "No beer," he muttered, almost under his breath.

It suddenly dawned on Kate that Lance hadn't said a word. He was sitting there like a petulant little kid, waiting for her to cajole him into better spirits. She didn't quite feel up to cajoling at the moment, but old habits were hard to break.

She put a hand on top of his. "Were you waiting long for us?"

Lance pulled his hand away. "Long enough. Where were you?"

The tone in his voice was definitely scolding, and Kate stared at him. "I beg your pardon?"

"You certainly took your time in getting here. What were you doing for so long?"

Any slight urge she had to appease Lance fled. "If you had taken me to the hospital, you'd know what I was doing."

"I didn't tell you to get in his truck."

"I didn't choose to get in his truck." Kate could hear her voice rising, but didn't give a damn. What had happened to all of Lance's fancy manners? "I was upset, and he took me there."

"You didn't have to let him."

"'I didn't have to let him.'" Every happily-ever-after movie, story and song that Kate had ever heard pushed her into horrified anger. "And what the hell were you doing, oh great protector of womanhood?"

They glared at each other, feeling the silence of the other restaurant patrons around them. Then, as if on cue, they both turned and looked at Jake. He just sat there with a big grin on his face.

"Ain't families wonderful?"

"Well, look what the cat dragged in," Granny Nan muttered.

Kate looked up as she poured herself a cup of coffee. "Morning, Granny. How are you?"

"Better'n you, I'd guess."

Kate slid into a chair at the breakfast table. She had managed to put on an old pair of cutoffs and a T-shirt, but had left the civilizing touches like shoes and makeup for those who felt civilized. Never in her entire life would she ever go on another date.

"Kate's got a hangover, Granny," Laura said.

"I do not." It was a severe case of the grumps, caused by the prospect of fifty years of solitude ahead of her.

"She's grumpy like she has a hangover."

"How do you know what a hangover feels like?" Kate basked in Laura's silence. It was a small victory, but better than nothing. Five seconds of silence was a treasure to hold.

After her and Lance's initial snarling fit, the rest of the evening had degenerated into an uncomfortable silence. In fact, Jake had been the only Jolly Roger at the table—so much so that Kate had spent the entire dinner nursing a strong temptation to smack him right in the mouth. Now she realized that she should have. At least she'd have had one pleasant memory to cherish in the dark, lonely nights ahead.

"Where's Mom?"

"She went to get the newspaper." Laura jumped when the doorbell rang. "I'll get it."

"Check first before you open the door," Kate called. Her mother's work as a librarian included teaching street smarts to a latchkey club of grade schoolers, but sometimes Laura acted as if she hadn't heard about the dangers around.

"Your mother told me you have a new boyfriend," Granny said. "Guess she should have said *had* a new boyfriend."

Kate glanced up with a frown. "What makes you say that?"

"Looking like you do, you couldn't have had a good time."

"Just because the evening was a little strained doesn't mean I'm dumping Lance," Kate explained.

"Lance?" Her grandmother said the word as if she'd discovered a cockroach in her pickles.

Voices floated up the stairs from the front door. Great. They must have company. Just what Kate wanted in her present state of mind. "I'm going to dash back to my room," she told Granny.

"Hey, look what I found," Laura said.

Damn. She was too late. Well, maybe she could just make an excuse and slip away. Kate turned. And screamed.

"He's a real-life cowboy," Laura went on, staring at Kate. "And he's got the two neatest dogs. I said they could sit in the backyard."

Jake stood there holding his hat in one hand. "Mornin', ladies."

"Morning, yourself," Granny said. "I've always wanted to meet a cowboy. Now I can die happy."

Jake looked slightly startled. "I hope not just yet," he said.

His eyes were the most incredible shade of blue, so deep and refreshing that Kate found herself longing to dive into them, to let the peace found there bring her alive again. The desire came on so strong and sudden that Kate found it hard to breathe. But when her breath came back, so did her annoyance at herself. She didn't like this man. How could she find anything attractive about him?

She frowned at Laura. "I thought you were told not to let strangers in," she said. Or wild beasts into the yard.

"He's okay," Laura replied. "Everyone knows good guys wear white hats."

Kate closed her eyes. Had she been that naive at ten? Was she any better now?

"I was worried about you," Jake said. "So I thought I'd drop by and see how you were."

Kate's eyes opened and delivered what she hoped was a dismissing glare. "I'm fine," she snapped.

"Sure you are," Granny said. "That's just what we were saying, wasn't it? That you looked just like a fine rose opening to the dawn."

"If I said I'm fine, I'm fine." Her grandmother's brow wrinkled in surprise and concern, causing Kate's resolve to crumple in guilt. "I'm sorry," she said. "But I am fine."

A moment of heavy silence hung over them all, during which her grandmother stared intently first at her, then at Jake. Finally the old woman turned back to Kate. "I presume this isn't Lance. Why don't you introduce us to your friend, dear?"

Because he's not my friend, Kate wanted to say. Because he's just some pushy old cowboy who strayed off his range. And the quicker we send him back the happier we'll all be, including him.

"This is Jake MacNeill," Kate said. "Mr. MacNeill, this is my grandmother, Mrs. Anna Mallory. And this is my—" damn, this was harder with each passing day "—my sister, Laura."

"Pleasure, ma'am." Jake bowed slightly at her grandmother and then turned toward Laura. "And a pleasure meeting you, little lady."

"I ain't a lady," Laura replied. "I'm a woman."

"Sorry," Jake replied with a grin. "My mistake."

"Would you like some coffee, Mr. MacNeill?" Granny Nan asked.

"If it wouldn't be too much trouble, ma'am."

"Not at all," she replied. "Sit down, please."

Jake sat down at the table, and Laura sat on his right. Kate considered running to her room, but then decided it would look like she was afraid of him. He was annoying, pesty and amazingly thick-headed, but she was not afraid of him, his blue eyes or his sweet-sounding laugh. She sat down across from him.

"Your voice says you come from out west," Granny said as she put a cup of coffee in front of him. "I don't suppose your initials really are JT?"

Jake looked momentarily stunned. Lost, Kate guessed, just as she was.

"No, ma'am," he finally said. "JM. Jake MacNeill."

Laura leaned forward. "It still could be the ring, Granny," she said. "Maybe he's got his name wrong."

Kate felt like she'd fallen from one nightmare into another. "What are you two talking about?"

Granny Nan grunted, then sat down herself. "Just some old nonsense," she said and looked across at Jake. "So what brings you to Chicago?"

"Kate did," Laura replied.

"I never met him before in my life," Kate protested. "I don't even know where he lives."

"I live in Montana," Jake replied. "I told you, remember?"

"You didn't tell me until yesterday," Kate snapped.

Tension filled the air until Laura's stage whisper broke in. "It's the legend, Kate. Granny Nan told me about it right after we found the ring."

"What legend?" Kate asked.

"Just a silly old story," Granny said. "Now tell us how you met, if you didn't know each other before yesterday."

While Kate longed to crawl under the table, Jake proceeded to tell them the whole sordid story. He was kind enough to spend most of his time dwelling on his carelessness and little on her spastic reaction or her and Lance's argument at the restaurant.

"My goodness," her grandmother said, after it was all over. "That certainly was exciting."

"Did your dogs get hurt?" Laura asked. "Were they scared?"

"No," Jake assured her. "They're fine."

"We never had any dogs." Laura's voice were so full of wistfulness and pathos that Kate felt like gagging. "Never in my whole life."

"Would you like to pet mine?" he asked.

"Yeah!" She sprang about ten feet out of her chair. "Can I? Can I?"

"Are they hungry?" Kate asked. She wanted Laura left in one piece.

"No," Jake replied kindly, as if he'd thought she was offering them breakfast. "But I'm sure they'd like a drink of water."

Laura went to the cabinet and took out the pot they used for cooking pasta. Kate wanted to tell her to choose something they didn't use for food, but the kid was gone before the words came out. Since Jake went with her, Kate let them go.

The room seemed awfully quiet once they were gone. Empty might be a better description. Kate picked up the cups. She actually preferred the peace and quiet, though she loved having Laura around. They didn't need some big, hulking cowboy to fill up the kitchen, to disrupt their lives.

She put the cups on the counter. She'd just clean up a little bit, then take a little nap. That was all that was wrong.

She was tired. It had been an emotionally draining day yesterday.

"So what kept you awake last night—thoughts of Jake or Lance?" Granny asked as Kate rinsed the cups.

"Neither." Kate dumped the cups into the dish drainer. It was a good thing they were plastic. "What's this legend Laura was talking about?"

Granny got to her feet slowly. "It's nothing much. Just some old story from your grandfather's side of the family. Rubbing that ring you and Laura found is supposed to bring some old love back from the west."

"Some old love?" Kate echoed. "I don't have an old love."

"Oh, not yours," Granny said with a smile. "Caitlin Mallory's. Your great-great-grandmother's."

This was becoming stranger and stranger. "Why would my rubbing a ring bring back an old love of my great-great-grandmother's?"

"I never said it would. Laura's the one who believes all this." Granny slid her chair up to the table and walked toward the living room door before she stopped and turned. "But don't you wonder why he's here a few days after you found the ring?"

The only thing Kate wondered about was what had happened to her family's sanity.

Chapter Three

Kate refilled the warming pan of stuffed flounder, then checked to make sure that the salads were still plentiful before she slipped back into the kitchen. She and her crew were catering a luncheon at a medical center on the west side of the city. The center, her first client when she'd started her business four years ago, was one of the few jobs that she personally supervised these days. But somehow concentrating seemed harder than it should.

She kept hearing a certain voice with slow, soft tones. And seeing those incredibly blue eyes.

One of Kate's assistants stopped loading up a dessert tray. "So did you go out with that Lance fellow?" Willie asked.

Kate was glad of the conversation. "Yes, I did, though it was pretty hectic."

"Didn't think hectic and that boy could exist in the same world."

All right, so Willie hadn't cared for Lance when he'd hired them to cater a brunch. Willie had her own ideas of what made a man, and Kate had hers. Getting into a dis-

:ussion on the subject was a no-win proposition for both of
hem.

"We had an accident on our way to the restaurant."

"I hope no one was hurt."

"No," Kate replied. "Lance's car got a few dents. We
weren't even bruised, just shook up a little. We were lucky."

"What happened?"

"We were going north on Lake Shore Drive when this
:razy cowboy—"

"A cowboy!" Willie's face lit up with excitement. "You
mean a real live cowboy?"

Kate looked away. Willie couldn't know anything about
he family legend, so it must be that cowboys were high on
ıer list of approved male occupations.

"Oh, he was real, all right," Kate said. "He had a big
white hat and was driving some kind of monster pickup
ruck."

"And he was tall, right?" Willie added. "With broad
shoulders, rugged kind of face and a crooked smile."

Kate shook her head, not certain whether Willie was into
he paranormal or whether Jake was just a standard-issue
:owboy. Somehow the idea of Jake being common and ordinary seemed impossible. "Yeah, and his nose was
:rooked, too."

"Mmm, mmm." Willie closed her eyes and hugged her-
:elf around her shoulders. "How come you have all the
uck?"

"Luck?" Kate shook her head again. Willie was a great
worker, but her romantic fantasies tended to dip toward the
:ar edge. "I was in an accident, remember?"

"What happened?" Willie made a face. "Lance screw
ıp?"

"No, he didn't. This stupid cowboy broadsided us. He
must have thought he was driving a team of horses."

Willie shrugged. "I'm sure the man had a good reason."

"Oh, sure." Kate snorted. "He just dropped by to say
ıowdy."

"Well, it is hard to meet people in the big city."

Kate had to fight to keep from gagging. "Willie, please go check the rolls."

"Did you guys go out after?"

For just the shortest of moments, Kate wondered if Jake had found Willie and had a little chat with her. It sounded ridiculous, but he had found Kate's home. "How did you know?" she demanded.

"Cowboys are always friendly."

"Go check the rolls."

"Friendlier than some folks I know," Willie grumbled as she ambled back out to the dining room.

Kate took a deep breath, held it for a few eons, then slowly let it out. She wished she could share Willie's enthusiasm and fervor. The woman took nothing seriously, certainly not her love life. Willie would act on the flash of attraction that Kate felt toward Jake. She wouldn't care that he was totally unsuitable. That he wouldn't follow any rules in a relationship. Or that he was a flash in the pan, here today and gone tomorrow.

Willie believed that her Prince Charming was out there someplace, and she wasn't going to stop looking until she found him. Kate wasn't sure such a species existed. And wasn't sure finding him was worth the risk of hurt.

"You're such a beauty, Princess. The boys will all be fighting over you." Kate could hear her father's voice as if that junior-high dance was just yesterday. She could still feel the love and pride in his hug, and the budding belief in her own soul that Prince Charming was out there for her. She shook her head to rid herself of the past and doubled her pace preparing the dessert trays.

Miguel had been her Prince Charming for a short time. With his passion and zest for excitement, he'd dared her to reach for the impossible. It had been hard, though—too hard with her father back in Chicago dying of cancer. Weekends were spent running home; weekdays she'd struggled to find meaning in useless classroom lessons. Weeknights in Miguel's arms were her only release, but they were too short. Dawn always came, and with it reality. Then reality came to stay, when Miguel left. Reality and the cold, hard fact that love was not enough to hold back the pain.

So she'd settled into a routine over the years, and it had been a mistake to try to change it. Just because Laura had made a remark that seemed negative, and just because it had echoed a dissatisfaction that had been emerging from the shadows of Kate's own heart, there had been no reason to rush into dating. Lance had seemed nice, seemed safe, but...

But nothing. Lance hadn't been the problem.

"It was that damn cowboy," she muttered under her breath.

"Kate?"

Startled, she jumped back, then began to breathe again. It was just Lance. She squashed the rush of guilt that followed the word *just*.

"Hi, Lance." She hoped her voice held a bit more enthusiasm than she felt. It was just that seeing him reminded her of the disaster on the weekend.

"Can I talk to you?" he asked.

Kate looked at her watch. It was an automatic action, but maybe more reflective of her feelings than anything. Guilt washed over her, forcing a smile to her lips. She was being unfair. Jake hadn't been Lance's fault any more than he'd been hers.

And whose fault was it that Jake, not Lance, had haunted her dreams the last few nights?

"Of course, Lance." She glanced around before nodding toward a small table in the corner. "Why don't we go sit over there?"

"I don't need to take up too much of your time."

"Oh, don't be silly." She looped an arm through his and led him to the table. "My staff has everything under control. I'm glad to see you."

He smiled shyly at her. Lance really was a nice guy. Saturday had been an aberration.

"I'm sorry about the other night," he said, once they were seated.

"Don't be silly," Kate replied.

"I was sitting there, waiting and waiting. And drinking too much. Then when you walked in with him..."

"Hey." Kate patted his hand. He looked so miserable she couldn't help herself. "Things just got out of control."

"I never should have let that man take you to the hospital."

"That was my fault," she said. "I should have just told him I was fine."

Lance took her hands in his, holding them firmly. "I want to make things up to you, Kate. I owe you a dinner."

For some reason, panic filled her heart. She felt like a bird trapped in a cage and wanted to pull her hands free. What had gotten into her lately? She hadn't been herself for the past week or so. It was like she had stumbled into the middle of someone else's life.

Or that some deep, hidden door in her heart had been newly opened.

It was all nonsense, Kate scolded herself. She was the same person she'd always been. She doubled the sweetness in her smile. "Don't be silly, Lance. You don't owe me anything."

"Please, Kate." He smiled.

He had a nice smile. It didn't exactly light up a room, but people had light bulbs for that. He had a nice, quiet, relaxing kind of smile. No threats, no wild, unrestrained passions. A safe smile.

"How about tonight?" he asked.

She was tired already, and by evening she'd be exhausted. But was it a physical weariness or a mental one? Maybe a good night out was just what she needed.

"Sure," she replied. "Tonight would be fine."

"Pick you up at seven?"

"Great."

Lance stood up and kissed her lightly on the cheek, then he hurried away, stopping at the kitchen doorway to give her a quick wave. Kate waved back, though a weariness threatened to settle over her.

Miguel with his passion and zest for life would laugh Lance out of the room. He'd tell her Lance had no soul, no spirit, and that his pretty little manners meant nothing. Her father would make a face and tell her she could do better. That he didn't trust somebody so smooth and polished. They'd both like Jake.

Damn it. Kate got to her feet, her fists clenched at her sides, though there was no one to fight. She didn't care what her father or Miguel would say. She didn't want someone better or different or more passionate. She wanted Lance. He was perfect for her. He wouldn't expect more than she was willing to give.

Going out tonight was a great idea. She'd have a good time. A hell of a time. And there'd be no cowboy getting in the way.

Kate's positive attitude took a slight hit with each passing hour. By the time she got home to change, her feet were dragging. There was no one around to welcome her as she climbed the stairs, and for a moment she wished they had a pet. A puppy, though, not some giant bear pretending to be a dog.

As she fumbled with her keys, the accumulated weight of the day pushed down even heavier on her shoulders. It would be so nice to fill the tub and lie in the comforting warmth until her tensions drained away.

But she didn't have time for that today. She barely had time for a quick shower before Lance came for her. Then they were going to have a nice meal and an evening filled with fun, fun, fun. Well, maybe not rip-roaring fun. Hell, it was a regular workday, not a weekend. But it would be comforting, relaxing. And that would be fun. At least some people thought so.

The door opened, allowing her to stumble directly into their living room. No one was there. Mom was probably helping Laura with her homework in the kitchen.

"Woof."

Woof? Was Laura being silly and playing some kind of game? Kate put her keys back in her purse and looked up toward the kitchen . . .

And screamed.

"You're gonna give these guys a complex."

Jake strolled in, following his dogs from the kitchen. He was wearing a light blue shirt, tight jeans and an altogether too easy smile. Kate just looked at him, feeling like she'd been hit by lightning. Like an earthquake was rattling through. Like her heart had stopped. Every time she saw him, it seemed that her reactions were stronger. More unsettling.

She had to stop seeing him.

"Every time you see them, you go 'eek'," Jake said.

She pulled her eyes away. "I don't go 'eek'."

"They have names, you know."

"I don't go 'eek'," she repeated.

"The black-and-white one is Nickolai and the brown one is Boris."

"I do not go 'eek'," she growled through clenched teeth.

"Did you have a hard day, dear?" her mother asked from the doorway. "I have some iced tea in the fridge. Would you like some?"

"What are those animals doing in here?" Kate asked.

"Why, they're visiting, honey."

Visiting? People visited. They stopped by and chatted about their families, the weather, how another year was winding down and the Cubs were in the cellar again. How could you carry on a conversation with beings whose vocabulary was limited to sounds like *grrr, woof,* and *arf?*

"Where's Laura?" Kate asked.

"I'm in here," Laura's voice sang out from the kitchen.

With a quick sideways glance at the dogs and not even a flicker toward Jake, Kate hurried into the kitchen, keeping her mother between herself and everyone else. It wasn't that she was afraid or wanted to sacrifice her mother, but these visitors weren't visiting her.

"Whatcha doing?" Kate asked.

"Science homework." Laura kept her head down as she concentrated on finishing a sentence. "I gotta do a paper on environmental stuff."

"Oh." Kate went to Laura and looked over her shoulder. There was a pad of paper before her and a number of photocopied magazine articles scattered about. "Need any help?"

"Nah, Jake's helping me."

Jake? One look at his complexion told her that he spent a majority of his time outdoors, but that hardly qualified him as an expert in environmental science. She would have to help Laura find other resources.

"We really shouldn't bother Mr. MacNeill," Kate said. "Why don't I plan on—"

"Jake's got a master's degree in environmental science," Laura said.

"Staying home tonight and—"

"She said time was a little tight," Jake murmured.

"We can go to the library right after dinner."

"Yes," her mother said. "Seems someone was waiting until the last minute." Her mother gently knocked Laura on her noggin. "Again."

Suddenly Kate's mind caught up with the conversation. Jake had a master's in environmental science.

"I don't have to go to the library." Laura indicated the pile of articles before her. "Jake had his secretary fax stuff to your office downstairs from some magazines he had at home."

"I'll be glad to pay for the paper," Jake said.

Dumbly, in slow motion, Kate took an article off the top of the pile.

"That's one that Jake wrote," Laura said.

Kate looked at the blurb about the author. Jake Mac-Neill, owner and operator of the J-Bar-T Ranch in Montana...master's degree in environmental science from the University of California at Berkeley...a renowned specialist on restoring chemically abused land to its natural state. She threw the article down.

"I have to take a shower."

She hurried out of the kitchen, barely noticing the dogs as she rushed past them to her bedroom. She got the door slammed shut behind her before the tears spilled over.

Damn it. She angrily wiped at her eyes. Painfully, over the years, Kate had come to see how much she'd given up by relinquishing her role as Laura's mother. A big sister, no matter how much older, had one kind of relationship and a mother had another. And no matter what the big sister did, she could never secure the respect that a mother could. Now it seemed she couldn't even secure the respect that came with a big white hat. Laura didn't need her for anything.

She'd learn environmental science from Jake, sewing from Mom and all about boys from her friends. Teen magazines would show her how to fix her hair and wear makeup. She'd go to high school, then college, and a few years later, she wouldn't even remember who Kate was.

One tear slowly made its way down her cheek, then another as a flicker caught her eye. Kate looked at the clock on her nightstand. Oh, hell. In fifteen minutes Lance would be here. Not only was a bubble bath out of the question, but she was going to have to rush through her shower.

She was glad she was going out tonight now. She really needed it. Needed to feel like a person in her own right, needed to have someone act as if she were special. The hell with Mr. Jake MacNeill and all his degrees and magazine articles and acres of wide-open land. The hell with his broad shoulders and blue eyes. He could stay here with his dogs and charm everyone, for all she cared; she was going to have some real fun. Some serious fun.

By the time her clock read 6:57, Kate was dressed, made up and ready to roll. From the minute she stepped outside to the minute she returned home, it was going to be one single, uninterrupted stretch of joy and laughter. She wasn't going to think about Laura or Jake or anything.

Disdaining a last-minute mirror check, Kate picked up her purse, set her shoulders back and strode out into the living room. Her mother was sitting alone watching television.

"Where's everybody?" Kate asked.

"Laura's still working on her report."

"Is Jake gone?"

"In a manner of speaking."

"Good." One less potential annoyance. Kate strode to the door then stopped and half turned. "Don't wait up for me, Mother. I have a feeling I might be late."

"Be careful, dear."

Her heels beat purposefully down the steps. Be careful. Jeepers. Have one little accident and you go back to being treated like some high schooler. Kate slammed the door firmly behind her and stepped out onto the sidewalk.

"You going out?" Jake asked.

Kate swallowed the rush of longing that desperately tried to surface. For a moment, she wished she were going out with Jake. That she'd spend the evening looking into his eyes and sharing his laugh. That she'd end the evening in his arms.

And leave her heart out for the trampling.

That shut the door on those wishes mighty fast. What she really wished was that Cowboy Jake and his two buddies would head on down the road home. They were starting to become intrusive.

"Good evening," she replied. "Though I can't see that it's any of your business, yes, I am going out. With Lance," she added, just for good measure.

He frowned at her. "I thought you weren't going to see him anymore."

"Where did you get that idea?" No, she was not going to invite Jake to share his opinions with her. "You know, if you fed your little pets once in a while, maybe they wouldn't eye every living thing quite so desperately."

"That's not hunger," Jake pointed out. "That's amazement. They can't believe that you'd go out with Slick again, either."

This guy really had butting in down to an art form. She thought of a million clever responses, but said none of them, as Lance was pulling up at that point. Kate moved toward the car, but as quick as she was, Jake was even quicker. He opened the door for her, and smiled ever so sweetly as she waited while his beasts checked out the interior.

Once she sat down, Jake reached in and fastened her seat belt. His touch was so gentle, so comforting. Her eyes misted over and she had to look away.

"Y'all be careful now," Jake said. "It's a rough world out there."

Didn't she know it? That was the very reason she had to avoid him. She looked over and found Lance staring in apparent amazement as Jake shut the door. After a moment of stunned silence, he pulled away from the curb.

"What was he doing there?" he demanded. The tone of his voice, the set of his brows said he wasn't too thrilled by the fact.

"Visiting my mother." She didn't want to talk about him, didn't want to think about him and hoped the tone of her voice said that.

"I didn't know he knew her."

Kate shrugged, not about to get into any sort of explanation. Her unsettling reaction to Jake was still percolating. Or was it anger at herself for not telling him off? Either way, she was rid of him for the time being and planned to keep it that way.

"I'm so glad you talked me into going out tonight," she said in her best party voice. "I'm in the mood to have fun."

"He just always seems to be around," Lance went on as if she hadn't spoken.

Kate leaned back and closed her eyes. Damn that cowboy. It didn't matter whether he was around or not, he was still able to spoil things for her.

If he wasn't nagging at Lance's thoughts, he was injecting dissatisfaction into hers. And she didn't want to be dissatisfied.

She was a wader, preferring safe, shallow water where she could keep her feet on the bottom. But since Jake had sprung into her life, she kept looking off toward the deep water, its mystery and promise of excitement calling to her more loudly. Her silly heart wanted to respond.

Kate shook her head, ridding her mind of any lingering thoughts of Jake MacNeill. This was going to be an evening of fun, fun, fun. Doubly so since there wouldn't be some pushy cowboy butting in every two seconds.

She pitied anyone who tried to derail the fun-train express.

* * *

"I can't believe she went out with him again," Jake said as he put the lid back on the garbage can. He stopped and frowned through the darkness at the dogs. "And I can't believe that it bugs me as much as it does. What the hell is with me lately?"

Neither of the dogs looked inclined to answer him, so he walked over to the water spigot at the side of the building to rinse off the shovel. Having to follow your dogs up and down the alley with a shovel at midnight was a good reason not to stay long in this damn place.

He leaned the shovel against the wall, walked around to the front of the building and sat down on the stoop. The dogs lay down on the sidewalk in front of him.

"This isn't like me," he said. Boris grunted at him, probably making some remark about Jake's intelligence, or lack thereof. "I mean, I came here because I thought I heard some voice telling me to, but why am I staying? Waiting for the voice to tell me to go home? And why do I care what Kate does?"

Boris was tired of solving Jake's problems and rolled onto his side.

"She's just so damn vulnerable," Jake went on. "I look into her eyes and I see a heart ready to break. And the damnedest thing is, I keep thinking I can somehow stop it from happening. Me. Can you beat that? Hell, if they were holding auditions for Superman, they wouldn't let me into the building."

Jake just stared out at the street. There was little activity here, but the sounds of the city wafted in over the trees and buildings. The constant hum of traffic, like the buzz of cicada bugs back home, was coming from expressways to the north and east of them. Interspersed throughout that constant were individual flashes of sound: the wail of a siren, the screech of brakes, shouts and screams. It seemed about as different from home as could be.

Maybe that was why he was acting so strangely—he needed the wide-open sky and the sounds of nature around him.

The dogs moaned, and Jake looked down to see them looking up at the sky.

"There's stars up there." Both turned to look at him. "Honest, guys. The same ones that shine in Montana. It's just that with all the city lights on they don't look as bright as they do back home."

Boris grunted and both dogs relaxed, putting their heads down on their front paws stretched out before them. Jake was fairly sure they didn't exactly disbelieve him, but he wouldn't bet the ranch that they entirely believed him, either. Poor guys. They didn't belong here in the big city. He snorted to himself. Hellsfire and brimstone. It wasn't as if he did, either.

"We're gonna be heading on back to the open range soon, guys." Neither dog acknowledged his words. "Real soon."

Maybe it was just the name, he decided. Maybe Kate was reminding him of Katie Delaney, the girl he'd sat behind in fifth grade. He'd had a major chip on his shoulder most of the time those days, and to prove it, no real friends, but she'd let him be in her group for their Indian-village project. He'd promptly fallen in love for the first, only and ever time in his life. He hadn't liked the feeling of vulnerability, the power that someone else had over his happiness. She'd moved to Los Angeles in seventh grade, and he'd been relieved.

Love sure wasn't something to be craved. It didn't exist where it should, left you open to attack when it was there and could be trusted about as much as a rattlesnake with a hangover. For proof, he just had to look at his mother and the bastard whose name was on Jake's birth certificate under Father.

"*Grrr.*"

Menace hung in the air like the potential of snow in the Rockies in October. A few moments later a car turned into their court—Lance bringing Kate home. Jake left the stoop and walked down to the edge of the sidewalk, followed by his big, fuzzy companions.

The car slowed to a stop in front of them, and Jake bent to open the door. He felt he owed a debt of some kind to the

Kates of the world and he would repay it. He would make this Kate see she could do better.

"Hello, Kate," he said. "Evening, Lance."

Lance nodded shortly. Kate did not reply at all. She was too busy trying to disentangle herself from her seat belt. There was something so fragile about her.

He stooped down. "Let me help you, ma'am."

"No." She shoved his hand away. "You're not my father."

The words came out with more than a hint of a slur and her movements were a tad uncoordinated. Looked as if Kate had taken herself a hearty sip of the old fermented grape fountain.

"Don't go fussing now," he said. "It's just stuck a little bit."

"You're not my father," she repeated, hitting at his hand.

"I'm not anybody's father." He gently pushed her hands aside, wanting to hold onto them instead. "Now let me unlatch this dang thing."

She quit protesting, and Jake quickly unfastened the seat belt. Then he helped Kate out of the car. Once on the sidewalk, she slumped against his chest, forcing Jake to put an arm around her trim little waist. She was so darn small, he could have swept her up into his arms and carried her off. A quiet cough from Lance reminded Jake where he was.

Jake looked over his shoulder. "I'll put the filly in the barn," he told him. "Save you the trouble of parking your vehicle."

"There's a spot in the next block," he said. "I was just saving Kate the trouble of walking." He leaned over to look at her out the open passenger door. "If you want to wait there, I'll—"

Kate waved at him like one would wave a bug away. "Oh, go home, Lance," she said. "All I have to do is walk up a few steps and I'm home."

"Kate," Lance protested. "I'll just—"

The lady had given the order, and Jake would enforce it. He slammed the door on Lance's words and waved him away. The car stayed there a moment, testimony to Lance's indecision, then sped away. Maybe if Jake couldn't get Kate to drop Lance, he could get Lance to drop Kate. The result would be the same, and maybe he could stop feeling so darned responsible for her. Maybe then he could go home.

The idea was not as alluring as it should have been.

He turned his attention to Kate. "Come on, Kate."

Jake put her left arm over his shoulders and tightened his right around her waist. She seemed to just fit against him, and the feeling that he'd been waiting for the chance to do this again came over him.

Again? Crazy notion.

Back to the task at hand. "One foot in front of the other."

"I'm not going in no barn."

Her body hung limp and heavy on his. Her legs kept breaking every which way, just like a newborn colt. The little lady must have had some Jim Beam chasers with her wine. Either that or she was too thin to hold more than a drop or two. Why had Lance let her drink so much? Had he had other plans for the evening that didn't include coming back here so early?

"Might help if we got those shoes off," Jake said.

"Hah!" Kate pushed herself away from him.

He wanted her back in his arms. "What's with the 'hah'?"

She stood there swaying, reminding Jake of an elk making a last stand against a pack of wolves. Lordy, but her eyes seemed to pierce him right through. They cut him up into tiny pieces so that he didn't seem able to do anything but try to take care of her.

"First it's the shoes," Kate went on. "Then what else would it help to get off?"

Boris and Nickolai sat back on their haunches and watched them both, heads swiveling from one to the other, looking for all the world like spectators at a tennis match.

"For cryin' out—" Jake clamped his mouth shut and glared up at the almost-starless sky. How could she lump him and Slick in the same basket? "I'm just trying to get you into the house."

"And then what?" she asked, her face twisting.

"Then I won't care anymore." Only a major lie, but then this woman would exasperate an Indian holy man. "You'll be safe in your beddy-bye and I can go to sleep in mine."

Suddenly her lower lip started quivering. Lord, he hoped she wouldn't cry. He'd seen that happen already and knew Noah didn't have enough arks lying around.

"My father was nice. Very, very nice."

The quivering moved up to her cheeks. She *was* going to cry. He knew how to put out a fire, but how did you put out a flood?

"He was the nicest man in the whole world."

The quivering degenerated into sniffles. Damn. Next she'd be wailing. Why was she hurting all the time?

"Here, let's get you inside."

"Leave me alone." She pushed against him. It was obvious she wanted to stalk off into her home on her own. Unfortunately, her heel caught in the sidewalk. "Oh," she cried. She didn't go down entirely, but she appeared to have twisted her ankle.

That was it. Cowboy rule number one: take control. Jake picked her up. "Let me take you downstairs," he said, "check the ankle, then get you upstairs."

"Damn shoes," she muttered as she kicked them off. They fell with dull thuds on the sidewalk.

He'd tried to tell her to get rid of the shoes, but no, Little Miss Know-It-All wouldn't listen to no cowboy. "Guys," Jake called over his shoulder.

The dogs each picked up a shoe in his mouth, and they made a little parade into the basement apartment of the Mallory's building. Kate didn't weigh more than a moth, so it was easy to balance her against the wall while he opened the door. He let the dogs in first, then turned on the light and followed with Kate.

Boris and Nickolai each spit out the shoe they carried and made their way into the kitchen.

"They don't like me."

"I think it's just the shoes they didn't like."

Her voice was still a tad teary, but the flood warnings seemed to have been taken down. Even so, Jake didn't say anything more as he followed the dogs into the kitchen. Besides, by the time he'd turned on the light, both were drinking from a little tub of water he'd put out for them. And when those two set their tongues to lapping, a body couldn't hear anything below a 7.5 on the Richter scale.

He set Kate on a chair at the kitchen table and went down on one knee to check her ankle. She didn't kick him or make any smart-mouth comments. Looked like the little filly was tiring. He let his fingers probe her neatly shaped little ankle. All tight without any swelling.

An answering tightness seemed to be growing in his belly and he stood up. She had on some kind of perfume that seemed to dance around him, making the air kind of shimmery. Making him feel kind of light-headed. Maybe a little distancing was in order.

"Everything looks shipshape," he said. "Don't look to be swelling at all."

"I'm sorry I got all blubbery out there," she said.

"Sometime you eat the bear," Jake said with a shrug. "And sometimes the bear eats you."

Kate rubbed a hand over her eyes. She looked so tired. Poor kid. Well, "kid" was wrong. There was sure nothing childlike about the woman sitting in his kitchen. If he was smart, he would send her on upstairs right pronto. Trouble was, he'd never been accused of being too smart.

"Want some coffee?"

"I guess it wouldn't hurt."

Jake went over to the cabinet. "Instant's all I got."

She just nodded, so he set to fixing the coffee. How was it a beautiful woman like this was sitting in his temporary kitchen without a boyfriend? Never mind Lance. She had to be in her late twenties; she should have been snatched up years ago.

And what was he going to do about it?

He waited, letting his mind go blank. No feeling or voices or whatever started to talk to him again; all he got was a lot of silence. Great. Bring him all this way, then they lose his number. Proof it was all nonsense, anyway.

"So how was the date?" Jake asked as he put two mugs of water into the microwave.

She just shrugged. "Okay." Nickolai came toward her, and she held her hand out for him to sniff.

"Lance is a jerk," Jake felt bound to point out.

"He's very nice. Very considerate."

Yeah, right. "He didn't see you to your door."

"You didn't let him." Boris came over also, his tail wagging.

"A real man doesn't let someone else take care of his woman."

"Not all men are as pushy as you," she said. "Lance thinks very highly of me. He even remembered seeing an article about me in *Chicago Business Woman* last year. Most men wouldn't have remembered that."

"What'd the article say?"

"Oh, just talked about my business. Made it sound a bit more prosperous than it actually is, but it was nicely done."

Jake got the jar of instant coffee out of the cabinet. "So he thinks you're rich, is that it?"

"No, that isn't it," Kate snapped. Both dogs jumped back slightly.

The buzzer on the microwave saved the day. Jake hadn't wanted to make Kate mad; he'd just wanted her to see how wrong Lance was for her. Trouble was, Jake was no good at this delicate, personal-type stuff. It was like a ballet dance—something foreign to him and not suited to a big bull of a cowboy.

And Jake wasn't sure he wanted to learn the steps. He took the mugs out of the microwave and stirred the coffee crystals into the water.

By the time he turned around, Kate had both her hands occupied petting the dogs. She was smiling and a lot of the irritation had slipped from her eyes. Critters had that kind of effect on people.

"They're so big they scare you at first." She worked both hands, vigorously scratching the tops of their heads. "But when you get to know them, you see how gentle they are."

"Depends on the folks and the situation," Jake said.

Kate continued smiling and scratching behind the ears of one dog and then the other. She seemed to be having fun, but Jake knew how merciless the buggers were. Your hands could fall off and they would demand that you continue.

"Go lay down, guys." They turned to glare at him. "I mean it."

He'd put a little more vinegar in his voice, but they hadn't moved. "Come on, let's go into the living room." He indicated for Kate to go before him. "I hate to see them pouting."

She laughed softly. It was a pretty sound, like a cardinal singing in the pine on a snowbound winter's day.

There wasn't anything to sit on in the living room except the loveseat that doubled as his bed. When he'd accepted Mrs. Mallory's offer to stay, he'd told her that he didn't need any furniture. He had his bedroll in the truck. But she'd insisted on moving down some odds and ends from their apartment. It seemed to please her, so Jake didn't object. And he had to admit it was more comfortable than a sleeping bag on a bare floor.

When Kate sat down, Jake handed her one of the cups and sat next to her. She seemed so tiny, so defenseless. It ate at him, making him feel somehow at fault for the loneliness leading her into dangerous relationships. She sipped at the coffee, then shivered.

There was no decision, no real thought. He just held his cup in one hand and put the other around her shoulders. It was just a neighborly thing to do when a body was chilled, as Kate obviously was. He pulled her closer to him and let his eyes close. That tightening need inside him was growing.

"I'm sorry," Kate said.

Jake opened his eyes. "Sorry? About what?" Surely she couldn't be reading his mind.

"For all the little scenes I keep causing."

"Oh, they're nothing," Jake assured her. "It wasn't like you were hitting me with a bottle or throwing up on my shoes."

Kate blinked at him over the edge of her cup. "You must have some very interesting friends," she said.

Those eyes tore at him, promised him glimpses of paradise, but he just smiled. "More coffee?"

She shook her head, and he was just as glad. Didn't want more himself. He put his cup on the floor, then put hers down also. But his arm stayed around her shoulder. Never could tell when a body's chills would come back.

Suddenly, though, she turned, and he found her eyes looking up at him. Wide and wonderful and blue as a summer sky, they were asking him to kiss her. Being an obliging gentleman, he touched his lips to hers.

They were soft and warm and ever so sweet to taste. He wanted to pull her closer and crush those lips beneath his, but they also felt as fragile as a butterfly's wings. He kept his touch quiet, undemanding.

Suddenly Kate jumped, her eyes open wide like a calf that had just been branded. "What are you doing in this apartment?"

"Sitting down. With you."

"Where did the furniture come from?"

Her voice had inched a tad closer to a screech. Jake had an uneasy feeling that the situation was rapidly moving toward being out of hand, so he stood up. Bo always said it was best for a man to be on his feet when trouble was moving in his direction.

"Your mother had me move it down here."

"My mother?"

"I told her I didn't need it, but she insisted."

Big, black thunderheads moved into Kate's eyes. If Jake were a sailor, he'd be tying things down about now, but he was a cowboy up against a little woman. And cowboy rule number two said the cowboy in this situation couldn't move anything but his mouth.

"Your mother's one fine lady," Jake said.

Kate's mouth stayed closed. A tad too tightly, but closed was better than open.

"Real nice," he continued.

She didn't reply.

"I bet she's as nice as your father was."

Kate let out a yowl like a female cougar telling a wolf to stay away from her kittens. Then she turned on her heels and stomped out of the apartment.

The noise had awakened the dogs, and they both reached the living room just as Kate slammed the door behind her. The three of them stared at her shoes lying on the floor, letting the sound of the still-vibrating door quiver in their ears.

"Well, boys," Jake said. "I guess the little filly doesn't like her shoes, either."

Chapter Four

Kate straddled him, strong thighs about his waist, strong arms holding his to the ground. Jake couldn't move.

Her eyes burned with the passion of a thousand endless nights, screaming for him to take her. His own loins cried out as she brought her mouth down toward his. Jake was pulled into her angelic beauty, drawn like iron filings to a magnet. She moved nearer. He raised his head, parted his own lips, and . . .

And quickly drew away. Her breath would curl a steel girder.

Jake's eyes flew open and focused on two fuzzy faces looking into his. Big fuzzy heads, attached to even bigger fuzzy bodies. They were lying on either side of him, holding down the sheet and pinning him against the bed. Nickolai's head was resting on Jake's chest, close to his face. The dog was panting and putting out fumes noxious enough to gag a goat.

"What are you bums doing up on the bed?" Jake hollered.

Two pairs of placid brown eyes blinked at him.

"Damn it. Get off. Get the hell off before I rip your guts out and feed them to the coyotes."

Nickolai looked ready to leave, but Boris just grunted. Damn him. He was always the argumentative one.

"I mean it. Get off!" He jerked at the sheet. "They got coyotes in the big city. You yahoos better believe it."

There was a lot of foul muttering, but both dogs eventually got off and ambled to the kitchen, from which a crescendo of lap-lapping soon echoed.

Jake sat up on the edge of the bed and put his head in his hands. His body was stretched tighter than a two-dollar drum and drenched in sweat. He couldn't remember the last time he'd awakened in this state. Sometime back in his early junior high days.

Shaking his head, he got up and went into the bathroom. The situation at hand was totally unbelievable. Here he was—single, in his thirties and having the erotic dreams of a kid entering puberty. Maybe Bo was right. Maybe he had been working too hard.

He splashed cold water on his face, refusing to look at his reflection in the mirror. That dream hadn't meant anything. He pulled the towel off the rack. Kate just happened to be the last attractive woman he'd seen. Jake was a garden-variety bachelor who liked women, but not any woman in particular. It was just a matter of right time and right place.

"What it really is is time to get back to Big Sky Country."

Suddenly there was a frantic scratching at the back door. "All right. All right," he snapped at the dogs. "Stop that noise."

Damn racket was enough to raise the dead, or at least everyone in the building. And he certainly could think of better ways to awaken Kate.

The tantalizing images that came with that thought danced in his heart, and he fled into the bedroom. What was the matter with him? He wasn't looking for involvement. Hell, Kate wasn't even his type. She was a city girl, through and through. Probably didn't even know the difference between a steer and a heifer.

"Let me get dressed and we'll do alley patrol," he called to the dogs.

He threw on some jeans and a shirt, then pulled his boots on over his bare feet. The city was making him loco, he told himself. That had to be it. Too many people all piled on top of one another.

The dogs raced into the backyard when he opened the door. It was early, not quite 6:00 a.m. yet. Maybe a good walk in the quiet morning air would snap him back to normal. He snatched up the shovel as he went to the gate.

"Cities are crazy places," he told Boris and Nickolai. "Ain't enough air for everything and everybody, so you breathe in other people's craziness."

The dogs ignored his wisdom, but that was all right. He was the one troubled and needing to clear his mind. He took a deep breath, shivering slightly. A jacket would have been nice in the cool of the early fall morning.

Fall, which for Chicago apparently meant pleasant days and cool nights interspersed with gosh-awful hot days, was sneaking into the area. Things weren't all that subtle back home. Autumn would be marching through the high-meadow country like Sherman through Georgia. The poplars would be turning yellow and the grass would be browning. Bears would be stuffing themselves for their big sleep, and the deer and elk would be heading for the low country.

The dogs reached the end of the alley and sat down to wait for him. A stomach-flipping sight greeted him there: traffic crawling along head-to-butt like a string of army ants. Jake sighed. There was just no denying it. His heart surely did pine for the big skies of home. Why in the hell had he ever come to Chicago?

Maybe he was just lonely. The advantage of living in a small town was that everyone knew everybody. But that had its flip side. Since folks had known you back when you were a little tad, everybody had pretty much made up their minds about who you were a long time ago. He was old George Tyler's bastard son.

Yep, everybody said that. Everybody, that is, except old George Tyler himself. Oh, he'd put his name on the birth certificate, making sure Jake wasn't a no name. And when Jake got older, he'd found out that old George sent money their way and even paid for a lot of Jake's education. But he never shook his hand, gave him hell or talked about the birds and the bees. Not one word. In short, old George totally ignored Jake.

His mother said that was why Jake had trouble entering into relationships. She said George's lack of acknowledgment left him with a low self-esteem.

That was a ton of bull puckey. He didn't have any trouble with his self-esteem. Jake was fine and he knew it. What it did leave him with was an appreciation for honesty. Total, absolute honesty. That was why he'd had his last name changed to MacNeill, his mother's maiden name. His father hadn't been a father; Jake had wanted no part of him.

A whine drew his attention back to Boris and Nickolai sitting before him. They were staring across the street, longing in their eyes.

"Ain't nothing to the other side but more of the same," he said.

Poor guys. They were just itching to stretch their muscles. And not just some teeny little walk. Heck. They weren't babies anymore, and they certainly weren't city dogs. Them two were range dogs. They wanted to pant and feel their muscles ache.

"Hey," he said. "What was that park Laura told us about? She said it was up north along the lake."

They continued staring across the street. Didn't look as if they were going to help him any. Probably figured they'd carried him enough and it was time for Jake to step out on his own.

"Lincoln Park. Yeah, that was it."

That got no reaction out of the two dogs. Lord, but they were a tough audience. You figured a little tail wag wouldn't pull all that much juice out of them.

"Come on," Jake said. "Let's get ourselves a good run."

He turned and hurried back to the apartment with his dogs bouncing perkily ahead of him. Damn. He should have thought of it sooner. The three of them were all used to hard work. They just didn't feel right unless they stressed their bodies. Unless they were in tune with nature.

The park wasn't all that hard to find, sitting along the lake as it did. Jake left the truck at the south end; then he and the dogs headed north along a jogging path. The path wove through trees and open space, past a zoo with smells that teased at the dogs and then all sorts of formal gardens. Nature it was, but made to conform to man's regulations. Still, it was better than the alleys.

When they came to the northern edge of the park, they crossed a pedestrian bridge over a busy road and jogged along the beach. Seeing as how it was getting close to eight o'clock on a workday, there weren't all that many people out. Finally, he and his buddies slowed down to a walk, then found a nice spot on the sand and stretched out to relax.

Lying here, staring out at the sky over the water, Jake felt almost at home. The sky was as immense and the breeze carried the smells of nature, not of the city. He felt the tensions flowing from his body, and for the first time since he'd gotten to town, he felt in control. There were no weird voices coming from out of the blue, no faces haunting him from a past he couldn't remember.

As for the dream, well, that was just the normal male re-action to an attractive woman. And Kate was attractive. Dreaming about her didn't mean anything more than that. No growing feelings, no lurking emotions.

He'd come to Chicago for a little vacation and that's what he'd had. A few days in the hustle and bustle of the city so that he'd appreciate home all the more. There had been no voices, no feelings from out of the blue. Just overwork and a load of tension that had triggered some need to relax for a while. Now that he had, it was time to start thinking about leaving.

Clearing his head also cleared his focus, and he discovered he was hungry. He glanced at his companions. They were always ready for food, but no restaurant would readily accept them.

"You guys interested in some doughnuts?" he asked.

Nickolai sat up.

"I thought so."

He should do something nice for the Mallorys before he went back. Maybe take them all out to dinner. After all, he wasn't even getting charged for the digs.

"Why don't we go for a walk, guys?" he said as he got to his feet. "Let's see if we can find us some doughnuts and a place to take the Mallorys to dinner."

They went back across the pedestrian bridge and through the park. Once they approached the western edge, the city came back with a vengeance. Old three-story buildings were cheek by jowl against high rises going up twenty stories or more. Jake shook his head. Even prairie dogs wouldn't live this close to each other.

"You guys stay up here with me on the sidewalk," Jake said. "I don't want you denting up somebody's car." Most of the vehicles appeared to be tiny, little toys that could zip in and out off traffic and park on a postage stamp.

They walked down a block or two, finding that most other pedestrians left a pretty wide path for them. That gave them a chance to check out the stores and restaurants.

"Lordy," Jake said. "There must be restaurants lined up from here to the Canadian border. Looks like room enough for half the world to eat along this street."

The problem was that there were too many nice restaurants. A person could starve half to death before making a choice. Maybe that was what made life so simple back in Cold Spring. You had a choice of eating at home, Randy's Roadhouse or The Blue Loon. Two flips of a coin and you had your decision. Life was sure simple back on the prairie.

"Let's pack it in, guys. Looking at all these fine eating establishments is making my head spin. Maybe we'd just better let the ladies pick."

Jake stopped at a bakery and bought a half-dozen doughnuts, then looked around. The side street looked interesting, lined with old-fashioned town houses. And there were even trees. The dogs would like that.

"Let's meander this way while we eat." Fortunately, there was a traffic light at the corner, so crossing the street was only semi-life-threatening. "We keep going in this direction and we should hit the park."

The dogs were more interested in the trees than his words. After they'd each had a doughnut, they ambled along while Jake gawked at the homes. They were obviously expensive and were probably beautiful inside, but he couldn't imagine living all squashed up like that against your neighbor.

A door opened a few buildings ahead of them, and a couple spilled out onto the stoop, their limbs entwined around each other. Jake and his dogs stared. After a moment, Boris snorted.

"Yeah, I know," Jake murmured. "Folks saw you and a lady friend wrapped around each other like that, they'd throw a bucket of cold water on the two of you."

The couple parted, and Jake could distinguish them as individuals. The woman was a long, lean blonde apparently wearing nothing but a robe, standing barefoot on the cement stoop. The man, dressed in a fancy business suit, was . . .

Holy moley. The man was Lance.

Lance bowed slightly as he stepped back from the woman, saying something that Jake couldn't quite catch.

The woman laughed. It had a hard tone to it, along the lines of a medieval tax collector who'd just heard his client on the rack say he had no more money. She reached for Lance and pulled him back toward her.

Jake wasn't wanting to spy on them, but Boris and Nick-olai had been moving up the block, checking out the trees, and Jake had to stay close to them. He leaned against a tree a house away from Lance and his lady.

Not that they noticed. They were locked in a clinch and kissing like they were drilling for oil. They finally pulled apart, and Jake looked away, watching the dogs, who were now sniffing at the tires of a BMW parked at the curb.

"Tonight," the woman said, her voice carrying easily in the relative quiet of the neighborhood. "Ten o'clock. And no excuses."

"Absolutely. Where else would I be?"

Lance then ambled down the street as the woman sauntered back into her house. Jake stared at Lance's back until he climbed into his car.

Should he ignore what he saw or should he tell Kate?

Poor Kate.

Forgetting what he'd seen might be the best thing. Just stay out of the whole affair. After all, he was a stranger in town and he really didn't know what kind of relationship Kate and Lance had.

Plus he'd heard that folks tended to be real private in the big city. A fella could get himself hurt putting his nose in other people's business.

"But that ain't the way I'm made," he told the dogs with a deep sigh. Honesty was the best policy. Always was, no matter what.

Damn. Why had he come down this street at just this moment? There were lots of streets around here. Why had he picked this one? For that matter, why had he suddenly thought about coming to the park? Where had these ideas come from?

The air seemed to hold a sudden chill. This wasn't the first time weird notions had come to him from out of the blue.

He picked up his pace, trying to escape his thoughts. This whole thing was just too weird for words—at least the ones his mama had taught him to use.

"Kate?"

"Yes, Sue?" Kate and Sue Catalado, her secretary, office manager and Jill-of-all-trades, had worked together long enough so that Kate didn't even have to look up. "What can I do for you?"

"There's the neatest hunk out front," Sue said. "And he wants to see you."

"What for?" Kate didn't need a description to know who was out there. She tried to feel annoyed, but her heart skipped a beat in pure anticipation.

"I don't know what he wants." Sue gestured with her arms. "But what difference does it make? He's long and lean and has the neatest drawl you ever did hear. And when you look in his eyes, you just know he'll be savage and gentle, all at the same time."

"So if I don't talk to him, you will," Kate said with a sigh. "And waste the whole afternoon keeping him company."

"Kate, if you don't talk to him, I'll take him home and keep him chained in the basement the rest of his natural life."

"Send him in."

Kate couldn't imagine what Jake would want, and she wasn't all that anxious to find out, either. After that little performance last night, she was ready to crawl into a hole. The only problem was, she wasn't sure just what part of last night had affected her most—the argument over Lance, the kiss or finding out her mother had let him stay in the apartment.

It wasn't Lance, she was pretty sure of that. And as for Jake staying in the apartment, she really could avoid him without too much trouble if she wanted. So that only left...

"Hi."

Kate's eyes went up, filling themselves full of a long, lean cowboy. A surprisingly gentle-looking cowboy. Her cheeks took on heat of their own and her heart was caught by strange yearnings to feel the strength of his embrace again. It was definitely the kiss. And she was definitely not going to let herself be interested.

"I'm rather busy, Mr. MacNeill. Will this take long?"

"It shouldn't," he replied as he sat down. He rubbed the back of his neck, seeming a bit uncomfortable. "Does Lance have relatives in town?"

"I don't know." Kate was confused, and then suspicious. Why was he always attacking Lance? Couldn't he pick on someone his own size? "What kind of a question is that?"

"Well..." He spent a moment rubbing his chin. "I took the dogs on a run in Lincoln Park this morning."

"And?"

"And then we took us a walk along Clark Street and the neighborhood around it. We were..." He paused. "We were just looking around."

"Mr. MacNeill, I really don't have—"

"We saw Lance."

She should have known it would be something silly. "So?"

"He was coming out a town house," Jake replied. "A woman was with him."

Kate laughed. "Lance has many clients and some of them are women. After all, men aren't the only ones with funds to invest."

"Their business looked to be on the personal side."

"He is a *personal* financial adviser," Kate replied.

The answers came quick and snappy off her tongue, but a nagging worry filled Kate's stomach. Like the time when she was twelve and broke her wrist during softball season. She hadn't been all that crazy about the game, but she wasn't sure she was ready to give up trying to be the star.

"Well," Jake said. "Lance and the lady were being *very* personal. I mean, they were one step away from being as personal as personal can be."

Kate knew what he was saying, understood the implications of it, but couldn't say a word. That worry was growing into fear, making her hands icy cold and her heart afraid. She hadn't cared about Lance, not really, but he was her safety net. He was someone she could hide behind until her heart stopped dancing around.

"And the lady must have appreciated it." Jake took a moment to clear his throat. "She was ordering him to come back tonight for a return engagement."

She closed her eyes for just a moment. She didn't want to hear these things, didn't need to hear them. What right did Jake have to destroy her little illusions? Anger filled her, and she flicked her eyes open. "Don't you have anything better to do than go around spying on people?"

"I—I thought you should know." His eyes turned soft and sorry, as if he wanted to make it all better.

God help her, something in her wanted to let him. She rose to her feet slowly, holding her heart in tight rein. "I'll decide what I want to know and don't want to know. Now please leave."

"Kate, I'm sorry," he said as he stood up.

"Get out." She took a deep breath. Her hands were shaking, or was it her heart?

"You deserve better."

"You deserve a kick in the head."

He turned quickly on his heel and left, leaving a heavy silence behind. She was angry now, really angry. Angry with Lance. Angry with Jake. But most of all she was angry with herself.

Lance was the only thing standing between her and long, lonely nights. He was the only thing between her and forgetting how to laugh. He was the only thing between her and the wild way her heart raced when Jake came into the room.

God help her, she needed Lance to cling to so that her thoughts and dreams wouldn't turn to Jake.

It took Kate awhile but eventually she sorted out her thoughts. It was possible that Jake was wrong, that he'd misinterpreted Lance's actions or that it wasn't even Lance that he had seen. And even if it was Lance, and Jake's interpretation was accurate, there still was no reason for her to be upset. It wasn't as if she and Lance had any sort of agreement. They'd had a few casual dates, that was all.

What it really came down to was her feelings, and to be honest, she didn't have all that many for Lance. She felt like a teen out on her first date, flattered by the thought that someone found her desirable, but not sure she returned the feelings. It had just been so long since she'd ventured out of her emotional hidey-hole that she had chosen somebody safe, someone who wouldn't be a threat to her peace of mind. So her heart hadn't been involved, just her pride.

As for her strange reaction to Jake, she had no logical explanation. Only relief that he wouldn't be staying around here much longer.

All in all, she found enough common sense to put her emotions in check and have a nice dinner with her mother and Laura. Then she even felt brave enough to go sit on the front step and enjoy the autumn evening, though risking another encounter with Jake. The next one, and all future ones, however, would be calm. No outbursts, no explosions.

She'd been out there only a few minutes when she heard Jake's door.

"Evenin'," he said as he and his beasts ambled over. "We were just about to patrol your alley."

His voice was soft in tone, but had a roughness to it that spoke of the mountains and forests and rushing rivers. It was the unyielding rock, the gentleness of pine needles beneath her feet and the life and energy of the west wind. She could feel them all in the dim light of the ending day and wanted to rush forward, to lose herself in the powerful sensations. Instead, she forced herself to listen for Miguel's laughter in the air and then to feel again the agony of being lost. It helped, and so did taking a deep breath. The city streets came back.

"That's very kind of you to take care of our alley for us," Kate said. "Me and my neighbors appreciate it."

The streetlights came on, and Kate risked a glance Jake's way. His craggy features were softened in the half-light, but the ruggedness came through. She could almost smell the sagebrush or whatever it was that grew out there. He seemed so strong, so sure of himself. She envied that. It seemed there was no one or nothing he feared, while she feared anything that took her off her little path, that wasn't written on her list of things to do. One of the dogs butted her with his head, demanding to be petted.

"Hey," Jake snapped. "That ain't polite. Now go over there by the sidewalk and lie down."

The dogs gave him a dirty look, but they obeyed.

"I don't mind, really."

"They'll push you to distraction, if you let them."

Kate smiled as she watched the dogs, after much grumbling, lie down on the sidewalk. They didn't look happy with Jake. Wrapping her arms around her knees, she leaned forward. "What kind of things does a cowboy do? I would guess you don't fight Indians and chase after cattle rustlers anymore."

"A lot of us are part Indian," Jake replied. "So, no, we don't fight with them anymore."

"I'm sorry. That was a dumb question."

"But we still have problems with cattle rustlers."

"Goodness."

"Wherever there's something of value, there's somebody who'll steal it."

"I guess."

"I'm a volunteer deputy," he said. "And I'm also a volunteer fire fighter. Most of our fires are on the range or in the forests."

"Isn't that dangerous?"

He shrugged. "Life's dangerous."

But there were ways to minimize the danger. They were quiet for a long moment, savoring the varied sounds of the city. At least she was. Or was she savoring the moment spent with this man at her side?

She sat perfectly still, almost not breathing. What was wrong with being attracted to Jake? Why was she trying to run from it? He was a good-looking man; she was a lonely young woman. She had no reason to be afraid of spending time with him.

She was so afraid of loving and losing again that she'd lost touch with her common sense. You can't lose what you don't have, and she would never have Jake. He was here for a few days, then he'd be gone. There wasn't nearly enough time for her heart to get involved.

She let her gaze slide over his hands. It was obvious he worked hard with them and out-of-doors. The backs were tanned, crisscrossed with some old scars. The palms, what she could see of them, were tough. He would do what had to be done and not turn away out of weakness or fear or uncertainty. Lance's hands had been soft, manicured.

"Some folks just don't understand about honesty."

"What?" She felt confused, her mind scrambling to return to some semblance of intelligence.

"Honesty," Jake said. "If you ain't got that, you ain't got nothing."

"I guess."

"Ain't no 'guess' to it." His words were definitive and sure. "It's the foundation for trust," he said softly. "So getting a con man-liar like Lance out of your life ain't losing nothing. It's more like a plus. A big plus."

Honesty was the foundation, and trust sat on it like a building. And without a good foundation, no building could last. She had trusted Miguel, but that hadn't lasted. Not exactly through his fault—he hadn't chosen to die—but neither had he chosen the safe path, to be there for her and their child. Trust might be a start, but was it enough? Was anything enough to guarantee something would last?

Suddenly Kate felt Jake's arm slip around her and pull her ever so gently toward him. He bent his head slightly and kissed her on the forehead. There was such sweetness in his touch, such promise of sunshine ahead. She wanted to close her eyes and bask in his strength, but he moved away.

"Now that you got that bum out of your life, your days are going to come up all sunshine."

She started at his words. Had he read her mind?

But he just got to his feet, the dogs jumping to theirs at the same time. "Well, off to alley patrol."

"See you," she murmured and watched as they disappeared around the side of the house. Then she let out her breath slowly.

The spot on her forehead felt as if it were melting her soul. He almost made her believe she could risk a real relationship, that she was strong enough to weather the storms that might come with it. Being with him seemed so right, so comfortable. As if she'd been waiting for the chance.

She could almost believe that she knew his innermost thoughts, that she could read his dreams in his eyes and that she shared them. It was as if they were two halves of a puzzle that could now be put together.

Summer, winter. Day, night. Man, woman.

Hold on there! she thought. What had happened to "Jake wouldn't be here long enough to get attached to"? Kate got to her feet and walked briskly down the block, as if her thoughts could easily be left behind. Her father's smile drifted into her mind.

He had thought she could do anything, be anything, and she had believed him. He'd said she was pretty, so she'd felt like the belle of the ball. He'd said she was smart, so she'd signed up for the toughest classes in high school. He'd said she was strong, so she'd made her own decisions instead of following the crowd. But then he'd died and with him went the rock that had plugged the leak in her self-confidence. Without him, the doubts flooded through and she didn't feel pretty or smart or strong.

Lance had almost made her feel pretty with his compliments and sweet lines. But then Jake had come along, making her feel somehow both fragile and powerful, dainty and capable. He didn't do it with words, but with a look in his eyes, as if he knew and respected all that she was behind her fears.

She didn't understand her reaction to Jake or the pull he seemed to have over her heart. She hardly knew him, just knew that he would be gone soon.

So which did she want—someone who was just reciting lines that could be said to anyone or someone who challenged her to come alive? Maybe it would be better if Jake left soon, before her heart started answering that question.

A car pulled up to the curb next to her, and Kate drew back slightly. She wasn't really afraid; she was only a few houses down from hers and she wasn't alone out here. Then she saw it was Lance, and her caution turned into annoyance.

"Hello, there," he said as he got out of his car. "I brought you that stock prospectus we talked about."

Maybe Jake was right and Lance thought she was rich, though how anybody could get that idea was beyond her.

But why else would he keep coming back? Jake had been downright rude to him, and she hadn't been much better.

Lance came around the car to join her, reaching over to plant a kiss on her cheek before she could move away. She was left with the urge to wipe it off. Not quite the same as Jake's kiss.

"I told you any number of times that I didn't have any money to invest," she pointed out.

He pushed the brochures into her hands. "Everybody has disposable income, and with a business as prosperous as yours—"

"Come a lot of expenses and an uncertain future," she finished for him. Was there really strength down in her soul? She took a deep breath, willing it to come forward. "Look, Lance, I don't think we're really hitting it off. Let's just both move on."

He frowned at her, obviously not about to bow out quietly. "That cowboy's not going to stay around forever, you know," he said.

"This has nothing to do with Jake," Kate said. "It's me. I'm looking for something else."

"I'll help you look."

His smile was so smooth, so polished. Covered with oil was what it was. And suddenly she knew that whatever her reaction to Jake, she was through with Lance. If protection was what she needed, she'd have to find some other method than hiding behind him.

It was difficult, but Kate kept a smile on her face. "Goodbye, Lance," she said softly.

He looked down at the ground. Kate could hear the gears of his mind grinding.

"I'll give you a call later," he said.

"Goodbye, Lance."

"Why don't I leave these brochures with you?"

"Lance."

The name came out through clenched teeth. Even he saw that she was getting irritated. Giving her a quick nod, he hurried to his car. The only indication of how upset he was came from the pealing of his tires as he drove off.

For just a split second, Kate felt that desolation wash over her, then she reminded herself she was strong. Still, the night seemed suddenly so quiet, so empty.

"Kate, are you all right?"

Jake was there at her side and she moved into his arms. No thought, no decision, no checking her things-to-do list. She just went where she wanted most to be. She felt his lips brush the top of her head and some of the hurt went away.

"You're lucky to be rid of that louse," he said.

"Yeah, I know," she murmured into his chest. His arms held her so close, so safely. She never wanted to move away from him.

"It's good that you know." He shook her shoulders gently, as if he were trying to waken a week-old puppy. "Now show it."

Shaking her head, Kate leaned back and wiped at her eyes with the back of her hand. She forced a smile to her lips, but he didn't seemed fooled by it.

Maybe because it was such a poor attempt, he leaned closer and covered her lips with his. His kiss was so tender, so comforting. It held all the healing of a mother wiping teary eyes, a father bandaging a scraped knee. But it held something else, too. Buried deep under all the healing and soothing and comforting was a hint of fire.

He moved away slowly to gaze down at her. She saw that his eyes looked dark and almost troubled, as if he had read messages on her lips that he didn't understand. Didn't he feel her awakening passions? Hadn't he felt that little tremor when her heart had come alive again?

But then he leaned closer again. This time the kiss left healing behind and moved into another territory. His mouth breathed hunger and magic into hers. His lips spoke of needing and wonder and springtime.

Kate moved closer to him, letting his arms tighten their hold. For the moment she felt pretty and smart and strong, and able to have anything she wanted.

And right now that was Jake MacNeill. She wanted to explore with him this garden that had sprung to life all around them.

They pulled apart finally, needing to breathe, and she lay against his chest. His heart was racing, and she smiled inside, knowing it was due to her.

"I'm okay," she said finally. "Lance was a jerk. I just held on to him because it was nice to have a boyfriend."

"I think you could do better," he said.

Could I? she wanted to ask, but instead pushed herself away so she could read the answer in his eyes. God, they were so deep and so blue. She felt like jumping into their depths.

"He knew how to make a woman feel wanted," she went on. "It was all the little things he did. The flowers, the candy. The way he pulled your chair out for you and helped you on with your coat. He did the whole nine yards." A crooked grin seized her lips. "Nine yards of what, I'm not sure, but that's what people say."

Jake nodded. "I've heard they do."

They settled into a comfortable silence, fitting together as if they were designed for each other. His arm was around her shoulders and Kate was leaning naturally into him as they walked slowly back toward the house. The dogs trailed along behind them.

"What'd you come to Chicago for?" Kate asked.

Jake seemed to hesitate, as if the question was harder than it appeared. "Oh, you know how it is. You get the urge to do a little visiting."

"You have friends in town?"

"Depends." His grin warmed something deep inside her. "Are we buddies?"

She just stared at him for a long moment. "Do you do this often?" she asked. "Come to new towns and run people off the road?"

"Ain't never done it before. And ain't likely to do it again. I'm not exactly known for my spontaneity."

Kate stopped walking to look up at him. "You mean the first time you ever got the urge to roam, you ended up in Chicago and saved me from the evil clutches of Lance?"

Jake had kept his arm around her shoulders, so got her walking again. "You would have seen through him on your own," he said, "just might have taken you a bit longer. But you're too smart a lady to let yourself settle for anything but the best."

Was she? They walked along in silence, but somehow, with each step, she seemed to feel stronger and freer. It was crazy, but in losing Lance she also seemed to lose her fear of being hurt. She didn't have to hide behind little weasels, she was strong enough to stand on her own and look for a man who was strong enough to stand by her.

She didn't know who he was or where she would find him, but she did know who she had to thank for her newfound strength—the cowboy at her side.

Chapter Five

"Hi, Bosslady."

"Hi, Willie. How's it going?" Kate was dropping by the last of three luncheons Kate's Katering was serving this noon. She rarely ran them herself anymore. She had a good staff and more than enough to do planning future jobs, but she still liked to check in on them and make sure everything was running smoothly.

"Everything's fine," Willie said, her grin wider than the Cheshire cat's in *Alice's Adventures in Wonderland*. "And how are you?"

"Okay," Kate replied with sudden caution. A smile that big on Willie meant somebody was going to have a hard time. And Kate was the only target in sight.

"Understand you're going to be learning some cowboy songs."

"Cowboy songs?" Kate shook her head. "Why do I want to learn cowboy songs?"

"Because cowboys like that kind of thing," Willie replied. "That's why they call 'em cowboy songs."

Sue must have been shooting off her mouth again. Lord, that woman hadn't even coordinated this job. She must have a network that would make the CIA envious.

"I take it things are wrapping up here." Kate peeked through the partially open door and pretended to listen to the luncheon speaker now expounding on the virtues of time-sharing condos.

"Yep," Willie asked. "We just have to clean up and we'll be through."

"Any problems?" Kate asked.

"Nothing we couldn't handle." Willie spent a few moments lighting up the hallway with her grin. "Sue said he's a nice guy."

"Sue thinks anything in pants is nice."

Willie snorted. "She didn't care all that much for Lance."

Kate clenched her teeth for the tiniest of moments. No one had cared for Lance, but it didn't matter anymore. Like the twenty-four hour flu, that man was gone.

"Cowboys are more fun, anyway," Willie said.

Kate was going to abstain from that vote. "I have to stop by the office, then Granny Nan asked me to drop in," she said. "I'd better get going."

"'Home On The Range' and 'Red River Valley' are good ones."

Willie's words stopped her. " 'Home On The—' "

"Cowboy songs." Willie's grin was about to break her face in half. "Remember?"

"I'll try to," Kate replied. Fortunately, an elevator arrived just then so she was able to escape.

This whole thing was becoming a bit much. People acted as if she had never dated, as if she was withering away on the vine and needed rescuing. By a man, of course.

She supposed she could save them all lots of trouble by explaining her new philosophy of life, but that would probably just start a whole other round of interference. And would they believe she was now going to enjoy life as it came along and not worry about its transitory nature? She thought not.

When Kate got to the office, Sue had a list of calls that needed returning, some letters that needing signing and a menu that needed revising. All minor emergencies.

"Oh, and Granny Nan called again," Sue said. "Wanted me to remind you to stop by. And you're supposed to bring the cowboy." Sue's grin was clear proof that this new tidbit would be all through her network in a matter of moments. Unless it had already been broadcast.

"What for?" Kate asked.

Sue just shrugged and pretended to get back to her work. Kate debated whether or not to press for an answer, but decided to give it a pass. Sue might not know what Granny was up to. Even if she did, it might be best not to show too much interest. Kate stopped by the kitchen and got the box of pastries she'd packed up for Granny, then went in search of Jake.

She found him hanging pictures for her mother up in their apartment. His shoulders seemed broader than she remembered, his eyes seemed bluer and his smile wider. And her heart seemed to beat a bit faster.

"Isn't it nice to have a man around?" her mother said.

They both looked at her as if expecting a negative reply. It was nice, she knew, nicer even when it was someone as easygoing as Jake. She just smiled. "It sure is." She turned to Jake. "I'm running over to see Granny Nan and she invited you, too. Are you free?"

Her mother took the hammer from Jake's hands. "Of course he is." She took Jake by the arm, as if herding him out. "Go on. Granny loves company."

"Is this some sort of command performance?" Jake asked as they went down the stairs.

Kate was conscious of his arm brushing hers on the suddenly narrow stairs. Instead of being afraid, she let herself enjoy the warm sensations. "Whatever Granny wants, Granny gets."

He stopped at the foot of the stairs to open the door for her. "And what about what Kate wants? Does she get it?"

His voice was light and teasing; it wasn't a serious question. But Kate rolled it about in her mind. "Kate doesn't know what Kate wants," she admitted slowly. "It's not as easy as I thought it was years ago."

"Hit the winning home run, ace that math test and change the world." He closed the door and followed her down the outside steps. "Never managed the first two, but I'm still working on the third."

She'd wanted silly things like a date for the prom and that hand-knit sweater with the roses on it, then not to be hurt again. She'd settled for a thriving business.

"But is that enough?" she wondered aloud, first about herself, then Jake. "Isn't there more you want from life than a healthy ranch?"

"That sounds like a pretty good accomplishment to me." He nodded toward his truck. "Want me to drive?"

After they got in, she directed him to Halstead Street. "What about your personal life? Don't you want a family?"

"I think healthy land's a better legacy."

But somehow an emptier one. She let the discussion drop, though. She didn't have any better goals for her life, so who was she to give lectures on personal relationships? Maybe she could point out how empty one's life was without them, but it was a new discovery and not ready for scrutiny. Instead, she talked about some of her clients until they pulled into the parking lot of the retirement home.

"St. Paul's Retirement Community," Jake read. "Somehow your grandmother didn't strike me as the retirement-home type."

"We've wanted her to live with us for years, but she likes it here. She's got lots of friends, bingo and canasta twice a week and day trips all over the area when she's in the mood. Plus she's only a short cab ride from us when she wants to visit."

"I guess there are advantages," Jake admitted.

A plan to combat loneliness seemed a real advantage. They went inside and found Gran waiting for them. The thin, white-haired old lady was frowning as she got up from a chair in the lobby.

"'Bout time you got here," she said as she led them over to the elevator. "I got something to show you."

She took them upstairs, through the halls decorated to look like a hotel, and into her apartment—a tiny three-room affair crammed full of favorite pieces of furniture, pictures and mementos. It smelled, as always, of ginger. Kate must have been ten or twelve before she realized that the scent could exist apart from Granny.

"I brought you some eclairs," Kate said.

But Granny was too excited to bother with them. She just waved her hand at the box as she led them into the living room. "I found out more about the ring."

She made them sit down, then picked up some yellowed papers on the end table. "I remember Patrick's grandmother—that was Caitlin—telling me about the ring when I was pregnant with Kate's father. How if I had a girl, the ring should go to her. But I knew there was something else, so I looked through all the boxes I have stored here. I found a letter Patrick's great-aunt wrote about it."

"And?" Kate didn't believe the ring had the powers Laura claimed it did. That was something out of a fairy tale, and Kate knew all too well that fairy tales didn't exist in real life. But still, a certain curiosity nagged at her.

Granny looked down at the papers. "Anyway, according to Maeve, it seems that Caitlin was going to marry someone else before the family lost everything in the Chicago Fire and she ended up marrying Kieran Mallory. Her real love gave her the ring before he went west, but vowed he'd come back someday."

"And did he?" Kate asked. Even Jake seemed touched by the magical story.

Granny snorted. "Not while Caitlin was alive, but she believed someday he'd keep his word. That's why she wanted the ring passed down to the oldest daughter in each generation, except that all the family ever produced was sons." Granny glanced up at her granddaughter. "You're the first Mallory daughter, so it really belongs to you now."

Kate felt her spirits sag. How sad it must have been for Caitlin, waiting for her lost love and finally finding solace only in the hope that he would come some distant day in the future.

"Must be a pretty old boy by now," Jake noted.

Granny gave him a look that would make a terrorist behave. "Maybe he is and maybe he isn't."

Kate looked up from her thoughts. *Maybe he is and maybe he isn't?* This was getting a bit too weird for her, even with her new positive outlook on things. "It's a sweet story, but no old lover is going to come knocking on our door."

"What if he already has?" Granny got a shrewd look in her eye as she glanced Jake's way.

"Whoa!" he cried, his face reflecting a mixture of horror and fear. "I never even heard of this Caitlin Mallory until just now. And I'm sure not a hundred fifty years old."

"And Kate isn't Caitlin Mallory," Granny said. "Haven't you two got any imagination?"

No, Kate wanted to answer, but didn't. The story touched her more than she would have expected. She would like to think that the sadness in Caitlin's eyes would someday be gone, that the man she'd loved all her life hadn't forgotten her. But it was impossible to think that somehow Kate and Jake were the final actors in her play. Not just impossible—terrifying. She had to dispel the very idea.

"The initials on the ring were JT, Gran," Kate told her. "And Jake's are JM."

Jake looked like someone had thrown him a life ring. "Thank you."

"Phooey!" Gran scoffed at the two of them. "Hell, how many generations were there between him and this Jacob Tyler? The name could have died out somewhere along the way."

"Yeah, but—" Kate stopped, for Jake looked like he'd swallowed a ghost. Or had become one. She felt something in the air, something she couldn't define or identify, but knew was there nonetheless. "What's wrong?"

He shook his head quickly, a grin coming back in almost full force. "Nothing. I was just thinking I wasn't the only one who came from the west recently. Maybe you really want Boris or Nickolai."

Granny had had enough of them. "Go on and get out of here, you two," she said. "But when Jacob and Caitlin start telling you what to do, don't be surprised."

"Lordy," Jake exclaimed. "Man spends a week watching stuff like this and he'd be a pervert before he got to church on Sunday."

He and the dogs were in their basement apartment watching television. Boris was asleep, but Jake and Nickolai were sitting on the floor, watching one of those talk shows that clogged the channels these days. This one was about men who fish naked or some such fool thing.

"It's bad enough to be weird, but why would a person want to tell the world about it?"

Nickolai, staring hard at the television, didn't have an answer, either.

As Jake watched the TV, his eyes glazed over. The picture became just a melange of color and the voices part of the city noise. Maybe the question he should be asking was different. Like why the hell was a grown man like himself watching this junk?

Boris rolled over and sat up. He looked around the room, then scratched behind his ear.

"Because I'd be climbing the walls if I wasn't," Jake said aloud. That little visit with Granny this afternoon had scared the hell out of him. Jacob Tyler. Voices telling you what to do. Old lovers coming back to find each other again.

"I think it's time for us to head back for the high country," Jake said. "Things are getting too tangled up here."

Neither dog responded. Nickolai appeared hooked by the show and Boris was slumped over on his side, asleep.

"See?" Jake said. "You guys used to be real active. Working dogs. Out running the range all day."

A commercial came on and Nickolai slumped over, joining Boris in dreamland.

"Now look at you. Got no more vim than a roadkill rabbit."

Boris grunted, but Nickolai, as was his way, just let that insult pass.

"We're square pegs in some extremely round holes." The show was coming to an end and the host was hyping tomorrow's presentation. Although not paying full attention, Jake thought it sounded like it would be about women who eat tree bark.

He shook his head. "We don't belong here. We were born and bred for the open range. We're safer there." Only this time he wouldn't listen to any voices that tried to speak to him. Not that there were any.

Both dogs were now snoring lightly. He glared at the sleeping, furry hulks. "I'd better get you two out of here before you forget what our life is like."

Neither bothered to reply—not a single ear twitch or tail thump. Shaking his head, Jake got up and pulled his duffel bag out of the closet. Time to quit talking and start doing.

It wasn't just the dogs that were getting soft, either. He wasn't doing any better, and it wasn't a physical sluggishness that was worrying him. It was mental. Or emotional.

He was not the type to settle down anymore than Boris was, but lately he'd been finding himself listening for a certain foot on the stairs, a certain voice in the air. Talk about irrationality. He had to get out of here before he went off the deep end.

Jacob Tyler. Jeez. He'd almost jumped out of his skin when Granny had rattled off his given name. But it was just too weird, too impossible, to think that he was here because some ancestor of his had sent him.

Nope, it was time to take back control of his life, and that meant going home. If he left now, he could be halfway through Wisconsin before midnight.

Since he'd hardly brought anything with him, he was packed up and putting his worldly goods into the truck in two shakes of a lamb's tail. Or any tail, for that matter.

"Jake?" Mrs. Mallory called out.

His stomach gave a quiver, but he forced a smile to his lips and slowly turned around. "Evening, Mrs. Mallory. And how are you?"

"You're not leaving us, are you?"

"My vacation is coming to an end, ma'am."

"Why, you've hardly spent any time with us." She came down the steps and stood in front of him. "There are so many things we'd like to show you."

"That's right kind of you, ma'am. But to a country boy like me, one concrete canyon looks like another."

"Laura's going to be very disappointed. You never did take her horseback riding, you know."

Oh, damn. The kid had never been on anything except a pony at a carnival and he'd offered one day to teach her how to ride. "I'm sorry, ma'am. I . . ."

Damn. He was breaking a promise. What was there to say? Nothing, actually. Bo always said breaking a promise was as good as a lie, any day of the week.

"Why don't you come up for some coffee?" Mrs. Mallory said.

Jake's mouth opened and then closed again. He wasn't running away, wasn't afraid of seeing Kate. He was just going back home. He could spare a few minutes to chat with Mrs. Mallory. "Sure."

"And bring your little friends along," Mrs. Mallory said. "We've bought a giant rawhide bone for each of them."

He'd heard a lot of descriptions of his two dogs, but "little" had never been one of them. "Ain't no need for that, ma'am. You'll just be spoiling them."

"Nonsense. We enjoyed picking the items out. Now go get the dogs and hurry on up."

There was no discussing things with that woman. She had this soft smile and sweet voice, but holding it all up was a backbone of pure steel. Once she set her mind to something, that was the way it was going to be. But that was okay. It wasn't as if she were some invisible voice forcing him to do something. He made his way downstairs.

"Boris. Nickolai." Jake called out as he stepped into the living room, but the only response he got was two fierce glares. "Come on, you bums. We're going visiting."

They dashed up the stairs ahead of him, without so much as a by-your-leave. Mrs. Mallory was waiting for them, standing at the open door.

"Hello, sweethearts," she cooed. "Look what I have for you."

She produced two rawhide bones, one in each hand. And, by gawd, they were giant ones, something like two feet in length and about as thick as a man's fist. Both Boris and Nickolai took their gifts as gently as if they were picking baby birds out of a nest. Jake shook his head and snorted quietly.

"Aren't they just too sweet?" Mrs. Mallory said as she beamed at the dogs.

"Oh, they are, ma'am," Jake agreed. "They surely are."

She turned back to him. "Why don't you sit down, Jake? I'll put the coffee on. You can start on the brownies. I think they're still warm."

Jake sat down and took a brownie from the plate in the center of the table. "Delicious," he murmured after his first bite.

He looked around the kitchen as he chewed the brownie. The room was on the small side, as one would expect for an apartment-house kitchen, but they had gone in for heavy wooden doors on the cabinets and butcher-block counter-tops. The whole effect reminded Jake of his mother's country kitchen back home. Mrs. Mallory hummed as she moved quietly about, fixing the coffee and getting out mugs. His mother often hummed as she worked around the kitchen, too.

She'd always had cookies and milk—hot chocolate in the winter—ready for him when he'd come home from school, along with an ear ready to listen and a tongue ready to pour out advice. Food for his stomach, food for his mind and balm for his heart. Just like Mrs. Mallory most likely did for Kate and Laura. If it weren't for mothers, they'd all be savages.

Jake shoved the last of the brownie into his mouth. It was definitely time for him to head back to the high country. There was no doubt about it. He was sitting here getting all philosophical and sappy over a single dag-gone brownie. Lord only knew what would happen if Mrs. Mallory gave him a glass of milk.

"You really should stay around a little longer, Jake."
Mrs. Mallory put a steaming hot cup of coffee in front of
him.

Jake wrapped his fingers around its warmth. He couldn't
tell her that there were things going on here he didn't understand. "I got a big place that needs a lot of care."

"I'm sure you have people who are doing that for you
right now, and Laura and Kate would really miss you."

"Oh, I doubt that."

"Ask them yourself," Mrs. Mallory said. "They should
be home from the library any minute now."

Jake looked at the huge pile of delicious brownies. "Why
don't I have me another brownie?" he said. "If they're here
before I finish, then we'll talk. If not, then I hit the highway."

Mrs. Mallory looked at him for a long moment, then
reached toward the plate of brownies. "That one's for me."
She put another brownie in front of him. "This one is for
Kate."

He looked at the two chocolate squares before him.

"And this one is for Laura."

Jake smiled and picked up the first one. He'd just taken
his first bite out of Laura's brownie when both dogs jumped
to their feet and rushed toward the front door. Excited
barking was mixed with happy squeals. Laura was home.

"Hi, guys." Laura walked into the kitchen.

"Hello, dear," Mrs. Mallory said. "Where's Kate?"

"Parking the car." Laura looked from one face to the
other, each of her arms around a dog's neck. "What's going on?"

"Jake's thinking of leaving," Mrs. Mallory said.

"Aw, you can't," Laura said. "You just got here."

The two dogs left off wagging their tails for a moment and
looked over their shoulders toward the living room. The
front door opened.

"Hi, Mom." Kate came into the kitchen. Her eyes turned
softer and a little smile curved her lips. "Haven't seen you
in ages," she said to Jake.

Her mouth was so sweet and inviting. Those lips tempted him like nothing on earth, and he had to force his eyes away. "Your mother invited me for coffee and brownies."

"Jake's talking about going home," Mrs. Mallory said. "We can't let that happen. Can we?"

He couldn't risk watching Kate. This had nothing to do with ancestors and everything to do with hormones. "They're great brownies," he said.

"But he promised Laura to take her horseback riding," Mrs. Mallory went on.

"If he has to go, he has to go," Kate said. "I'm sure Laura will understand."

Her voice was as gentle as the touch of her lips had been, yet it almost broke something within him. He felt like the tall grass that grew on the prairie, bending and bowing to the whims of the wind. He had no will of his own. Kate's voice drove it from him.

"Jake wouldn't break a promise. Certainly not to a child." Mrs. Mallory turned toward him, tough eyes hiding behind soft cheeks, like a harsh summer sun behind some high clouds. "Would you?"

His eyes found Kate, the forbidden fruit. He read nothing in her eyes, not a desire for him to stay or impatience for him to leave. But there was a glow there, the flickering embers of a fire that he longed to warm himself at.

"I guess I could stay a few days longer," he said.

"You ought to do what you want," Kate said as she leaned back against a kitchen counter. She sounded pleasant, unconcerned.

Yet, there was something. In her eyes? Maybe her face? He didn't know. Just something about her that was so...so vulnerable.

Yeah. That was the word. Vulnerable. It described a tenderness rather than a weakness. It called for protection, rather than someone taking charge of her life. Maybe Lance had taken a bigger bite out of her confidence than Jake had expected.

Mrs. Mallory turned toward him. She didn't say anything, just looked at him. It wasn't too hard to read the message in her eyes.

"A few more days sounds great," he said. "We can decide when and where we want to go horseback riding."

"You and me?" Laura asked.

"Kate, too."

"Kate?"

"Me?"

"Your mother said I'd promised both you ladies."

"He did," Mrs. Mallory said, nodding her head.

"You're not afraid?" Laura asked Kate. "Are you?"

"No, I'm not."

Jake took another brownie. No use going home yet. Wait until things were a little more settled around here. Especially for Kate.

It was the gentlemanly thing to do, that was all. Old Jacob wasn't directing his actions.

"Are you sure you wanted to stay?" Kate asked him. "You didn't let Mom pressure you into it, did you?"

"Hey, I'm a big boy. I do what I want, when I want."

"Sure."

It was dark out, almost ten o'clock, but the sounds around them said the city was still alive and kicking. Trucks from the expressway not too far away. A baby crying nearby. An ambulance in the distance. Funny how she never noticed all these sounds until she was walking down the alley with Jake and his dogs. Being with him made everything come alive, everything more vivid.

"How can you sleep with all this racket?" Jake asked.

She just laughed and linked her arm with his. Could he really read her mind? Or was it just coincidence?

When she'd been eight, she and Tammy Kelleher had decided to become blood sisters. They'd hidden in Tammy's garage, screwing up their courage, then pressed pricked fingers together. It had seemed so serious, so sacred, so adult. They were going to be bound together for life, perfect friends forever. No one and nothing would come between them. Except then Kerry Michinski had moved into the neighborhood and Tammy became her best friend instead. But in those intervening months, when she and Tammy had done everything together, Tammy had never read her mind.

No one ever had until now. But Granny's story was crazy. Wasn't it?

"What'd you think about Granny this afternoon?" she had to ask. "Have any lost JT's in your family?"

"Pretty wild," he admitted, then turned to keep an eye on the dogs. "Come on, you bums. We don't want to be out here all night."

She pulled in a little closer to him. "Why not?" she teased. "It's kind of cozy, don't you think?"

He looked around them, and she knew he was seeing the overflowing garbage cans, the weeds sprouting out of odd corners and the peeling paint on the garage doors. "I think brownies have a strange effect on you."

"Silly." She waved her free hand around at the alley. "What better place for Caitlin and Jacob to appear and give us our directions."

"Why here?"

"Well…" She wrinkled her nose at him. "I suspect some of this garbage has been here since their time."

He slipped an arm around her waist, imprisoning her against his solid chest. "You are in a strange mood tonight."

"Yep."

She was, and ready to admit it. Last night she had shut the door on one part of her life and opened the door to another. No more settling for the Lances of the world; she would take her chances with the Jakes.

There'd been no rush of fever when Lance had touched her arm, no hunger for more. But when Jake touched her, the stars grew brighter in the heavens and the night a little sweeter.

Granny used to tell her that the stars were angels with lanterns. Her angel must approve of Jake.

"Not missing Lance, are you?" he asked.

"Not for a minute."

"You can do better than him."

"I suppose."

They reached the end of the alley and turned around. The dogs didn't stray as far, their sniffing and patroling done already. Jake kept his arm around her, soft and comforting. She was glad he was staying, even though it was just for a few days. He brought a peace to her soul, a sense of completion that she didn't understand, but wasn't ready to give up, either.

They reached the gate to her backyard and stopped, letting the dogs go into the yard. Jake looked down at her, his eyes dark pools in the dim light, but she could feel a question in them, a searching.

She moved into his arms, as if the searching was over. His lips came down to hers, their meeting a joyous reunion. His touch was gentle at first, making her feel as free as the clouds. She was drifting, her heart alive and singing.

Somewhere in the distance a car honked, brakes squealed and angry voices shouted. As if one, they moved closer. Together they were safe from the world's anger. Sheltered in each other's arms, they tasted the joy of heaven.

One of the dogs began to growl softly, and she pulled back. Boris was staring out at the alley.

"Boris," Jake snapped. The dog retreated slightly, and Jake closed the gate. "You ever have any days off?" he asked, his arms encircling her once more. "I have to see some open spaces before I go crazy."

Spending a day with him sounded almost too wonderful, yet she jumped at the chance. "The leaves are starting to turn. We could take a ride in the country tomorrow, if you'd like."

He pulled her closer once more. "I like," he said.

Chapter Six

A young mother guided a skipping child toward a car with one hand, while she carried a package of groceries in the other. Kate watched the simple scene with a sense of envy. It was all the little things she missed with Laura that hurt the most. Sometimes what hurt was just a nagging ache; sometimes it was a pounding agony. Today it was somewhere in the middle.

She and Jake were at a combination gas station-grocery store in a little no-name hamlet west of Chicago. They had enough gas, but Jake wanted to check in with Laura, who was dog-sitting.

Kate smiled as she watched him fidgeting at the pay phone. It was obvious that he was getting a whole lot of flack from the person at the other end. It wasn't as if Kate hadn't warned him. She leaned back, closing her eyes.

She hadn't expected Jake to be so concerned about his two companions; it showed a side of him that was both unexpected and endearing. He usually seemed so tough and independent. His little speech yesterday proved he thought he was, but his calls about his dogs showed something else. The man had a soft side; he just kept it well protected.

"Laura getting a little testy, is she?" Kate said as Jake threw himself into the truck.

A dark frown filled his face and tried to overflow out into the cab. "She said if I didn't quit bugging them, she was going to hire a couple of guys from the neighborhood."

Kate flashed him a smile. "I guess you'd better quit bugging her then."

"I'm not bugging her."

He looked so cute, like a little boy told to get out of the way so the grown-ups could take care of things, that Kate had trouble keeping laughter away from her lips.

"She said I called her three times already," Jake said, glaring out at one of the few cars that were using the little country road this Saturday morning. "I never did no such thing."

"Yeah, you did," Kate replied.

He turned his glare at her. "Whose side are you on?"

"Truth."

His eyes snapped forward again.

"Not to mention justice and the American way."

There was still no reply.

"How can you be worried about those big beasties?" Kate said. "They're not babies, you know."

"They've never been alone in a big city before," Jake murmured.

"They're not alone," Kate pointed out. "Laura and Mother are with them."

He just grunted.

"I think next time I'll ask Lance to come along," she said.

The look he gave her would have curled paint, but Kate just laughed.

"He ain't nothing but a lop-eared liar."

"Oh, he's certainly that and more," Kate replied. "But he is a fun kind of a guy."

"I'll show you fun," he growled as he put a powerful arm around her shoulders.

"Hmm. Is that a threat or a promise?"

Suddenly his eyes turned hot, a hard light dancing in them like flames in a forest fire. She felt his strength turn to steel. Her own desire grew and filled her body near to exploding.

Then, just as suddenly, Jake pulled his arm away and turned to face the road. "My stomach says it's getting on to lunchtime," he said.

Kate closed her eyes and took a deep, deep breath, hoping to cool the heat within her body.

"How about you?"

From the sound of his voice, Kate knew that he'd turned to look at her. But she didn't turn herself, didn't even open her eyes. She just nodded.

"Maybe we can ride along until we see a good place for a picnic," Jake said.

"Yeah."

Her voice felt hoarse. She was sure it sounded awful. Fortunately, Jake concentrated on getting them in motion. He turned on the ignition, put the truck in gear and eased out onto the road. Kate fought to bring her heartbeat back down to normal.

"Quite a few of the leaves are changing already," Jake said, after they'd been on the road awhile.

"Yeah," Kate replied.

"I told Laura that I found a stable where we can go riding one day next week after school."

"She'll enjoy that."

She wanted to reprimand herself for being such a marvelous conversationalist, but she was too shaken to do anything. Here she was, a big-city, sophisticated kind of woman. And for just an instant, as she'd looked into Jake's eyes, time had rolled back a few eons. It was as if she were in a cave and a big, strong, virile male had come for her. It had to be the truck. The darn thing was so big she felt as if she were in a cave.

"How about over there?"

"Huh?" Kate blinked rapidly and tried to return to the real world—a world where even modern cowboys were somewhat of an anachronism.

"Lunch." He looked at her quizzically. "You said you were hungry."

Kate spotted the quiet little picnic area off to their right. Towering oaks cast their shade over the table and onto the rippling river right next to it. "Oh, that looks great," she said.

Jake turned into the narrow gravel lane and pulled the truck up close to the river. She got out and walked over to the water's edge. It was cool and peaceful here, and so quiet. She had forgotten just how quiet it could be.

Jake came up behind her and slipped his arms around her waist, pulling her back against him. His solid strength kept the world at bay, letting nothing but the beauty of the scene reach her. She could stay that way forever, she thought, and closed her eyes. Above her, in the branches of the big old trees, birds sang. And at her feet, water laughed and played as it ran over rocks and fallen branches. Inside, her heart sang and laughed also, shouting out the joy of the moment.

"Nice here, isn't it?" Jake asked, his breath tickling the back of her neck as he spoke.

"Wonderful."

"See what you're missing by living in the city? You should move out here and hear nature instead of honking all night long."

It would be heaven to be so free. Just the mention of the idea teased at her, promising her glorious days like this to feed all the needs of her soul. "And how would we live?" she asked. "I have a business that takes care of us pretty well, but I need to be around people."

"So you start a new one."

Was it the possibility that made her weak or Jake's closeness? She pulled out of his arms and walked back to the truck for the picnic lunch she'd packed. "Kate's Katering," she said. "I can see it now. Gourmet Hay for Epicurean Bovines. Probably be a big moneymaker."

"Might be."

"Right," she called over her shoulder. "If there are farmers out here that don't know the first thing about cows."

Jake came over and pulled out the cooler, carrying it to the picnic table. Kate spread out a tablecloth, then began unloading sandwiches, fresh fruits and vegetables, cans of juice and little containers of condiments.

"Hope you're hungry," she said.

"Always."

She glanced at him. His voice was different, as if he'd suddenly gone far away from her. Had he suddenly been overcome with homesickness? His mind seemed to be far away, at least out beyond the gravel lane. Probably out in his wide open prairies.

She watched him as he picked up a sandwich and began to eat, staring out over the river. Jake was a real man of the land—honest, straightforward and no nonsense. What made a person that way? Was it the land and the environment, or was it in his genes? He had told Laura that his family had been among the early settlers in Montana, and he'd also said he was part Indian, so some of his ancestors had been there even before the settlers came. He wasn't at all like Lance.

"How come you never liked Lance?"

He slowly brought his eyes around to look into hers. They were hard, yet Kate was somehow positive they hid a gentle soul.

"Never said I didn't like the man."

"You didn't trust him," Kate said. "How come?"

"He was too smooth," Jake said. "All the rough edges had been planed off."

Kate began to work on her own sandwich. "I guess you don't like political figures then."

"Nope."

"Do you know any?"

"My father." His face had turned to stone. There wasn't a trace of gentleness left anywhere—not in his eyes, not in his mouth. "I mean, he never said he was my father, but everyone in town knew he was."

There was such raw hurt in his voice that Kate couldn't help herself. She reached over and put her hand on his. "I'm sorry."

He didn't take his hand away, but he didn't move toward her, either. "No need to be," he said. "Weren't no fault of yours."

"I'm sorry you're hurting."

"I'm not hurting," he replied. "I'm just aggravated."

Through that veneer of hardness, Kate saw a little boy, pretending so hard to be tough, to be strong and above all, not to care.

"My father's family liked to show off. Liked to tell folks how honest and straight shooting they were." He took a gulp of his juice. "What they don't like to talk about is how they cheated my mother's father out of his land."

Had he ever talked about this before? The pain was so strong, so much on the surface that it seemed as if his words were ripping open a wound that had never healed.

"Oh, what they did was legal," Jake went on. "But it wasn't right."

Maybe this was why he seemed to keep himself distant, why he said that, instead of a family, he wanted to leave the healed land as his legacy.

"The only way to judge a man is by his actions," he said. "Words were made for liars to decorate the garbage they want to feed the rest of us."

"But you got the land back, right?"

"Eventually." But his tone said all too clearly that it hadn't been without a high price.

Kate just squeezed his hand. They'd both locked away parts of themselves, trying to keep the hurt at bay, but you could never really do that. She felt a sudden longing to share her own secret with him, to tell him how she, too, had lost something that should have been hers to love and take care of. But the losing had been her own choice. She had chosen not to tell Laura she was her mother....

Kate suddenly froze, the warmth gone from the day as surely as if clouds had covered the sun. Was what she'd done the same as what Jake's father had? And would Laura hate her as much as Jake hated his father when she found out?

Kate leaned back in her chair, stretched her arms high overhead and yawned. Once that set of exercises was done she slumped forward and glared at the paperwork scattered about her desk. She'd had a hard time concentrating on business lately. Whenever she had a quiet moment, a certain cowboy rode into her thoughts. This wasn't what she'd had in mind when she'd decided to enjoy life as it came along. Maybe it was time he moseyed on home.

That thought didn't cheer her up any, so she wandered over to the window. The dogs were in the backyard, playing with a thick piece of knotted rope while Jake watched. A smile came over Kate's lips, and she felt a need to be in their sunshine. Work could definitely wait.

She slipped out of the office and down the back stairs, coming silently up behind Jake. She slid her arms around his waist.

"Hello there," she whispered into his ear.

Jake turned. "Howdy yourself," he said with a smile as he wrapped his arms around her.

Since his lips were so near and so available, she brushed them lightly with her own. Then, since that was so delightful, she went back for a second helping, a longer sampling this time. Though his lips took hers with seeming eagerness, something cooled her heart slightly and she pulled back.

"Is anything wrong?" she asked.

"No."

The answer came quickly. Maybe too quickly.

"Well, not really," he said. "I got a call from my ranch foreman. I need to get back home by Sunday night. Early Monday morning at the latest."

Back home. Kate's throat tightened up. She'd been thinking it was time, but when he said the words, it felt different. They hurt.

"A bunch of us are trying to get the state legislature to move on some environmental issues." He shrugged apologetically. "And a committee of citizens and lawmakers is taking the next couple of weeks to tour various outfits. They're gonna be at my place on Monday."

"I see," Kate said quietly.

"It wouldn't be a good idea for me not to be there."

"Of course not," she agreed.

"These kinds of events are a good chance to go one-on-one with these people. You know, get their heads screwed on right."

"Oh, sure."

He paused to look around the yard, and Kate could feel her spirits going down, down, down.

"I'm going to need to fly out," he said. "No way could I drive back in time. I don't know what to do about Boris and Nickolai, though. They've never flown before. I'm not sure how they'd take it."

She could feel him slipping away from her, like sand through her toes at the water's edge. She jumped at any way to have him stay just a touch longer.

"You're going to have to leave your truck, too," she said. "Why don't you leave Boris and Nickolai here? Laura would love to take care of them."

"They're a lot more trouble than the truck," he said, shaking his head.

"She's already taken care of them when we went out." Once Jake was gone, there would be no more dates. And even if he came back, it would only be to get his dogs and truck. Not to stay.

"Yeah, she has," Jake agreed.

"Then it's okay for us to take care of them."

"I don't know," he replied. "Let me think about it."

She wasn't really trying to hang on. She just wasn't quite ready to let go.

Jake needed time to think, and he couldn't do that surrounded by concrete. He needed wide open spaces and the wind whipping by him. He needed quiet. After making a few phone calls about planes and schedules, he packed up Boris and Nickolai and went to the lakefront.

They jogged along the water's edge for a mile or so, until his heart was pumping and his mind grew clear, then they started walking back. The breeze had a briskness that felt good, woke up his spirits as it stirred up the water. He took a deep breath of the damp air and felt strength surge through him.

"She's a nice lady," he told the dogs. "Well, nice doesn't quite cover it. She's special. She deserves better than that Lance, but I'm not the answer."

They agreed.

"I don't have the slightest idea why I came here, but it's definitely time I went back."

They agreed to that, too.

"Trouble is, I don't think you guys will like flying, but if I leave you here, I'd have to come back to get you."

They looked up at him.

"And I get the feeling it would be best not to come back."

They were growing bored.

"Not that I'm afraid to, mind you. It's just that a clean break would be best for all."

Boris gave him a look that said he saw through all of Jake's arguments.

"All right, a clean break would be best for me. I'm not into getting tied down, but there's something about Kate that really makes it hard to go."

He'd had girlfriends before, but it had just been good times and then drifting apart. No broken hearts, no hard feelings, no regrets. But he didn't think it would be that easy with Kate. He was drawn to her more strongly than he'd been drawn to any other woman. She dominated his thoughts awake or asleep, and the longer he stayed around, the harder it would be to leave.

"Thought you'd be here."

Jake looked up from his musing to find Kate in front of him. Had he conjured her up? No, the sun seemed to have suddenly come out; the air grew warmer, almost springlike.

His lips broke into a smile that his heart felt before his mind could stop it. How could he not want to come back? How did he dare even stay another day?

"What are you doing here?" he asked.

"Looking for you." She gave each of the dogs a scratch behind the ears, then fell in next to Jake as they walked. "A travel agent called. Said he could get you on the early flight tomorrow, but he needed to know right away about the cages for the dogs."

"Oh." So much for wondering how to break the news to her.

She looked out over the water. "You going to miss all this?" she asked, her voice calm and even.

"I guess." He didn't have a clue to what she was feeling.

"It remind you of your wide open spaces back home?"

"I guess." Jeez, great dialogue. He forced his mind to start working. "It's got the same big sky we have in Montana, but the range smells a lot better."

"Well, excuse us!" Kate said, coughing out a short laugh.

"We got grassy and woodsy smells. The lake is mostly dead fish."

"How about I buy you a gas mask?"

He slid his arm around her waist and they continued walking. She felt so right next to him, close to him. Yet he knew himself too well. It was like a dream being here; nothing seemed real. But sooner or later he'd wake up and remember all the reasons why being alone was better.

"How'd you find me?" he asked.

Kate just shrugged. "What around here's the closest thing to a prairie?"

"I guess I'm easy to read."

"Only in some things." She stopped to pick up a thick stick and tossed it into the water. Boris barked at it, while Nickolai just watched, his tail wagging slowly. She patted their heads as she stared out at the stick, floating away from shore.

Jake felt left out. Like the stick, he was drifting farther away. He told himself it was what he wanted, but he couldn't help the feeling.

Kate turned. "So you aren't leaving Boris and Nickolai with us, are you?" she asked.

"No, I think it's best that we all go back at once."

Kate looked away from him, the breeze gently mussing her hair. "Laura's going to be very disappointed."

"I know. We never went horseback riding." There was something so still about her, so fragile. He had to bring back her smile. "Maybe you could all come out to the ranch. During the summer, or even over Christmas."

"What about your truck?"

Was that a refusal? He called to the dogs, and they started walking again. "The travel agent gave me the name of a service that'll find a driver to bring it back."

"So everything's all settled." Her voice reminded him of a gentle fall rain. No wind, no rage, no crashing thunder, but the silent end of summer.

"Yep. Everything's settled." It was best this way; it really was.

Yet he wanted her to stop him. Or to go back with him. For one wild, impulsive moment, he wanted to throw off the coat of isolation he'd always worn and to let those dreams become reality. But he knew better.

They reached the parking lot and, it seemed, the end of the road. "Well, I'd better be getting on home," Kate said.

Perversely, though he was ready to leave, he didn't want to say goodbye. "You want to stop anywhere for a bite to eat?"

"I really have a lot to do."

There was no opening in her tone or her words. Well, this was it. The end of this little gig.

Hell, he should never have come. Bo always told him that a cowboy shouldn't ever spend time in the city. A buckaroo can't ever get the open range out of his system, but once he gets used to the soft life, he's never satisfied with what he has.

Jake got the dogs into the truck, then followed Kate's car back to her house. He wasn't one for permanent-type relationships and now he could see why. Find yourself a reasonably nice gal, and then when you parted, which cowboys always did, it left one hell of a big hole in your life.

"Maybe I could get a pizza," he told the dogs as they rounded the corner and turned onto Kate's street. "We could—"

Kate had slammed on her brakes and stopped her car in the middle of the road. She was out of the car running as if all hell had broken loose. What the—

"Holy smokes," he said.

And that was exactly what it was. Smoke. The damn stuff was pouring out the windows of Kate's office. He screeched the truck to a stop in front of the building and flew out the door.

A million fears were warring in his stomach as he raced after Kate. She couldn't go in there. He had the training, the experience that would keep him safe. He caught up with her at the doorway and pulled her back.

"Call the fire department from across the street!" he shouted. "I'll get your mother and sister out."

He didn't wait to argue with her, but rushed into the smoke-filled entryway.

Chapter Seven

"**Y**ou folks were pretty lucky."

Kate looked at the fireman, then back up at her house. Sooty streaks of smoke stained the wall around the windows, and broken glass littered the sidewalk. The air held the stench of wet ashes. Something had happened to the furnace when the basement had flooded last week, and when the heating system had switched on this afternoon, the building had filled with smoke.

"Smoke damage upstairs," the man was saying. "And water damage to the floor below. Looks awful, but it could have been worse."

"I know. No one was hurt." Kate knew they'd been lucky, but somehow she couldn't stop trembling. She would never forget that clutch of pure terror that had grabbed her heart when she'd turned into the street and seen the smoke. She'd thought she was going to lose Laura and Mom.

The fireman patted her on the shoulder. "Get a good contractor and this place'll be as good as new in a few weeks."

Kate nodded and the fireman left. Others passed her, carrying equipment back to their trucks. It was an awful-looking mess, but the man was right—there was no structural damage. Some cleaning, some new drywall, and the place would be as good as new.

The problem was that she'd never be as good as new. All these years of telling herself she was getting strong, that she could handle life's ups and downs had been just a lie. She was about as strong as a baby bird. She couldn't handle anything. Not one damn thing.

"Kate," Jake called.

She could hear his cowboy boots on the pavement, but didn't turn around. He was another loss she was about to suffer. All right, she hadn't let herself get that attached to him, but she didn't feel that she had the strength to break even those threadlike bonds.

"Your mother's got things fixed up with your neighbor across the street," Jake said.

Kate took a deep breath before she turned around. He was so close and his arms seemed so safe and secure. All she wanted was to fall into them and let him hold her tight. Her eyes got weepy and she looked away quickly.

"Yes, Mr. Mendoza," Kate said. "He has an empty flat on the second floor. And he has room in his basement for your dogs."

He slipped his arm around her shoulders and looked up at the house with her, not knowing that she was only feeling, not seeing. Why was life a series of losses?

"Yeah, that's the guy," Jake said. "They're getting some cots and stuff from some of the neighbors."

"Everybody's been really nice."

"Hey." His hold on her tightened and his lips brushed the top of her hair. "It could have been worse."

She closed her eyes and leaned against him for just a moment. "I've been told that."

"Don't you believe it?" he asked. "You look so glum."

Kate pulled her heart back into place and toughened her armor. "I'll be fine tomorrow," she said, "after a good night's sleep and a hearty breakfast. It's just..."

Her words dissolved into near tears and she had to swallow hard. So much for being tough. She tried again. "If we hadn't come home when we did..."

"Hey, but we did," Jake said, shaking her slightly. "And if we didn't, they would still have gotten out all right. They weren't in any immediate danger."

But any danger was too great. "I'll be all right," she assured him. "It was just a shock."

She didn't know whether he believed her or not, but he did leave his arm around her shoulders. She tried to let his strength seep into her.

"Will this screw up your business?" he asked.

"A little." She was grateful for the change of subject. Concern for her business ranked pretty low on her list after Mom and Laura. She could talk about it without ripping open her fears. "I'll need to make some calls. Maybe beg a few favors to get the next couple of jobs done, but we'll be back in business in a couple of days."

"You got folks that can help you get everything up and running?"

"Sure." A slight shiver raced through her, and Jake's hold tightened once more. She tried to pretend she was fine. "Sue can run the business as well as I can."

"Maybe you ought to let her."

Kate frowned up at Jake. He frowned back.

"What are you talking about?" she asked.

"You're obviously shaken," he said. "Maybe you shouldn't be rushing back to work."

"I have responsibilities," she pointed out.

"That others can handle."

He didn't seem to understand. "And just what am I supposed to do while everyone else works—loaf around Mr. Mendoza's?"

"Come to Montana and visit."

She stared at him. Maybe he'd inhaled too much smoke. "Montana?"

"Yeah, it's one of the fifty states."

"I know that," she snapped. Why was he suggesting this?

"Bring Laura and your mother along."

"Laura has school."

"It would only be for a week or two. The teachers can give her a load of homework. We can help her."

"I don't know...." Her heart was starting to smile even as logic tried to throw cold water on the idea. Going out there would only make the eventual parting more difficult. She needed to stay here and concentrate on her business. That was the safe thing to do.

"We might still be able to get seats on my flight tomorrow."

"Tomorrow?" she cried. That was too soon. "I'd have to get things set up. I couldn't just leave."

"All right, so we get you seats on a flight on Monday."

Life was speeding downhill, out of control. "Wait a minute. I haven't decided anything yet," she said. "And if we did go, wouldn't it make more sense for us to drive out in your truck? Maybe even bring the dogs."

"I didn't suggest it to help me out." He sounded annoyed.

"But it would make more sense," she argued.

"So you're coming?"

What was she to do? The fire trucks were all packed up and leaving. Kate watched them go as if wisdom might be written on their backs. She'd love to go visit Jake's ranch, but she was afraid to. Afraid of getting too close, of losing again.

"I just don't know."

"Talk to your mother about it. I'll take the dogs on an alley patrol, and we can discuss it when I get back."

Kate nodded absently, her eyes going back to the house. Their insurance agent was sending over some workers to board up the broken windows and had said he'd get them a list of contractors in the morning. She couldn't go; she had to be here to supervise not just her business but the repairs. Maybe Mom and Laura could go.

Kate felt a presence behind her and turned as her mother slipped a jacket onto her shoulders.

"Don't you think it's time you came inside?" she said.

Kate pulled the jacket closer around her and turned to walk with her across the street.

"Mr. Mendoza said he'd keep an eye out for the people Mr. Allen was sending over," her mother said. "I think we could use a nice strong cup of tea."

"A cup of tea?" Kate couldn't help but laugh. "After all this, you think a cup of tea will help? I was thinking of a pint of bourbon."

"No, you weren't," her mother gently scolded. "And a cup of tea will do just fine. We need to return to our normal habits if we want things to feel normal."

Would things ever feel normal for her? What was normal, anyway?

They went into Mr. Mendoza's apartment on the first floor. It was so different from their own place. It smelled like a greenhouse and looked like a jungle in the corners. The old man obviously had a green thumb. Plants were everywhere, some quite large and old looking. A row of tiny pots were lined up on the front windowsill with seedlings in them.

Strangely enough, the wild abundance of growing things seemed to lift Kate's spirits. A cup of tea would taste good. With a bit of lemon, maybe it would take the taste of the fire from her mouth.

"Jake wants us to come to Montana to visit while the house is getting fixed," Kate said.

Her mother turned in the kitchen doorway. "That's a wonderful idea. You haven't had a real vacation in ages."

"He wants all of us to go. You, me and Laura."

"That's very kind of him." The older woman paused. "But somebody ought to stay here and oversee the repairs. You and Laura should go. I know she'd love the trip."

Her mother went over to the sink to fill the teakettle. She made it seem so reasonable, so possible. Didn't she see all the problems? Didn't she understand the risks involved in spending more time with Jake?

"I wasn't sure about Laura's school."

"Oh, for heaven's sake, Kate." Her mother put the teakettle on the stove. "She's in fourth grade. A couple of weeks away won't hurt. Besides, the teachers can give you all her assignments and you can teach her.''

"I could teach her?" Kate had never thought of that. Sure, she helped Laura with her homework on a reasonably frequent basis, but teaching was different. It had to be or there wouldn't be specialized training for the profession. "I don't know about that."

"Those board guys are here," Mr. Mendoza called from the living room. "I'll go down and make sure they do it right."

"All right, Carlos," her mother called back.

Kate glanced over her shoulder, then back at her mother. "I ought to—"

"You ought to stay and have some tea. Someone else can handle things for a change." Her mother took Kate's hand, drawing her gently over to the kitchen table. "You take on too much, Katie. You always have, whether it's work or responsibility or guilt."

"What's that supposed to mean?"

Her mother's eyes grew sad. "That you're still punishing yourself for things that are long past."

Kate looked away, staring at the faded curtains that framed the kitchen windows. Mrs. Mendoza had probably made them years ago—at least ten years back, since it was almost that long since she had died. Yet here they still hung, tired looking but still serviceable. Was it right to hang on to the past? Or was one supposed to chuck it in favor of something newer or brighter?

The teakettle began to whistle and her mother got to her feet. She poured boiling water into the mugs, then dunked a tea bag first in one, then in the other before carrying the steaming mugs over to the table.

"The trip would be good for you," she said.

"I know I could use a vacation," Kate said. "But—"

Her mother set a mug in front of her with a sigh. "That wasn't what I meant."

Kate stared at her, a queasy feeling dancing in her stomach. Something in her tone of voice made Kate consider running. She felt like a little girl, unsure of what she'd done, but certain it was wrong.

"I'm more interested that you and Laura spend some time together."

"We do, Mom. I help her with her homework. We go to the zoo. I help coach her—"

"I mean alone with each other." Her mother's voice was firm, her gaze steady. "It would be the perfect time to tell Laura the truth, dear."

That queasy sensation in Kate's stomach turned into full-fledged nausea. "Mom, there's no reason to tell her anything. Everything's fine the way it is."

"I'm not getting any younger, Kate."

Kate felt as if her vocal cords were paralyzed. She could only shake her head. "I just thought—"

"Katie, Katie!" Her mother's voice was soft and gentle, but there was no denying the steel in it. "I'd have to say you aren't thinking at all. You've been denying that Laura and all of us are changing. That the circumstances are changing. That Laura has a right to the truth."

Truth. Honesty. There were those words again. Had her mother and Jake had discussions about life and how things ought to be?

The front door slammed and light, running footsteps echoed in the hall. "Mom. Kate. Are you guys in here?" Laura popped into the kitchen. She looked from one to the other. "Hey, guys. What's going down?"

"We were talking about a little trip to Montana for you and Kate," her mother replied.

"All right!" Laura shouted, raising her arms high over her head.

"That's if Kate says it's all right."

Laura's face twisted into a frown. "If Kate says it's all right? How come she gets to say? Just because she's older. That's not fair."

Her mother gave Kate a look she remembered well. The one that said, "You broke Mr. Jacoby's window, now go tell him."

"Life isn't fair, kid," Kate said, trying for lightness but knowing she failed.

Laura started to argue, but just then the front door opened. Cowboy boots clunked down the hall, accompanied by the clicking of dogs' nails.

"Howdy, ladies." Jake doffed his hat and looked around at them. "Well, am I going to have company in Montana or not?"

Three pairs of eyes stared at Kate. She didn't look up, but she knew they were there, staring and waiting. Should she follow her head or her heart?

"Yes," she murmured. "Yes, you are."

Laura squealed with delight and that set both dogs to barking furiously. Kate wanted to bring some control to the situation, but it was like trying to bring back a raft that was halfway down the rapids.

It was too late, much too late.

"I could have taken a cab," Jake said. "You had enough on your mind without having to drive me to the airport."

Actually, Kate was driving him—in his truck—to a hotel near the airport. He'd have a chance for a few hours of sleep, then he could literally fall out of bed and board his plane. He had decided not to stay at Mr. Mendoza's, since the dogs weren't flying back with him.

"I need to practice driving this thing," she said.

"It's not that hard. Not much different from a car."

"It's just so big." Kate couldn't imagine driving it all the way to Montana, but then she still couldn't quite believe she'd agreed to go. It was pure insanity. It was utterly nuts. It was like jumping into a live volcano.

Jake got something out of his pocket, and for some silly reason, Kate almost expected to see that old ring in his hand. But it was just a piece of paper.

"I wrote down a route for you to take," he said. "Mostly interstates. Not exciting, but safe and fast."

She kept her eyes straight ahead, not chancing any more weird suppositions inspired by the sweetness in his eyes.

"Safe, I'm not worried about," she said. "With those monsters of yours along, no one's going to bother us."

"I suppose not."

Kate saw the hotel up ahead and slowed down, then turned into the parking lot. It felt empty and desolate.

It was absolutely crazy, but her eyes watered up. She was going to miss Jake. And she was going to see him again in less than a week! Lordy, the fire had taken more out of her than she'd realized.

She pulled up in a spot beneath the flashing hotel sign. Jake's face alternated between being fire red and disappearing into the shadows. Sort of like how he'd come into her life—charging in and then about to vanish. She leaned over to look at the paper in his hand.

"So what's this route?" She tried to sound businesslike, but her voice was wavery. When she looked at the sheet, the words seemed all wavery, too. But she didn't think it was her eyes. "What did you write this with, your spurs?"

"Very funny." He frowned at the paper, which was also jumping in and out of the darkness because of the sign, and began pointing out words. "Take I-90 north through Illinois to—"

"Haven't you got a map?" she asked. "That would be a whole lot easier."

"My list is fine."

"Your list is chicken scratchings."

"I'll have you know chickens don't write."

"All right, buffalo scratchings."

He started to laugh, a wonderful, warm sound that surrounded her and melted away all the fears and tensions and indecisions of the day. Like a flower coming to life again after the winter, she felt joy creep into her fingers and toes, and mostly into her smile. And like spring melting all of winter's snows, the ice in her heart turned to water—tears, actually.

"Hey, what's all this?" Jake asked, pulling her into his arms.

It was so absolutely safe and warm there that she couldn't move. She couldn't pull away, couldn't even talk for the moment. She just lay her head on his shoulder and breathed in the peace. What was happening to her? She'd reached for Lance, wanting a peek into the world of belonging, and instead fell headfirst into a well of emotions and needs and incomprehensible attachments.

"You okay?" Jake asked, his voice caressing her ear.

"Yeah. Fine." She pulled away slightly and found a watery smile to prove the truth of her words. "Just a little delayed reaction."

His frown said he wasn't convinced that was all it was. "I'm not sure I like the idea of you driving back by yourself tonight. Or driving across the country. It's not too late to make other plans, you know."

"It may not be too late, but it's not necessary." She leaned over and looked again at the scribbled directions. He wasn't holding them in a patch of light from the hotel sign anymore and they were totally unreadable. "A map really would be a whole lot better."

He sighed and opened his glove compartment, rummaging through it until he took out a well-used map. "It's really very straightforward." He tried to open the map, but there wasn't room in the truck.

"Maybe we ought to go inside," he said. "We can spread out the map and go over the route better."

"Okay." Somehow going to his room seemed safer than staying here. It would be bigger, so she wouldn't have to lean so close to him. They could be on opposite sides of the map, so her hand wouldn't brush his. And there'd be lots of light, so she wouldn't have this feeling they were the only two people in the world.

Where had she left her brain? Kate wondered a few minutes later as she followed Jake into his hotel room. It was bigger than the truck, but dominated by the king-size bed in the middle. And if the truck had seemed cozy and cocoonlike, the room was even worse. With the drapes closed and the hum of the heater going, they were totally alone. The world didn't exist anymore.

"You okay?" Jake asked.

Kate realized she was standing in the doorway and took a step inside so he could close the door. "Yeah, sure. I'm fine." She swallowed hard, trying not to look his way and failing miserably. "Nice room."

He looked around as if searching for something that lifted it above ordinary and shrugged. "I guess."

He took the map over to the bed and opened it up. She dragged her unwilling feet to join him. It wasn't that her feet didn't want to move. It was that her heart was suddenly so very heavy. Jake was leaving and this irrational fear that she would never see him again ate at her.

"See, you just take 90 until you reach 94 and then take that all the way across to Montana."

She forced herself to look at the map, but all she could see was his finger pointing the way. He had such wonderful hands, so strong. Roughened by hard work, but they could be surprisingly gentle.

How did she know that? she wondered.

"Kate?"

She blinked, focusing on the map. "Looks easy," she said.

"It gets a little more complicated once you get to Montana, but not much."

She reached out to take the map at the same time Jake was picking it up and their hands brushed. A jolt charged through her, a lightning bolt seeking grounding. Her heart shuddered. Or was it shattered?

Jake had turned, his eyes locked with hers. She couldn't read what they were saying, at least not in words, but her heart began to race. There was something in the air, some magic promising springtime and sunshine and forevers. But all she cared about was now—that hunger growing in her heart to be held and caressed and loved.

"Jake?" she whispered as she stretched her hand toward him.

He took it in his own, clasping it lightly as he brought it to his lips. His kiss was gentle, but she felt it race through her. His hold on her hand tightened even as some wonderful twisting tension tightened inside her. He brought her fingers to his lips again, then reached his other hand out to slide it behind her hair.

"You look so incredibly fragile," he said. "You look like some piece of fine china, and I feel like the bull in the china shop."

She laughed and let his hands bring her closer. She slid her arms about his waist, leaning back to look up into his face. The feelings churning inside her were anything but dainty and delicate. Fires, hungers, a need to feel really alive.

"I feel pretty tough," she said. "Not at all in the breakable mode."

"Us cowboys sometimes forget to say please and thank you," he said.

"Us tough businesswomen sometimes don't even bother with talking."

Since he was so close, she reached up to brush his lips with hers, then went back for a longer, deeper helping. His lips gave her strength and power, gave her heart a steadiness and certainty that it had lost. There was no more worrying and fretting in his arms. That weepy little girl who had shied away from desire out in the truck was gone. The confident woman here in Jake's arms was the real Kate, the one who knew that she needed to come alive under his touch.

Their lips still clung, their hearts speaking in words that only the soul could hear. Kate closed her eyes and rode the tide of passion farther and farther out. She would let it carry her wherever it went. She would not stay in the shallow water tonight. There were too many mysteries to explore in the depths, and with Jake leading the way, there was no reason to be afraid.

His hold tightened, his arms drawing her ever closer. Kate let her senses steer her course. She could hear Jake's breath coming as hard and fast as her own. She could smell the faint lingering smoke in his clothes mixed with the scent of him and his woodsy after-shave. And she could feel the steel bands of his muscles as her hands slid over his back.

Jake was the forest and she was lost in his vastness. He was the sea and she was drowning in his depths. He was the heavens above and she was soaring into eternity.

His lips still locked to hers, he slid her jacket from her shoulders and off her arms, then his hands loosened her blouse from her skirt. The cool air in the room rushed over her skin, but his hands followed, bringing heat and passion and fire. They slid over her back, turning her skin to flames and making her heart race.

She pushed his jacket off, then tugged at his buttons, wanting to feel the warmth of his skin beneath her fingers. Then they both stopped, and his smile sent sparks all through her heart.

"Maybe we need to work together at this," he said, and he undid his buttons while she pulled her blouse off over her head.

Skirt, pants, bra and panties fell onto the floor; then she and Jake were back in each other's arms. The hard male length of him against her body woke up her hungers, sent her desires dancing in a frenzy. Jake pushed aside the map as they fell onto the bed and then she was surrounded by warmth—quilt on one side, Jake on the other.

His hands never left her, stoking a fire in her heart to burn through the ages, to destroy all shadows and past hurts. She needed him, wanted him with a fierceness that she'd never known before. Her hands, her lips, coursed over his length, daring him to meet her heat with a rage of his own.

Their lips met again, to cling with an urgency that made her tremble. It was now, it had to be now. She opened her heart and took him in, pulling at his fire to ignite them both in one blazing explosion. The world stood still as the fire raged around them, caught them and threw them up to the heavens.

They held their hearts, their breath, each other as if the splendor would stay just a moment longer, then they slowly floated down from the heights. Ragged breathing was the only sound in the room, that and the pounding of Jake's heart next to her.

"My, my," he said in a jagged whisper.

"Yeah," she breathed into his chest.

They lay still, wrapped in each other's arms for a life-time. She had no desire to move, to let reality intrude where it had no business. Her eyes started to close, sending her drifting to a land of peace and utter contentment, until she heard the sound of a car honking outside.

She opened her eyes and found an unfamiliar ceiling above her. She was at the hotel. She couldn't fall asleep. She had to drive Jake's truck back home. Mom and Laura would be waiting.

"Something wrong?" Jake asked as she tried to slip from his arms.

She took a moment to kiss his lips, to wander back for just a moment to perfection. "Just reality," she said. "I need to get home. Mom'll be waiting up."

"Damn." He sat up, running his fingers through his hair. "I shouldn't have—"

She pressed her fingers over his lips. "Maybe we shouldn't have, but we did."

He ran a finger lightly over her shoulder, coming around to cup one breast with his hand. Leaning forward, he let his lips touch it, nuzzle it. She wanted more—much, much more—but pulled away and reached for her clothes.

"I don't like you driving alone at this hour," he said.

"I'll be fine." She tugged on her underwear.

"You should stay. Drive home in the morning."

"I'll be fine." Blouse on and quickly fastened, since she hadn't bothered to unbutton most of the buttons. "Honest."

"I could drive you home and then take a cab back here."

"Don't be silly." Skirt on, then shoes and jacket. She leaned over to plant a last kiss on his lips. "I'm a big girl. I'll be fine."

He grabbed his pants. "I'll at least walk you to the truck."

"Okay."

But the walk turned out to be strained and silent, as if once outside the room, doubts came rushing at both of them. What had she done? Kate asked herself as they went along dreary, carpeted halls. This man had no place in her future, not her real future. Had she lost her mind?

She was relieved when they got to the truck and she could worry about something important—like driving this monster.

"Take care," Jake said. "If you have any problems, you call me."

What kind of problems—like she was setting herself up for a broken heart? "The truck'll be fine," she assured him. "And so will the dogs."

And so would she, she vowed silently.

Jake walked slowly back to his room. The halls were empty and still, all doors closed. He felt isolated, alone, shut out. It was what he had chosen for his life, but at this moment, it hurt. Behind one door, he heard voices, soft laughter, and it made him hurry on even faster to his room, though only more emptiness awaited him there.

Emptiness with the scent of memories.

Damn. He shouldn't have invited them all to Montana. He shouldn't have agreed to let Kate drive him to the hotel. He should never have suggested they go up to his room. It was as if he had no sense lately, no control over his actions. He was doing things totally out of character again. He had to get back home.

He opened the door to his room and was met with the memory of Kate and the love they'd just shared. Her scent still lingered in the air, her voice seemed to hover just out of hearing.

Damn, but he missed her.

That was out of character, too, and the very realization of it got his feet moving. He went into the bathroom, stripped and showered quickly.

It was being away from home, that was all. Away from the prairie and the wide open spaces that allowed him distance, he was responding in ways he wouldn't back home.

It was not Jacob and Caitlin. It couldn't be.

Feeling calmer, more in control, he dried himself off and went into the bedroom. Once settled into bed, he turned off the light. Images wanted to crowd into his mind—of Kate and the passion they'd shared—but he refused to let them.

He was used to the darkness, though this wasn't exactly dark by prairie standards, and to shutting out the day from his thoughts. He was overly tired and needed sleep. Sweet, mind-numbing sleep.

He closed his eyes and willed sleep to come. He thought of the ranch and the smell of the prairie just after a rain-storm. He let his mind play back the sounds of the night—grass rustling in the breeze, animals calling in the distance and insects chirping.

Sleep started to overtake him—sweet, blessed drowsi-ness. Just before it claimed him, though, he felt suddenly awake to the smell of smoke clinging to his clothes and a terrible, unbearable loss about to break his heart. Then he fell into a dark, dreamless sleep.

"I'm so glad to see you going," Granny Nan said.

"Thanks, Gran," Laura said with a snicker. "You and Mom going to party while we're gone?"

Kate just listened to their byplay as she loaded the cooler into the truck. This whole thing reminded her of the one-and-only time she'd been on a roller coaster. When they'd paused at the top, she'd wanted to get off, but couldn't. She'd had to hold on tight and just finish out the ride. Well, she was at the top of the hill again, and could only hold on tight and finish out this trip to see Jake.

"I think we've got everything," she told Laura. "Want to get the dogs?"

Laura ran off, leaving Kate with Granny Nan. The older woman took Kate's hand and patted it.

"This trip is such a good idea," she said.

"I don't know." Kate looked across the street at their home, windows boarded up and sooty stains on the walls. "I ought to be staying here and Mom ought to be going."

"Oh, stop being such a chicken. This is a trip somebody should have made a hundred years ago. If it hadn't been for some of us Mallory brides passing down letters and diaries, we'd have never known about the ring and Caitlin might never have had this chance to find Jacob again."

Kate sighed. "Gran..."

"Patrick's grandfather lived only for three years after he married Caitlin. Why didn't she send for Jacob?"

"Maybe she didn't know where he was."

"She had the ring. If it worked now, it would have worked then."

"Gran, it didn't work now."

"Then why did that young man come barging into your life?" Granny asked. "And why are you going out there to see him?"

"Because I got talked into it."

Kate was relieved to see Laura and her mother coming down the steps, followed by the two dogs. Kate opened the door and the dogs jumped in. Laura bounced in after them, her eyes shining with excitement.

"Drive safely," Kate's mother said. "And give us a call when you get there."

Kate hugged her. "We'll be fine, Mom."

They were inching forward, about to race down that hill out of control, and Kate didn't want to let go. It wasn't just that this whole trip seemed out of her control, but that everything seemed to be on the verge of changing.

Her mother stepped back, putting her hands on Kate's arms and looking into her face. "Talk to her, Katie. It's time."

It was time to leave, that's what it was time for. Kate gave Granny a kiss and a hug, then climbed into the truck. Nickolai gave her a wet, sloppy kiss on the back of the neck, and they were off. Laura leaned out the window, waving, until they turned the corner.

"What are you supposed to talk to me about?" she asked as she sat back.

"Your common sense," Kate said. "Put your seat belt on."

Laura grumbled some, but did as she was told, then settled in with the road map to be navigator.

Illinois passed in a slow haze. Traffic was moving well and the dogs were snoozing, so that left Kate's mind to ponder all the problems facing her. How was she supposed to tell Laura the truth? Should she just blurt it out or lead into it gently? And how was she supposed to act toward Jake after their last night together? What had possessed her to make love with him, anyway?

They stopped for lunch in Wisconsin, pulling off the highway at a deserted roadside rest area. Laura took the dogs for a quick romp around the trees while Kate got their lunch from the cooler.

"This is so cool," Laura said as she knelt on the picnictable bench across from Kate, pouring water into a big bowl for the dogs. She put it on the ground for them. "Just think, everybody else is in school. Jake is such a better boyfriend than geeky Lance."

Kate's heart practically stopped. "Jake is not my boyfriend."

Laura frowned around her sandwich. "Sure he is. I saw you kissing him."

"That doesn't make him my boyfriend."

"You kiss guys who aren't your boyfriend?"

Yeah, Kate, a little voice asked. Do you? And do you sleep with them?

"It's different when you're a grown-up," Kate tried to explain, both to Laura and to herself. "You sometimes do things that are hard to explain."

"You never did before," Laura pointed out.

It was Kate's turn to frown. "Since before when?"

"Since before we found the ring," Laura said, pulling the onyx-and-silver ring from her pocket. "Granny said Caitlin and Jacob are making you and Jake do stuff."

Kate didn't know which to argue about first—Laura's statement or the presence of the ring. "Caitlin and Jacob have been dead for sixty years. Granny's joking."

"Then why'd you kiss Jake?"

"Because I felt like it."

"Then you do like him?"

This conversation was becoming too twisted for Kate. She wrapped up the remains of her sandwich. "We need to get going if we want to make Minneapolis tonight."

The rest of Wisconsin passed along with the help of license-plate bingo and an alphabet race. They stopped here and there to exercise the dogs, but made it past St. Cloud before Kate decided to stop. In order to keep Laura's conversation off the ring, they spent an hour on her math homework, then watched TV until they all fell asleep.

The next day's agenda included the rest of Minnesota and North Dakota. As each stretch of pine forest began to look like the last, Kate wondered if this wasn't a good time for talking to Laura about the past. Just how would she start, though?

"Remember that old boyfriend of mine I told you about?" she asked.

Laura had been half lying on top of Boris and looked up. "You mean the one that died?"

Kate nodded, but found she couldn't glance Laura's way. "Miguel," she said. "That was his name."

"Oh." Laura sat up straighter. "Did you like him better than Jake?"

"Laura..." Kate sighed and bit back her impatience. Why was she turning everything around to Jake? "They were very different. I was very different."

"Like how?"

Kate thought a moment and felt Nickolai shift his position. Was everybody listening? "I guess I was more ready to fall in love back then," she said. "I didn't yet know how much it hurt to lose someone you cared about."

"Do you have to be ready to fall in love before you fall in love?" Laura asked. "I thought you just saw somebody and it happened."

Kate laughed. "Only in the movies."

"It happened to Jake," Laura said.

Kate turned then to frown at the girl. "To Jake?"

"Yeah. He said he saw you in Lance's car and the next thing he knew he was zipping around to stop you guys."

"That was him falling in love?"

"Yeah."

"Did he tell you that?"

"He didn't have to. I just knew."

"You just knew?"

"Well, not at first," Laura admitted. "But when I found out about the ring, it all made sense."

"Laura, that ring has no power."

The girl glared at her. "Don't you want to fall in love and get married?" she asked. "This is your big chance, and you keep telling me it's crazy."

"I don't know what I want," Kate admitted. "But this isn't my big chance. This isn't any chance at all. Jake lives way out in Montana. We live in Chicago. They're not exactly commuting distance apart."

"So we move."

"Laura, Chicago's our home. You have your friends there. I have my business. Mom has her work."

"We could make new friends and get different jobs."

"It's not that simple."

That pretty much ended the discussion, and they rode on in silence. Minnesota stopped and North Dakota started, endlessly stretching out ahead of them. It was hard to tell if they were making any progress, since nothing seemed to change. Oh, buildings came and went, but the horizon was unchanging.

It suddenly seemed like her life—endlessly the same, never changing, never making any progress. Was Jake her big chance at love? Not because of Granny's story, but because there was some kind of electricity between them. Was it the beginning of love?

An urgency seemed to propel Kate forward, a need to get away from these silent scoldings. They drove longer than she'd planned, not stopping for the night until they were into Montana.

By morning, she'd regained her sense of equilibrium. North Dakota wasn't an analogy of her life, and Jake wasn't her one-and-only chance at happiness.

"They know they're almost home," Laura said.

Kate stopped packing up the truck and looked at the two dogs, standing like statues pointing off to the west. Boris put his nose to the air and sniffed. Nickolai looked at his partner as if asking what the winds were telling him.

"Almost is a relative term," Kate said. "We still have more than three hundred miles to go."

"But it probably feels more like home," Laura said.

Kate just looked around them, breathing in the crisp, early morning air. It did seem different from Chicago and it wasn't just the silent emptiness. Everything was so immense out here, no neat little blocks or neighborhoods or even towns. Everything just sprawled out as if there were no walls to keep things tightly locked in.

Strangely enough, she felt freer out here, too, as if her spirit had all sorts of room to expand. The walls she locked herself behind had vanished, blown down by the winds and reduced to ashes. Yet even as the wide open spaces gave a sense of freedom, they also left a hint of fear in her soul. Things almost seemed too uncontrolled, too free.

"Come on, guys," Laura called to the dogs. "Into the truck."

Glad for the diversion, Kate turned to watch her handle the dogs. She was amazed at how docile they were with Laura and how they obeyed her every word. It couldn't be fear. The animals could break the girl in half with one snap of their monster jaws. It had to be love.

Love. It seemed to have more forms than the sky had stars. Made you do all sorts of things you'd never dream of doing if you were sane. Like crash into the car of strangers? Like drive halfway across the continent to see some guy you'd only known for a week or so?

"Kate."

She turned. Laura and the dogs were already in the car. She climbed in, too. Some weariness was settling on her shoulders and it took an extra effort to pull herself into the cab. She inserted the key and started the motor. After checking the long stretch of empty road behind them, Kate pulled onto the blacktop and headed down another long stretch of empty road toward the horizon. She shivered. All this space made her seem even more insignificant than she thought she was.

"I can hardly wait to get to the ranch," Laura said. "Aren't you excited?"

"Oh, yeah." Kate wasn't sure what she was. She wasn't sure about anything anymore.

Chapter Eight

The new barn was almost done. A few more days and it'd be all set to weather a hundred winters. More than he would, Jake thought. But then, everything had its place. Some plants lasted only a season, man for seventy years or so and the hills and prairie forever.

He stopped short, halfway between the house and the horse pens. And where did love fit in with all that? According to Kate's grandmother's strange story, it rivaled the mountains for longevity.

Jake shook his head, trying to shake off the eerie feeling that returned each time he thought about that afternoon at Granny's apartment. Jacob Tyler, indeed. Not that he believed any of it, but it sure was one hell of a coincidence.

Like running into Kate in Chicago.

Like being on the right street to see Lance.

Like having a backbone of melting snow when Kate looked into his eyes.

"Hearing voices again?" Bo asked.

Jake didn't bother to turn around. "Go to hell."

"I imagine she'll be along anytime now," Bo said. "So don't go running off before then."

"What are you talking about?"

"What am I talking about?" Bo shook his head. "Some folks sure got a short memory. The last time you stood around gaping off toward the east, you took yourself on a sudden trip to Chicago."

Jake clenched his teeth. He really should ignore the old buzzard. It probably was the only way to make him go away. "I was just worried about the dogs, that's all."

"Next thing you know, you'll be running off to Cleveland or Altoona, even."

"Altoona?" He turned to face the old man. This was getting to be more than ridiculous. Sure, dashing off to Chicago had been a tad irrational, but it wasn't as if Jake was some kind of nut. He'd just needed a vacation.

"That's in Pennsylvania," Bo said. "If you forgot your geography, too."

"No, I haven't forgotten my geography." It looked as if Bo was going to hang around until Kate arrived. "I know where Altoona is." Come to think of it, it seemed that a lot of the hands were hanging around the main house. "And I know Schenectady is in New York. And I know there's a Portland in Maine as well as Oregon."

Jake turned back to glare off toward the eastern horizon. This was a stupid, stupid conversation. He should just walk away from it. And he would, if this wasn't his ranch. He was the owner, so why should he let his employees push him around? He should tell the bums to get to work. All of them hanging around like this would scare poor Kate half to death.

"For your information," Jake said, "even though it's none of your damn business, along with worrying about my dogs, I was just looking over my land. Us owners do that, you know. See how things are going."

Bo took the hay stalk out of his mouth, spit to the side and returned the chewed stem to his mouth, all without saying a word. Well, two could play that game. Jake leaned back against the oak tree nearest him and stared off at nothing.

The longer he was back home, the worse this little visit of Kate's was looking to be. His ranch hands were walking around with junior-high smirks plastered on their ugly faces. And the whole county was acting like it was the Queen of England coming to visit. He should have flown the dogs out with him and hired somebody to drive the truck back.

"The little lady must be sumpthin'."

"What little lady?" Jake knew who Bo was talking about, but he'd be damned if he'd give the old coot any satisfaction. "Chicago is full of beautiful women. They got more ladies than Montana has cows."

"You interview all of them before you found this one that can drive a truck and likes dogs?"

"Ain't nothing to driving the truck," Jake replied. "She already knew how to drive a stick shift."

"But she got on good with Boris and Nickolai."

"Not especially." Jake squinted. A dust cloud was moving up the road. He gave his heart a swat so it would sit still and quit hopping around. "Actually, they sort of scare her."

"Hellsfire," Bo muttered. "Those two monsters scare the devil."

"Her little sister came along to take care of them on the trip."

"How old is her little sister?"

"What? She's ten years old. Just had—"

"That's your momma comin'," Bo said.

Jake's eyes snapped back toward the road and the approaching cloud of dust. Hell. His mother never came out to the ranch. She'd lived in town all her life and said she planned to die there. Wasn't even interested in visiting out here except on rare occasions.

It could be no accident that she was coming out today. He should never have invited Kate to Montana. It was putting the wrong idea in everyone's mind.

The Jeep careened into the lane and sped toward them. Jake wondered for a moment if he should step behind one of the big oaks until his mother stopped, but that would have been showing fear and he figured that a fella should stop doing that by the time he left sixth grade. No matter how he really felt. The Jeep stopped a few yards short of them.

"Evenin', ma'am," Bo said, doffing his hat.

It wasn't quite four o'clock yet, but it was long after lunch and that was evening in Montana. Jake didn't say anything as he watched his mother stride toward him. She was the epitome of the Western woman—medium height, slender and muscular, with piercing eyes that saw the distant mountain peaks as well as the depths of a man's soul.

"Jake, quit pouting." Her eyes flashed as she stopped and spread her arms wide. "Come here and give your momma a big kiss and a cowboy hello."

"I'm not pouting."

"Don't give me no lip and just do as I say," she snapped. "I can still put you across my knee if I have to."

"Excuse me," Bo said, putting on his hat. "I've got some chores that need doing over by the barn. This lovey-dovey stuff chokes me up."

Jake barely nodded at Bo's departure, concentrating instead on glaring at his mother. He was a whole lot bigger than she was, but cowboy rules said a momma was bigger until she'd been buried for a year. And then the odds weren't no better than even. He closed the gap between them, gave her a big hug and kissed her on the cheek.

"We ought to set you up a room of your own." Jake stepped back out of her reach. "I mean, since you come out here so often."

His mother shook her head, disgust curling her lips. "All the Tyler men that ever breathed air could charm the drawers off a spinster schoolmarm. I don't know what happened to you."

"I'm not a Tyler," Jake snapped. "My name is Mac-Neill."

"I don't give a tinker's damn what you got some judge to do." She wagged a finger in his face. "I know who your father was."

Jake turned and looked off across the prairie. When he was young, a student in college, he'd toyed with the idea of leaving Montana and never returning. He figured there were too many memories here, the kind that would pull him down into a deep, dark depression.

But when summer came, he would always go home. Home to this land that called to him whenever he was away. He wasn't always happy here, but this was where he was going to live and die. No way a two-bit old ghost was going to drive him away.

"I'd appreciate a little something to wet my tongue," his mother said, her voice having dropped almost to the soft range of gentle.

"I could get you some iced tea."

"And I could kick your butt," she replied.

"I thought the doctor talked to you about moderating your life-style?"

"He also told me not to get aggravated," his mother replied. "And the longer I stand here without my bourbon and branch water, the more aggravated I'm getting."

There was no use arguing, so he turned toward the house. "Come on. I'll mix you up a glass to wet your whistle."

She thrust her arm through his and matched him stride for stride. "Boy, you're chock-full of the Tyler charm. I bet you had to beat off the women with a club back in old Chicago."

Jake just continued walking toward the house. He hadn't talked about it with his doctor, but he was sure that aggravation wasn't doing him any good, either. His mother pulled away when they stepped onto the porch and walked over to a swing hanging from the ceiling.

"Bring my libation out here," she said. "I want to enjoy the fresh air as long as I can. Winter's going to be on us soon enough."

"You ought to go south for the winter," Jake said.

"Does it sound like I'm quacking?"

This had to be one of those trick questions that mothers liked to ask, the kind where one answer got you a whop on the head and another got you a kick in the butt. His best bet was to just wait her out.

"Ducks go south for the winter," she said. "In case you haven't noticed, I'm not a duck."

Jake pulled open the door.

"Oh, Jake?"

"I know," he replied, without bothering to look at her. "Don't go overboard on the water."

"We need to conserve our resources, boy. You should've gotten at least that much out of all that book learning you had."

"Yes, ma'am," he replied, then he hurried into the house.

He took his mother's personal bourbon bottle down from the cabinet and poured her a good three fingers of liquor, splashed some water on it and dropped in a couple of ice cubes.

How was he going to get rid of everybody before Kate arrived? He'd just been acting neighborly when he'd invited her out. He'd never thought about how everyone back here would misinterpret it. He returned to the porch, where he silently handed his mother the glass.

While she took a long sip, Jake sat down by her side. Inviting Kate out was an even more irrational act than going to Chicago in the first place. That was just taking a trip, having a little fun. Inviting Kate to Montana was inviting disaster.

His mother smacked her lips in satisfaction. "Someday you're going to make some lucky girl a fine husband," she said.

Jake didn't bother to reply. They'd had these nowhere conversations before. He just stared out over the acres of his front yard toward the road. Where the hell was Kate? She should be here by now.

"This lady know your real name?"

His mother's words pulled him out of the netherworld his mind had been wandering in, but his ears felt stuffed with cotton as he gaped at her.

"Did you tell her who you are?"

"I told her my legal name."

She sighed and took another deep swig from her glass. "You lied to her."

"I did not." Whatever he was, Jake knew damn well that he wasn't a liar. He would never be like his father. "I always tell the truth."

"The whole truth?"

"I told her my correct name," he said. "The name that's on all my legal documents."

"The one you paid some shyster lawyer to change."

"I didn't do anything illegal."

"That could be. But it wasn't right."

His anger faded like a pricked balloon when his own words—words he'd spoken to Kate in Chicago—came flying at him. He put his elbows on his knees and dropped his face in his hands.

"Why are you always standing up for him?" he asked.

"Because I loved him."

He turned to look at her. The softness building up around her eyes made his stomach hurt.

"And I always will."

"But he had no respect for you."

The fire returned to her eyes, chasing the gentleness from her face like thunder chased the baby lambs in the spring. "You're just a punk kid and you don't know anything."

"He never took you anyplace. Even after his wife died, he still didn't bring you out here."

She drained the last of her drink and put the glass on the floor. "That was my doin'," she said softly.

"Aw, come on, Ma. I'm sick and tired of you—"

"My mother warned me."

Jake snorted. "You should have listened."

She frowned at him momentarily. "He was a good man." She looked down at the ice cubes in her glass. "A good man who carried a heavy sorrow."

"Yeah," Jake replied. "He didn't own the whole state. Just a good part of it."

His mother gazed for a moment at her empty glass. "The first Tyler came out here in the 1870s. A man named Jacob."

"Jacob Tyler?" All other thoughts were shoved out the door. The eeriness returned. He knew all of this, of course. Every school kid in town knew the history of Cold Spring, but still . . .

"He was a man who carried a heavy sorrow in his heart," his mother went on. "He married and had children, but the pain never left. And that sorrow carried on down through generations of Tylers."

Jake wanted to speak, but no words came out.

"The old women said it was a curse. They said it would continue until a Tyler married a woman from the land of the morning sun."

Good lord. That's all he needed—a crazy Indian superstition to go along with Kate's grandmother's superstition and that damned ring. He stared dully out toward the road. If he were a praying man, he'd ask the gods to open up the earth and swallow him whole.

"Oh, my gosh, Kate," Laura squealed. "Look!"

Her screech brought Kate up short and she slammed on the brakes, fighting to keep the big pickup on the road.

"What in heaven's name are you hollering about?" she asked once she'd brought the truck to a complete stop.

The closer they came to the ranch, the more nervous Kate was becoming. She was more and more positive that she should never have come out here. Why had Jake invited her? What if he was having second thoughts? Laura's screaming didn't help her nerves at all.

"That." Laura pointed at the gate to the ranch. "Do you see that?"

Kate stared. They'd been riding along, in the middle of this vast, open prairie, when the gate appeared on their left. Exactly where Jake had said it would be.

"J-Bar-T." Laura's voice came out in a whisper.

"I see it," Kate said. "So what? That's the ranch's name. It was on that article Jake wrote that you used for your environmental report."

"Don't you get it?"

"Get what?" Kate was close to screaming herself. "I'm really not in any mood for games."

"Take the Bar out and what do you have left?" Laura asked.

Kate shook her head. "JT?"

"Yeah."

Kate gripped the steering wheel harder. "So?"

"The same initials that are in the ring."

"So what?" She tried for a bluffing tone, a tone that said it was all a joke, but her heart was starting to quiver. This whole thing was beginning to scare her. "I mean, it's not like those are uncommon initials."

"It's the legend."

"Laura, this is—"

"It's all going to come true."

"What's going to come true?" Kate asked.

"I don't know," Laura replied. "I just know it is."

Kate suddenly felt very tired and slumped back in her seat. The dogs whined softly. She had control over her life. She really did. She just had to keep telling herself that.

"I mean, this is all gonna be, like, really awesome," Laura said.

"Laura," Kate said quietly. "I don't want you to talk about this to anyone."

"Why not?" she asked, all wide-eyed innocence.

"Because I don't want to be locked up until someone decides whether or not we're dangerous." That wasn't quite it, but it would be enough to keep Laura quiet, Kate hoped. Her heart was feeling wound up tight enough because of this trip without the added burden of dealing with the Jacob Tyler story.

She put the truck back in gear and pulled through the gate of the J-Bar-T Ranch. It should be a relief that the long drive was over and that she wouldn't have the responsibility of the dogs anymore, but it seemed the closer they came toward the buildings ahead, the darker her heart became.

"Boy," Laura said. "I wonder if something's wrong."

"Why?"

"There's a whole crowd of people over by the house."

The long, one-story ranch house was straight ahead at the end of a long lane, and even from this distance, Kate could see that it had been built in bits and pieces, probably at different times. The main part looked like it had been a log cabin, the other parts looked semirustic, but modern. A covered porch ran the whole length. The other buildings, ones of various sizes and shapes, were scattered behind the house and to the sides.

And there were people standing around. Actually, quite a few. As she got closer, she saw that Jake was standing off to the side. Her stomach tensed.

"I hope they don't shoot us," Laura said.

"Laura, don't be ridiculous."

"Lean out the window and wave so they know who we are."

Since Kate kept her hands firmly on the steering wheel, Laura followed her own order and leaned out her window, waving wildly. This was dumb, Kate thought. No one was going to shoot anyone. The days of the Wild West were long over. These were probably just ranch workers doing ranch work.

The truck rolled to a stop near a Jeep, and she could see that everyone was smiling. She turned off the motor and pulled on the hand brake. Why didn't Jake come over and welcome her, show the natives she was friendly and that they should be nice to her?

But Jake didn't come. He remained standing, separated from the crowd. She could almost see the walls around him that said "stay away." A stocky, gray-haired man came toward the truck.

"Howdy, Kate," he said as he pulled open the door. "Welcome to the J-Bar-T."

For an instant, Kate's eyes flickered toward Jake and the crowd of almost all men. Within that blink of an eyelash, things turned from dead quiet to exciting. The men shouted greetings of welcome, the dogs leapt out of the truck, howling and barking, and Laura ran around, wearing a huge cowboy hat that somebody had slapped on her head.

As Kate struggled to shake hands and smile at everyone, a woman pushed herself forward and took her hand. She was about her mother's age, with salt-and-pepper hair, dark piercing eyes and a manner that brought a respectful quiet to the multitude of boisterous men.

"Hello, Kate," she said. "I'm Faith MacNeill."

"I'm pleased to meet you, Mrs. MacNeill."

"Not Mrs.," the woman replied, a big smile covering her face. "I'm just Jake's mother."

Kate didn't know what to say. "I'm pleased to meet you," she repeated.

"We'll talk later," the woman said.

She slapped Kate sharply on the shoulder, then strode toward the Jeep. After gunning the motor, she spun around, cowboys dashing every which way, and sped on toward the road, leaving a heavy cloud of dust hanging over them. The men all laughed, making remarks about how old Faith was going to kill everyone in the damn county before she was through driving.

"All right, you lazy, side-winding coyotes," Bo called out. "Get your butts back to work. This ain't no charity farm."

The men shouted insults back, but began to move on toward the barns, away from the house. It would be a good guess that Bo was the ranch foreman who had been in charge when Jake came to Chicago.

Kate looked again toward Jake. He hadn't said a word to her. One would think that Bo owned the ranch and not him.

"Hey, Buckaroo." Bo was leaning toward Laura. "You want to see our remuda?"

"Yeah," Laura responded.

Remuda? Kate found herself blinking in bewilderment. "Laura—"

"That's their horses," Laura told her.

To Bo's credit, he didn't laugh, but his eyes glowed a little brighter. "I'll take care of her, ma'am."

"I can take care of myself," Laura protested.

"How about we be partners?" he said, taking Laura's hand.

"Okay."

Kate watched as the bowlegged old man ambled off, hand-in-hand with a bouncing Laura. Maybe she ought to go with them. Laura wasn't used to being around animals and—

"She'll be fine."

Startled by the nearness of Jake's voice, Kate spun to find he'd come closer. Very close. Close enough to see the flecks of fire in his eyes and close enough to be in his arms if she just leaned forward slightly. But one semifriendly remark wasn't a welcome.

She took a step backward. "He seems to get on well with children."

"Yeah, he does that."

"Does he have many of his own?"

Jake shook his head. "None anyone admits to."

"That's too bad."

"He always said he made a better uncle than he would a father."

Bo looked like a man who had come to terms with his life. Her father always said that was what made a person happy. Kate wondered when she would come to terms with her life.

"How was the trip?"

This was worse than a first date. Next they'd be discussing the weather. Where was that passionate man whose arms she'd lain in less than a week ago? Where was the bossy, take-charge guy who'd run Lance to the ground? When was the soonest they could leave?

"Fine. Just fine."

"It's a long drive," he said. "Especially when you're the only driver."

"Laura and the dogs were good company."

"That's good."

There was a slight softening in his voice, a slight lessening of the prairie's desolation in his eyes. She hadn't really wanted him to come running over and sweep her into a passionate embrace, but a little pleasure at seeing her would have been nice.

"The dogs give you any trouble?"

"No. They and Laura got along well with each other."

"Good."

"It was great to have them along," Kate said. "They kept Laura from getting bored."

He smiled, and she suddenly felt his welcome. Like a fire smoldering unnoticed, something flared up in her heart. She wanted to be here, wanted to be close to him again.

"Thank you for inviting us. This country is so beautiful."

"I'm glad you could come," he said softly. "I hadn't planned on such a big welcoming party, though."

She just glanced around her, taking in the house and surrounding buildings, which probably covered at least the area of her city block, and then the whole open area around them—immense stretches of grass covering the gently rolling prairies. Everything was bigger here, wilder here. Stronger here. She grinned at him, feeling strangely bold herself.

"They aren't around anymore," she pointed out.

"So they aren't."

Even as he reached for her, she moved into his arms. Their lips touched in a joyous greeting as his arms surrounded her. His kiss told her all the things his words hadn't—they welcomed her, told her how he'd missed her and how glad he was to have her here.

When they finally pulled apart, she felt alone and abandoned. The brisk winds blowing across the prairie seemed to enter her heart, and she shivered.

"Hey." Jake put an arm around her waist. "Let's get you inside afore you get the deathly chills."

Any contact with him sent that shiver packing. "Sounds scary," she said.

"We'll get ourselves a nice fire inside," he said. "And good hot drinks. Coffee. Chocolate. Whatever."

"Sounds good."

It did sound good. It felt good. It was good.

Kate watched as Laura, sitting up on the sand-colored horse, waved her hat at them. "Are you sure we shouldn't stay around here? She hasn't really been horseback riding before."

"Bo's just going to walk her around the yard," Jake replied. "And I thought you wanted to see some of the ranch."

Yeah, she'd said that at breakfast, but that was before she'd known Laura wasn't going to be tucked safely alongside her in the carriage.

"What if that horse starts bucking and Laura falls down?"

"Sandy wouldn't buck if you lit her tail on fire," Jake said with a chuckle.

Apparently tired of her indecision, he took Kate's arm and helped her up into the carriage, then climbed in himself.

"Let's go, babe," he said, lightly snapping the reins on the horse's rump. The animal moved forward at a leisurely trot.

It hadn't taken Kate and Laura long to get settled in their rooms last night—though Kate would never get used to the spectacular view of the mountains out her window if she stayed here a hundred years—and then they had dinner with Jake and his ranch hands. Everyone had been so friendly that Kate wondered why she'd been nervous about coming.

Once the steady stream of food had started winding down, so had she. The drive, the tension of arriving and seeing Jake again all caught up with her and she turned in early, falling asleep almost as soon as her head touched the pillow.

After breakfast the next morning, Jake had offered to show them around the ranch. After Kate had accepted, it had turned out that Bo had already promised Laura her first riding lesson. It had quickly been decided by everyone else that Laura would go riding and Kate would go touring. Kate had tried protesting, but had given up when she'd sounded wimpish even to herself.

"This is our main barn," Jake said, pointing toward a large, new-looking building. "It should be done in a few more days."

Kate dragged her eyes away from Laura and looked over at the barn. "This replaces the one destroyed in the fire?"

"Yep."

She watched for a moment as workers hung a small side door. "You must have had to put something up fast," she said. "Since winter's not that far away and all."

"Bo took charge of it."

"I just expected one of those steel-sided pole barns," she said. "I thought they went up real fast."

"And come down real fast," he said. "I don't go for speed. I only want things that will last."

There was more to that philosophy than barns, she knew. Did he view relationships as the pole barns of emotions? In spite of the warmth of his kiss when she'd arrived, he seemed more distant here in his home than he'd been in Chicago. They went past the barn and around some smaller buildings.

"This is where we raise our chickens," he said, indicating a couple of small, slant-roof buildings sitting within a fenced-in yard.

"Isn't that like blasphemy?" Kate asked. "A rancher raising chickens?"

He shrugged his broad shoulders. "We like the variety as well as being more self-sufficient."

"Is that some code of the west?" Kate asked. "Depend on no one but yourself?"

He looked at her, his eyes still. "I don't think it has anything to do with the west," he said. "But everything to do with being smart. No one's going to look out for me the way I am."

"I suppose not, but no one can be totally independent."

"You can try."

Kate said nothing, but watched the chickens pecking about the little yard as they passed. Jake seemed different here, more determined to stand alone. Or was it that in her own environment, consumed by her normal routine, she just hadn't gotten a clear view of him?

"Anyway," he went on in a normal tone, "Mary Redwing takes care of the chickens, not me. That makes them hers."

Kate tried to match his light tone. "Is she the cook?"

"Yup."

"I think she used up half her egg production in breakfast."

"Mary's used to feeding cowboys."

"I keep eating like that," Kate replied, "and I'll turn bowlegged, too."

Jake laughed and patted her on the knee. "Your legs are just fine."

"Thank you, kind sir."

They drove on, leaving the complex of buildings behind as they followed a trail through the grass. They heard Laura's laughter in the air behind them.

Jake smiled at Kate. "She's enjoying herself."

"Wouldn't you be—ten years old and out here instead of in school?"

A cloud seemed to pass overhead, darkening his eyes and bringing a line of tension to his lips. "At ten, maybe I would have liked it out here," he said slowly. "I don't know. Maybe my anger wasn't as strong then and I would have welcomed any overtures."

"You mean from your father?" Kate asked. "He lived out here then?"

"Until he died twelve years ago."

"And where did you live?"

"In town with my mother."

"Did you see much of him?"

Jake shrugged. "Off and on when he came into town. Never talked to me, though, even though I tried to get him to once or twice when I was younger. Never acknowledged I was his son."

"But he left you the ranch, didn't he?"

Jake glanced at her, then concentrated on driving the horse. "He died without a will. I had to go to court to get it."

His voice was stiff and tight, as if years of anger had risen to the surface. Silence reigned for the next few minutes; then he turned toward her with a smile.

"Warm enough?" he asked.

"Oh, yes. I'm fine." She looked at the miles of prairie flowing out in endless waves around them, and tried to put Jake's story of rejection behind her. "The air is just great. It's so clean and pure."

"I thought you big-city folks didn't trust air you couldn't see."

"Be nice," she said as she slugged him on the arm.

"You call that nice?"

"I'm just responding in kind."

"Weren't you taught to turn the other cheek?" he asked.

"They talked about it in Sunday school," Kate replied. "But us big-city girls learn real quick that turning the other cheek just gets you hit again."

He smiled with real amusement, and Kate felt herself relax. She looked at the expanse of blue sky and prairie surrounding her, then looked behind and was surprised to see that the ranch complex now appeared below them.

"I thought this land was flat," she said. "But it's actually hilly."

"Yeah, General Custer made that same mistake. Unfortunately for him, he didn't get a chance to put what he learned to practical application."

"Custer?"

"The guy that got him and his troops ambushed at the Little Big Horn."

"I know my history," Kate replied. "I just don't see how it applies to what we were talking about."

"The land here's filled with dips and hollows," Jake said. "The Indians hid there and waited for Custer to march him and his troops right smack dab into the middle of the warriors."

"Oh."

"You have to know the land," Jake said. "If you don't, it'll turn on you."

"I'll try and remember that," she said.

He was so much a part of his land. Separate him from it and you separated him from his life force.

Or would you separate him from the shield he was hiding behind?

"So what do you think of the place?" Jake asked.

They'd had a wonderful day of seeing the ranch, of riding over the prairie and delighting in the richness of nature, of just being together. Kate felt more relaxed than she had in days and at the same time more alive.

"It's wonderful," she said. It was after dinner and, as the sun was setting over the hills to the west, they were walking across the grounds near the ranch house. Boris and Nickolai were around somewhere and various ranch hands were in sight, but somehow she felt very alone with Jake.

"It's different from the city," he said.

She laughed, and laughed again as her voice seemed to echo into the shadows. "Only slightly. It's so quiet here. How did you ever stand the noise of the city?"

He took her hand and led her around an outbuilding. "The crowds were worse," he said. "A person needs space to breathe. I don't know what keeps you from going crazy all cooped up like that."

"You tend not to think about it," she said. "And sometimes the crowds are energizing. There's so much happening around you. You just sort of catch an excitement in the air."

She wanted to make him understand, to see the good side of living in the city, though she doubted she could. They walked along a path that led through a stand of trees.

"Can you see okay?" he asked.

"It's not that dark yet."

"But it gets a hell of a lot darker here than in the city."

That was sure true. She'd woken in the middle of the night and gone to sit at the window for a while. The blackness had astounded her. It was thick as black felt, like someone had draped a cover over the ranch as they'd slept.

The trees stopped suddenly, their canopy of branches like a hallway leading them into a wild and untamed arena of nature. The sky rose like a huge vault above them and a river raced at their feet. The little light that was left in the sky danced on the water, leaving it glittering as if with laughter.

"Oh, this is beautiful," Kate cried as she moved closer to the water's edge. It looked so shallow as it raced over stones, but she could see it was the clarity of the water that made it seem so. She spotted flashing amid the ripples. "Are those salmon?"

"Probably."

Jake picked up a stone and skimmed it across the water's surface. His tone seemed suddenly quiet and melancholy. Not that he was prone to constant chuckling, but she had thought this afternoon he was losing some of the tightness she'd felt in him since they'd arrived.

"You fish much?"

He shook his head and skipped another stone.

Where had he gone? What made him go into this mood? She stooped down at the water's edge and fished a stone out. It had looked so clean and bright and smooth, yet as she watched it dry, it became ordinary.

Was that like Jake? Take him out of his surroundings and he changed? Yet here he was in his home, swinging from one mood to another. She tossed the stone back into the water and stood up.

"This a favorite hangout?" she asked. "If I lived here, I think I'd spend most of the time here."

"This was my father's favorite spot, Bo says."

Kate shrugged and walked through the long grass to where Jake was skimming another stone across the waters. The shadows were growing longer; some of the glitter was gone from the air.

"Doesn't mean you can't like it, too," she said, turning slowly to gaze around her.

It was almost as if they were in a cavern, with the trees like walls, the sky high above and the water below. A person could feel safe here and at peace. There was abundant life here, the constant pulsing of nature. She walked over to a fallen tree and sat down.

"I'd bet this was a favorite spot of everybody who lived here," she said. "Maybe it's why the house was built so close by."

Jake came to sit at her side. "A generic favorite spot, is that it? Divorce it from my father so that I can let myself enjoy it?"

The shadows were creeping closer across the land, fingers reaching out to touch her, steal her sunshine. "You can't dance around him forever," she said. "He was a lousy father. Accept it and let it go."

He took her hand in his, intertwining their fingers, then staring down at them as if there were some wisdom in the weaving. "It's not that easy."

"Easy, no. Possible, yes."

"Are you speaking from experience or being pompous and know-it-all?"

She smiled softly at him, her heart growing lighter with the looking. His eyes asked for reassurance, for release from the demons that chased him.

"I didn't have a lousy father," she said, turning to look out at the river. The sound of the water splashing along somehow reminded her of her dad, though they'd never been together along a riverbank that she could remember. "He was wonderful. So loving, so kind. So accepting. He loved me no matter what. But when he died, I had to learn to live without his support."

The past seemed to be lingering in the shadows, waiting to pull her back into the sorrows of long ago. She shook her head as if to will them away. "About the same time, I lost someone else very close to me and I felt that I had lost everything." Her voice grew small. "It was so hard to go on day after day, so certain that anything I grew to care about would be taken from me."

His hand tightened around hers. "What helped you get over all this?"

She shrugged. "I didn't," she said. "Sometimes I still miss them incredibly. My father more than Miguel, but I let time wear away the sharp edges of the pain until it was bearable. I still fear losing, but I've gotten to the point where it's not keeping me from caring."

And you did that for me, she wanted to say, but didn't. She glanced his way and found him staring out at the water. It was darker now, both the water and the sky, as if it was done with laughter and filled with sorrow. The sound of the river rushing over stones and logs and along the banks no longer seemed a happy one, but rather purposeful.

Jake slipped his arm around her shoulders, and she lay her head against his chest. "Putting things aside must be the hardest of chores," he said. "Like calling off a fight that you've spent years training for."

"But what a waste of energy it is," she said. "I think of all the years I stayed in my little cocoon, hiding away because I was too afraid, and all the friendships I missed."

"Well, I for one am glad that you didn't get too involved earlier," he said.

"You are?" She was puzzled and turned toward him, only to find him smiling at her.

His lips were so close, so warm and so welcome. She reached for them and met them with her own. The touch was soft and gentle at first. A cleansing of shadows and bad dreams and all the aches they carried with them. Then it grew stronger, like the river speeding along, bringing life. His arms pulled her closer so that their hearts pressed against each other, beating as one.

She felt his warmth, inhaled the sweet scent of his body and was surrounded by safety. It was like coming home. The wind rustled the leaves of the trees overhead, a lullaby for all the hopes and dreams that her heart cherished.

They pulled apart slightly, and Kate lay her head against his chest, letting his arms stay around her. It was almost night, but there were no bad dreams or monsters in her closet waiting to get her. Jake had brought her tomorrow, and with it came hope and laughter and just a touch of delicious fear.

"We should be getting back while there's still a little light," he said.

She let go of him and got to her feet. There'd always be light around him, a light in her heart. But she just took his hand and walked with him in silence back to the ranch.

Chapter Nine

"You're doing real good," Jake said.

"Thank you," Kate said. A gentle warmth touched her cheeks, but she concentrated on maintaining unity with her horse.

Its name was Molly. Jake had called it a paint: white with broad splotches of brown on the rump and shoulders, it was a descendant of ponies that the Plains Indians had bred before the white man came. The mare pulled at the bit, so Kate let it move ahead of Jake and his horse.

"We've been out almost an hour," Jake called out.

"So?"

"We don't want to overdo anything. An hour of riding on your first day is more than enough."

"This is fun," Kate said. "What am I supposed to do? Go back to the house and sit around like some old lady?"

She looked about her with awe—at the mountains in the not-so-far distance, the immense blue sky over them and the ocean of rolling prairie around them. She couldn't imagine being in such splendor all the time. It made her feel free as the winds on one hand, and tiny and insignificant on the other. It was so different from the city, where you looked inward to gain a sense of peace.

She felt Jake pull up next to her. "Tell me about your house," she said.

"My house?"

"Yeah. It looks like it was built in pieces. How long ago was the first part built?"

He shrugged. "Oh, I don't know. More than a hundred years ago."

"Wow. Your father's family was here a long time. Oh, wait. You said something about him taking the land from your mother's family. So it was the first MacNeill that built the house?"

Jake stared off into the distance for the longest time, and Kate wondered if she'd pried too much. "No, my father took land from my mother's family—doubled the size of his ranch—but the house and the outbuildings were on his original ranch."

"Your family's been here a long time then," Kate said.

"Not so long compared to the hills."

"Ages when compared to stuff in Chicago. Few buildings have been around for a hundred years, and even fewer still have the same family living in them. I think it's really great to have such a sense of belonging."

Jake's face got that shuttered look. "It's not what my father intended."

"But maybe it was what fate intended."

He stared at her, his eyes unreadable, and she didn't know whether he was thinking about her words or amazed at her audacity in saying them. She was feeling brave out here where the winds would blow any shadows from her heart, and that bravery let her look directly into Jake's soul.

There were too many hurts imprisoning him and she wanted to set him free. He'd come to Chicago and pulled down the battlements that kept her from really living. She wanted to do the same for him before she went home.

"How about we head back?" Jake said. "We could jump in the Jeep and take a ride up into the mountains."

"I like being on a horse."

She touched Molly lightly in the ribs and the horse took off up the trail, but they hadn't gone many yards before there was a piercing whistle and the mare stopped dead. Kate tried encouraging her, but nothing would make Molly budge. Kate turned around.

"That's not fair," she shouted at Jake.

"Maybe not," he said, as he trotted up to her. "But it is effective."

"I'm not going back to the barn."

He sighed and looked off toward the mountains. Kate wasn't sure what he was contemplating, but she thought it would be better if she exerted some control on the situation.

"You said this was a working ranch," Kate said. "So why don't we do some work?"

He made a face, and frown lines creased his forehead.

"Come on," Kate persisted. "Laura's out helping Bo. Why can't I help with stuff?"

A grin spread across his face and totally eliminated the frown lines. "She's less trouble than you are."

"Like heck," she replied. "That kid's ornerier than any six people."

"All right," Jake said. "Let's go see how Bo and the boys are coming along. Maybe we can help them repair some fence."

He turned his horse around and moved down the trail. Without waiting for direction, Molly quickly fell into step behind him.

"I thought the horse was supposed to obey her rider," Kate said.

"Sometimes," he said over his shoulder.

"Sometimes?" Kate said. "That's real swell."

"She's a smart horse," Jake said. "You're just a visitor. She has to live with me."

It was true. Kate was just a visitor. But that thought didn't bother her in the least. It gave her a sense of purpose, a sense of direction. She had a job to do in a short amount of time, and she would do it. They walked along at a gentle pace.

"How long has Bo been foreman?" Kate asked after a moment.

"I don't know," Jake said. "Ages. He was foreman when my father ran the place."

"Really? How old is he? Sometimes he looks like your grandfather. Other times he looks like your older brother."

Jake shrugged. "I don't know that, either."

Kate just stared at him. "The man's worked for you forever and you don't know how old he is?"

"Hey, some things we don't ask out here. A man's got a right to privacy."

Yeah, but which man was the one wanting it? Bo, to stay mysterious, or Jake, to stay apart? As they crested a ridge, Kate saw the fence crew and Laura down below them.

"Come on, honey." She nudged the horse in the ribs. "Let's put your feet in gear and shake these darn doldrums."

They zipped by Jake and his mount.

"Hey," he called after them. "Take it easy."

Take it easy? Kate had been taking it easy all her life. Playing it cautious, close to the vest. Being careful. Minimizing the risks. And what had it gotten her?

"Last one to the wagon is a rotten egg," she shouted as she and Molly raced down the gentle slope.

The cowboys laughed and cheered as she and Jake came racing in. Kate won, but she had a sneaking suspicion that he hadn't really been trying.

"What are you doing, riding around like some kind of nut?" Laura demanded, standing tall on the wagon, hands on her hips.

"What?" Kate gave her one of her best glares, but the kid was impervious. "Who died and made you boss?"

"No one died," she replied. "But Bo said I could be boss."

Kate looked toward the grizzled ranch foreman. His broad face was like stone. He shrugged. "Kid was the most qualified," he said.

"For what?" Kate asked.

"I gotta tell them which post to take next. And I tell them if they're making the fence straight."

Bo nodded solemnly while the other ranch hands chuckled good-naturedly. Kate tried glaring again at Laura. The kid already thought she ruled the world. There was no need for anyone else to tell her she was in charge of anything.

"We came over to help you," Kate said to Bo.

"Gotta talk to the boss," he said, tilting his head toward Laura.

Oh, this was ridiculous. "Laura, get—"

"Can I work on your crew?" Jake asked.

"Sure," Laura exclaimed, grinning widely.

This was not helping matters any. Kate tried to get Jake's attention, but he studiously avoided looking at her.

"And how about my pard?" Jake asked.

Laura's grin quickly melted. "You mean Kate?"

"Yup."

Laura took a long moment, face twisted in concentration. Kate sat on her horse, frowning. If that kid said no, she would take the whole group of them across her knee, one at a time.

"All right," Laura said, reluctance pulling at each word. "She can help."

"Golly gee," Kate said. "Thanks a heap."

"But you're responsible for her," Laura told Jake, shaking a finger at him for emphasis.

"Right, Boss," Jake replied, snapping the brim of his hat in salute. He dismounted from his horse and came toward Kate.

"Thanks." She paused a moment. "Pard."

"That's what partners are for," he replied.

Kate thought his grin needing a little toning down, but there would be time enough later for that. Right now she was going to show everybody that she could be a big help. That she wasn't some kind of a tenderfoot.

Jake put out his hand to help her dismount.

"Thanks again, Pard," Kate said. "But I can take care of myself."

* * *

Jake slipped on his jacket, picked up a chocolate-chip cookie from the plate on the counter and stepped outside into the darkness. The day had been pleasant, but the night was quite chilly. He turned up the collar on his jacket.

A red ember winked at him from the far end of the porch, like a good-time girl beckoning a sailor to come hither. Jake stuffed the rest of the cookie into his mouth and walked toward the invitation.

"You know those coffin nails are going to kill you," he said.

Bo's sardonic laugh bubbled around the gravel in his throat. "Boy, you college kids know everything," he said. "I quit smoking and I'll live forever."

"Not forever," Jake replied, sitting down in the chair next to Bo's. "Just longer."

"I've lived too damned long already."

Jake looked out into the blackness and the canopy of stars above them. It was a clear night, which was why it was especially cool, but there was only a quarter moon out, which made things on the dim side.

Kate's questions this afternoon had set Jake to wondering. Near as he could tell, Bo was somewhere between fifty and a hundred. The old foreman never talked about his past nor said how old he was. Bo was like the mountains—he hadn't been born and didn't grow old, but had always been there. At least, he had been for Jake. And that was why Jake wasn't going to pry.

"The world keeps changing, and I don't." Bo ground out the cigarette and flicked the remains into an old coffee can he kept by the porch railing. "Every day me and the world drift farther and farther apart, like folks that's been married too long."

Normally Bo didn't talk all that much. And certainly not about himself. Jake felt himself growing uncomfortable and didn't know quite how to respond. Cowboy rules said you should respect every man, even if he was crazy—so long as he didn't show the mess that was in his soul.

Might be a good idea to divert Bo about now. Take him off this heavy track and put him on to something lighter. "You and Laura sure are getting along."

Old Bo made a growling sound in his throat that Jake knew was a chuckle. "Having a kid like that around is like having a new puppy."

"Don't be too nice to her." Jake smiled. "She'll get right attached to you and won't want to go home."

"Wouldn't mind that one bit," Bo growled. "Sorta like getting a second chance at having a family." He leaned forward, resting his arms on his knees. "You never think as you watch the ladies come and go that one day it's gonna be too late. That you're gonna be an old man and all alone."

"Hey, you're not alone," Jake protested.

Bo glared at him through the darkness. "I'm exactly what you're gonna be if you're as stupid as I was."

Jake scrunched back into his chair, trying to hide in the darkness. In all the time he'd known Bo, they'd never had one of these bare-your-soul kind of conversations. It made him feel like a point man leading an infantry unit through a mine field. Everything was kind of quiet now, but Lord only knew what would happen the next time he moved his foot or tongue.

"Kate's a fine lady," Bo said.

"Yeah." Jake was not going to say more, but Bo's silence pushed at him. Damn it. He was sorry Bo was feeling a bit down and regretful, but that didn't mean Jake was going to make his and Kate's relationship into something it wasn't.

"It's nice having them here," Bo said. "Place needs ladies around."

"What's Mary Redwing?" Jake asked.

"She's a grandmaw," Bo replied.

"My mother comes out once every blue moon."

"She's a wannabe grandmaw," Bo said.

Jake's mouth was open, ready to snap out a reply, but this time no words came. What the hell was this stuff about his mother wanting grandchildren? She'd never said anything to him about it. Besides, she knew that kids weren't something you went out and bought like kittens or puppies. There was a whole lot of baggage that came with a child. The kind of baggage his father hadn't wanted to carry.

The chair next to him scraped and Jake felt, more than saw, Bo get up and stretch.

"Best get these old bones to bed," the foreman said. "Got us a couple of full days ahead of us. We got to get those calves all checked out and vaccinated."

"Damn, I forgot about that," Jake said. "I'm supposed to take Kate into town one of these days. My mother wants to visit."

"I imagine she does," Bo replied.

"What the hell is that supposed to mean?"

"Go whenever's convenient," Bo said. "You ain't all that much help anyways."

"Thanks."

"You're going to leave the young one here, aren't you?"

"I guess."

"Appreciate that. Kid's a good worker."

Without another word, Bo stepped off the porch and strode toward his little cabin down under the willows near the creek.

Jake stared at his back long after it had disappeared into the darkness. Why hadn't Bo had any children of his own? From his talk tonight, it sounded like maybe he'd just never gotten around to it. But the fact of the matter was this was none of Jake's business. He forced all thoughts out of his mind, pushing them to where they could drift into the evening mist.

Whatever his age, Bo was getting on in years. He was out of touch with some things, but he was right about Kate and Laura. It was nice having them on the ranch. Most likely it was their fresh enthusiasm for anything to do with the prairie, the animals and everything else connected with the place.

And it wasn't just what they did to the atmosphere. Kate also brought a special light into his life. She had a good sense of humor and a soft charm that stoked his fires at the same time as they soothed his nerves. She was new to the

ranch, yet she fit in so well it was as if she'd been there forever.

Jake sighed and slumped down in his chair. She hadn't
been around forever and she'd be around less than that in
the future. She wouldn't be here more than another week or
so, then she'd be homeward bound. Home to her business,
her family, her friends. Home to the big city by the lake.

Good thing it was already dark. The thought of saying
goodbye to Kate would have sent the sun scurrying, and then
everybody would be madder than hell at him.

"You could close the door, you know."

Just as soon as the last word was out, Kate clamped her
teeth over her lower lip to keep herself from hollering out in
pain. Oh, my. Every single teeny tiny muscle in her body
hurt. Actually, hurt didn't come close to describing how she
felt. Every cell within her screamed in agony.

"Good morning to you, too."

Laura's words came out blurred, having to make their way
around a toothbrush, but they were loud enough to make up
for that. Kate groaned to herself.

She and Laura had separate rooms, but they shared a
connecting bath. Laura had gotten up first and had been
clanging around the bathroom for ages now.

"You going to stay in bed all day?"

Kate shut her eyes, wishing she could shut her ears to
Laura's demanding voice. She would have preferred being
able to break the kid's neck, but in her present state, that
was not something she could accomplish on her own. And
the darn kid had made a zillion friends on the ranch, so Kate
knew she wouldn't get any help there.

"I'm just resting my eyes," she replied.

"You look like a corpse."

"Thank you. You're charming, too."

"What do they called it when a body is dead and gets all
stiff?" Laura asked.

"Rigor mortis."

"Yeah, that's it."

Kate could feel Laura staring at her. "Don't you have anything to do?" she asked. "Like going up into the mountains and jumping into an ice-cold lake?"

"Don't you feel good?" Laura asked.

"I feel fine. I just don't want to play bunny rabbit and go hop-hopping out of bed."

"You overdid things yesterday."

"Go away."

"Jake warned you about that," Laura said.

Clenching her teeth, Kate forced herself to sit up. Oh, Lord. Now she realized what pain was. Pain was when you lay real still. Excruciating agony was when you moved.

"You should listen to him, you know. He knows a lot about a lot of stuff."

Kate thought about throwing something at the kid, but knew it would hurt her more than Laura. "I want to use the bathroom," she said.

"I'm done," Laura replied, leaning against the wall.

"Don't you have anything else you want to do?"

"Uh-uh."

"Then get out of here anyway," Kate said. "Get out while you're able to walk."

"Jeez." Shaking her head, Laura went to the door and pulled it open.

"Good morning, Laura."

Kate's hand dashed to the throat of her nightshirt. What was Jake doing at her door?

"Hi," Laura said. "You better not go in there. Kate's got a super grump on."

Jake stepped into the doorway and stopped there, leaning against the door. "Good morning."

For an instant, Kate felt a deep, burning annoyance at his cheerful attitude. But just for an instant. "Good morning," she said, proud of how light and pleasant her tone was.

"Little stiff, are we?" he asked.

"I don't know about you, but I'm fine."

He had a nice smile. But sometimes it was just a little too much for her tastes.

"You need to move slowly," he said. "Warm up and stretch a little."

Kate nodded. "I'll do that."

He stayed in the doorway, looking disgustingly pleasant. "Need any help?"

"No."

Jake still didn't move. It was obvious she was going to have to get up to assure him that she was fully able to care for herself. Clenching her jaw, she put her hands on the bed and pushed herself up.

"Oh!" The cry escaped her lips and she would have fallen if Jake hadn't dashed in, wrapping his arms around her. The door closed softly behind him.

"I told you that you were overdoing things."

"Shut up." The words were satisfactorily harsh, but Kate was disappointed in the tone. It was too soft and mushy, not having near the emphasis she'd meant to convey.

But she hurt so much that she just gave up and sighed. It was so comfortable in his arms, but her pain wouldn't let her relax completely. That was probably a good thing. It would keep her out of trouble.

His lips ever so gently took hers, touching them softly over and over again. "That hurt?" he whispered.

"Nope."

He let his lips wander along her chin and down her neck so that she felt little, tingling sparks all along her spine. "How about that?"

"Nope. Just fine."

His hands moved slightly, roaming across her back, leaving a trail of heat under her thin nightgown. Down her sides and along her waist those hands kept moving. "Any problems?"

"Only when you stop," she murmured, hungry for his lips to return to hers.

"Maybe then I'd better not stop."

His lips came back to hers, so she could quit longing for them and just enjoy their sweet taste. His hands were so gentle they eased away the ache in her muscles. Her heart forgot to be wary, forgot its cautious nature and rushed ahead.

She gloried in the touch of his hands, in the fire that his caress awakened and in the delight growing in her heart. She wanted to come alive in his arms again, to feel like a complete woman.

There was something about these last few days, of living in the vast expanses of the prairies, that seemed to have freed her heart of its silly constraints. She was ready to accept the challenge of passion as well as the promise of it.

There was no hesitation in her touch or caution in her lips as she invited Jake to share her love. She let her hands be bold and brash, her lips demanding. A fire grew in Jake's eyes that she felt in his caress. An answering fire flared up inside her.

When their needs could no longer be denied, they lay together, letting their passions consume them both in a wild, raging storm. It was better, hotter, stronger than the first time. Kate felt her heart explode in wonder, and then later, as she lay in Jake's arms, she wished she could stay there forever.

She was alive with him as she'd never been before. Her heart was free to soar, her dreams free to grow unhampered. She let her eyes drift closed and listened to the rhythm of Jake's heartbeat, the rhythm of her life.

The day crawled by. After sharing breakfast with Kate, Jake had gone off with the ranch hands and Laura to round up some calves. Kate had wanted to go, but Jake decreed otherwise.

"Stay here and take it easy," he'd said. "This is supposed to be a vacation for you."

She'd argued, but he'd won in the end. Laura's smirk as they left hadn't helped.

So Kate had spent the day reading, walking around the buildings close to the house and generally going stir-crazy. In the middle of the afternoon, she found Mary Redwing on the back porch.

"Want some help?" Kate asked.

Mary was snapping beans with her hands while her eyes gazed out at the prairie. She turned at Kate's words and nodded at the bench next to her.

"You're a guest. Our guests don't work."

Kate sat down with a sigh. "Laura's out working with the calves, I'd like to feel at least semiuseful."

Mary shifted the bushel basket of beans into the space between them and gave Kate an empty bowl to toss the beans into. "Anything to keep a guest happy."

Kate smiled at the older woman and began to snap the stems off, tossing them to one side, the beans into the bowl. They worked in silence for a time, the sounds of the ranch washing over them. Birds. Men calling to one another. The wind in the trees. Man and nature all mixed together.

"At home, you can't hear too many nature sounds," Kate said. "Sometimes birds chirping in the early morning, but not much else. Unless you go to the lakefront, of course."

"Must be hard to hear your soul then."

Kate snapped the stem from a bean and stared at it a moment. "I guess. I mean, we do have quiet times. I like to listen to music, and that's kind of like nature."

Mary nodded. "Music is man's nature."

Kate thought of the George Winston piano instrumentals she liked to listen to. The soft rhythm of the music seemed to free something inside her, put her in touch with herself.

"Me, I like Garth Brooks," Mary said.

"Oh?" Soft classical music was what Kate viewed as revealing man's nature, not cowboy hats and guitars.

"And T.G. Shepherd," Mary went on. "Know what the T.G. stands for?"

Kate shook her head.

"The German." Seeing Kate's blank stare, Mary continued, "He needed a stage name and he was looking out the window and saw a German shepherd, so he picked T. G. Shepherd after The German Shepherd."

"Weird."

"But true." She went back to her beans. "Jake likes you a lot."

"Oh?" Kate wasn't quite ready for the shift from names to personal feelings. She snapped a few beans with great concentration. "Have you worked here long?"

"No. I came ten years ago, after Harry died. I needed a place and Jake needed a cook. It's worked out." She snapped the last few beans in her hands. "I knew George, though. Jake's father. Very unhappy man."

Kate bit her lip. She'd like to ask a million different things, but somehow couldn't. "It sounds like it," she said.

"Jake is very like him. He has a hard time being close, but you can trust him. Just be patient."

Kate reached down into the bushel basket, which was becoming alarmingly empty. How would she occupy her hands then? "We're really just friends," she said.

"He's had girlfriends, but never ones that could see inside him," Mary said as if Kate hadn't spoken.

And she could? "Neither of us is looking for anything lasting."

Mary pulled out the last handful of beans. "The heart decides how long something will last."

"Well, I hope it's listening to the rest of me then. I have a business back in Chicago. Laura and I will be here for only a few more days."

"For now," Mary said, her fingers snapping the beans as if for emphasis. She finished the last and stood up. "Want to help me bake pies? The men'll be back in a couple of hours for dinner, so we haven't got much time."

"Sure." Kate got to her feet also, feeling strangely content.

Baking pies for the menfolk? This sounded like something out of a 1940s western. She looked out over the prairie, wondering where Jake was. A nineties woman she might be, but she missed him.

Chapter Ten

"I could drive myself into town, you know," Kate said. "It can't be all that difficult."

"That's okay." His tone was clipped and curt.

Kate watched as he thoroughly checked the two-lane highway before pulling out onto the road. He was either at his limit in traffic violations, an extraordinarily cautious man or he didn't really want to go visit his mother. Kate searched for some clue as to Jake's sudden mood change, but found none.

"Your mother seems nice," she finally said.

"Yeah, she is." He sighed. "She likes to act as if she's tough as nails, but she's really a pushover." His face darkened. "People have been known to take advantage of her."

Kate suspected he was referring to something in the past and made no comment. No matter what they'd shared over the past few weeks, there was still this barrier between them. Pieces of himself that he'd locked away and wouldn't let anyone touch. They rode for a while in silence.

"Did you grow up in this town?" Kate asked as the city limits came into view.

"Yeah," he replied. "My mother still lives in the same house."

"You have any brothers or sisters?" Kate asked.

"Nope."

"Your mother live alone?"

"With a bunch of cats and an old mutt."

Jake slowed down as they came to the outskirts of town, passing through the usual hodgepodge of discount stores and fast-food outlets interspersed with small motels. The older part of town had a certain rustic beauty. Old trees, probably planted by the first settlers, lined the streets of simple old homes.

They went a short way down Main Street, which could have served as a movie set for a western, and turned left. There were sidewalks in front of the homes but no curbs. That privilege appeared to have been reserved for Main Street.

Jake pulled off the road into the driveway of a simple one-story home. The house, garage and shed in back were all neat, clean and recently painted. And the yard, although it had a rustic, natural appearance, was also tidy.

"Well, here we are," Jake said.

He seemed to be steeling his soul, and Kate started to worry. Didn't he like his mother? Or was he concerned about what she might say or do?

They moved slowly up a walk made of railroad ties and bricks, and onto the porch. Kate thought he paused when they came to the door, but she told herself it was her imagination. Jake knocked lightly on the door.

A baying sounded from inside the house and suddenly the door swung open. Jake's mother stood in the doorway, fixing them with that same hard gaze Kate remembered from their last meeting. A medium-sized hound stood by the woman's side.

"Damn it, Jake," she snapped. "What are you moping about now?"

"I'm not moping about anything," he snapped right back.

"Then why in the world are you knocking on my door? Everybody in the county knows I don't lock it."

"Sorry, Mom," he replied. "I was just trying to be polite."

"Poor old Lucille here thought you were some kind of damned salesman." His mother indicated the gray-whiskered dog at her side, who was now wagging her tail in welcome.

Kate stared. The woman lived here all alone and never locked her doors? Good heavens, that would have been asking for trouble back in Chicago, or anywhere else, for that matter.

"Come in. Come in." Jake's mother stood back from the door. "I don't want to spend good money heating up the out-of-doors when the Good Lord intended for it to be cool."

Jake took Kate by the hand and pulled her into the house, where they waited for his mother to close the door. She did so, then turned to Kate.

"Jake's a nice-enough boy," she said. "But he gets himself into a grumpy spell now and again."

"Kate," Jake said. "As you already know, this charming person is my mother, Faith MacNeill."

"It's nice to see you again, Faith."

Faith took Kate's hand. "You best wait until you know me awhile before making that kind of a judgment. And you certainly never want to say anything like that in public. Less'n you're looking for a good fight."

The flippancy was similar to Jake's, but somehow Kate had the idea she was looking into Faith's soul rather than being distracted from it.

Kate smiled at the woman. "The public be damned," she said.

"Lordy," Faith exclaimed. "A woman of principle. No wonder you and Jake here get on so well."

Kate looked toward Jake and smiled. Poor guy. He looked like a high-school boy whose mother was telling his football coach how well he could sew.

"So what's your plan, Jake?" Faith asked. "You coming back when you got your supplies or you want me to bring Katie back to the ranch later today?"

Jake grew a tad more uncomfortable looking. "Uh, I thought I'd stay and visit, too."

"You're going to stay and visit?" Faith gave him a look, then turned to Kate. "He can't be worried you'd shock me, so he must be afraid I'm going to misbehave."

"I can't believe that."

Faith gently pushed the two of them farther into the house. "Oh, I can misbehave real good. But he ain't got cause to worry. I can be polite when I put my mind to it."

She took their jackets and led them into the living room. It was decorated in a Western kind of a style with the same Spartan charm as outside. Three cats already occupied the room—a calico sat on the windowsill looking out, a black one with one white foot and its eyes closed sprawled on the sofa's backrest and an orange tabby relaxed in a recliner and glared at them.

"Sit in the recliner, honey," Faith said. "It's the best chair in the county. Just put Toby on the floor."

Kate looked into the cat's eyes, so fierce they seemed to be burning. "That's okay, I'll just—"

"Nonsense." Faith marched up to the chair and swept the cat onto the floor. "Kate here is a guest, you old reprobate. Go find someplace else to laze around."

Then she grabbed Kate by the arm and plunked her down in the chair. Just as quickly, Toby jumped back up and onto Kate's lap.

"Oh, he's a stubborn one," Faith muttered. "You bothered by cats?"

"No, ma'am," Kate replied.

"Scratch him under the chin," Faith said. "He just loves that. I'll get us lunch."

About two seconds later, she was back with two plates, each piled high with a sandwich about a foot thick, nacho chips and an assortment of raw vegetables. She handed one plate to Kate, then kept the other as she sat down.

"Your plate's in the kitchen," she told Jake. "Why don't you get us some coffee while you're there?"

As Jake marched off toward the back of the house, Faith smiled over at Kate. "Your coming here is quite an event. Jake never had a woman staying out at the ranch with him before."

Kate suddenly saw the reason for Jake's uneasiness. The town matchmakers were busily at work. "Well, he stayed with us in Chicago, so it's kind of a payback."

"Oh?"

"Our furnace went haywire and we had some smoke damage in our house. Since it was going to take a few weeks to fix, he suggested Laura and I come to visit."

Faith looked disappointed. "That's what he told us." A thoughtful gleam appeared in her eyes. "But he trusted you with the dogs."

"Actually, he trusted my sister with them," Kate said. "And it was more because he didn't think they'd take to flying."

"Huh."

Jake walked in at that moment with three cups of coffee. He let his mother take one, gave one to Kate and then put one on the table next to the wingback chair to her left. He went back for his lunch.

"So," Faith said. A healthy gulp of the steaming-hot liquid seemed to revive her spirits. "How'd you two happen to meet?"

Kate had just taken a bite of her sandwich—mounds of tender roast beef between slices of homemade bread. Since she didn't want to talk with her mouth full, she had a moment or two to think. Jake came back into the room, and it was obvious from the scowl on his face that he had heard his mother's question.

"Jake sideswiped my date's car," Kate said.

Faith's eyes narrowed as she frowned at her son. "Nobody hurt, I hope?"

"No. Just a few scratches on the car," Kate said, then grinned. "And a few scratches on Jake where I walloped him with my purse."

Faith let loose a burst of laughter. "Good for you. Always hoped someone would come along and wallop some sense into him."

"Thanks, Mom."

They settled down to lunch, Faith barely touching her food as she recounted story after story from Jake's youth for Kate. They were the typical stories a parent told—fights Jake had gotten into, funny things he'd said, accomplishments Faith was proud of. But through them all, Kate saw the same stubborn, hurting little boy she could still see in his eyes when he let his guard down. Was there any way to help him let go of the past and look ahead?

"Whatcha got planned for your lady here?" Faith asked Jake once they were done eating. "Gonna visit some folks here in town?"

"We're visiting you," he replied.

"Jake," Faith snapped. "Don't go word dancing with me or I'll set you in a corner and leave you there until you're all happy and cheerful again."

"There isn't anyone else I wanted to visit in town."

"You're still as ornery as you were back in high school," Faith said.

Jake's mouth took on a grim, stubborn look. He and his mother traded glares for a moment. Then she shook her head and finished the rest of her coffee.

"Damn Tylers," she told Kate. "They hold a grudge like a miser holds his pennies."

Kate had her cup halfway to her mouth and froze in that position. Damn who? her mind sputtered. She couldn't have heard right.

"Ain't no grudge to it." Jake was busy arguing with his mother. "We're just going to sit a spell with you, then head back to the ranch."

"Oh, that sounds real exciting." Faith snorted. "Almost enough to make a girl all giddy and giggly."

"Wait a minute," Kate said.

Jake apparently hadn't heard her. "I got me a bunch of calves to get ready for the winter."

"Hellsfire, boy. At least take her to the museum."

"Who holds grudges?" Kate asked.

Jake went on again. "I'm not taking her to some dusty old shack filled with useless junk."

"Shouldn't that be her choice?" Faith snapped. "No wonder you never have company out at the ranch. You haven't got any manners."

"I've got enough manners not to bore her to death with dust and old tales."

Kate stopped trying to get Jake's attention. He'd been acting weird all day. He wasn't not hearing her interruptions; he was ignoring her. And now he was getting into an argument about a museum. She had a strange suspicion and suddenly knew where she wanted to go. She got to her feet.

"I'd love to go the museum," she announced in a voice loud enough that no one could pretend to ignore it.

Jake parked the truck on Main Street in front of the museum and sat staring at the sign advertising beautiful girls and cheap drinks. The museum was housed in the old Longhorn Saloon building, and its original signs had been repainted to contribute to the atmosphere around the place. He didn't know about the atmosphere in the museum, but that in the truck combined annoyance, suspicion and resignation.

"You could've come into Bobbie DeVeaux's office with me," Faith said to Jake. Annoyance speaking.

"Why?" he asked. Resignation. "The keys too heavy for you to carry by yourself?"

Kate gave him a look. Suspicion. He knew that one with his eyes closed. Knew it would be there as a prelude to anger before the day was out if they went visiting his mother. There was no way the Tyler name would be left out of things.

"It wouldn't hurt for you to be sociable with your neighbors once in a while." Faith put the key in the lock of the saloon door. "It's folks working together that gets things done."

"I don't have any problems getting things done," Jake replied.

"Wouldn't know it from all the complaining you do."

"I don't complain." Jake knew he sounded snappish and tight, but didn't care. "I tell you about the things that I do. If that bothers you, then I won't talk to you anymore."

Shaking her head, Faith pushed the door open. Kate followed, ominously silent.

"Never met a Tyler man yet that wasn't as bullheaded as all get out," Faith said, reaching in and flipping on a set of light switches to the right of the door. "If it weren't for the fact they're so all-fired good-looking, the line would've come to a dead stop back with old Jacob."

Jake steeled himself for the explosion, but Kate just smiled at his mother and wandered into the room. Photographic displays lined the outer walls, while maps and a diorama were held in a case in the middle of the room.

"This place is really unique," Kate said.

Why didn't she just blow up? All right, so he hadn't acknowledged that Jacob Tyler was an ancestor, or that his own given surname was Tyler, but he hadn't actually lied about it.

"Probably the only town in the lower forty-eight that has its museum in an old saloon," he grumbled.

"This was the center of Cold Spring's social, political and business activity back in the old days," Faith put in. "Weren't no other building that rightfully could be the museum."

"Yeah," Jake said. "This was where the best fistfights, knife fights, gunfights and plain all-around brawls took place."

"Them were the good old days," Faith murmured. "Things are a hell of a lot duller now."

"And I'm talking about the women," Jake said. "The men took all their fights outside."

"The western states were always more progressive in their treatment of women," Faith replied, trying to outdo him.

"Wyoming was the first state to give women the right to vote, you know."

Kate didn't appear to be listening as she wandered over to the diorama. It was a model of the town in the year 1900. The saloon was in the heart of the town, a church on one side, the railroad station on the other. The saloon, the caption told her, was the only building still standing, though a rebuilt version of the church stood on the same plot over near the river.

She stepped back after a moment. "This smells like an old saloon," she said, sniffing.

"That's just the sawdust you smell." Faith snorted. "A real western saloon would mix whiskey, beer and sweat in with that pine smell."

It was just that he didn't put any stock in that silly old story about Caitlin and Jacob. To acknowledge he was a Tyler seemed to give it credence.

Kate walked on to a nearby table holding artifacts. Old six-shooters and knives filled up one display; ropes, spurs and other cowboy paraphernalia filled another.

"So who founded the town?" she asked.

"Calvin Loughern," Jake's mother said, coming over to join her. "Back in 1853."

Jake turned to stare at some old newspapers on the wall. They started in the early 1900s and chronicled major events in the town: several fires, a sheriff's son killed in World War I, the closing of the railroad station.

Would his murder here in the museum one day join the list of stories? The waiting was making him stir-crazy.

"I really ought to be getting back," he grumbled.

"So go," Faith said. "I can drive Kate on out."

He just leaned against the doorway, feeling like a man awaiting hanging. Maybe he should announce the truth now. Confront Kate with the news and see how she acted.

"I just love old pictures," his mother said. "Don't you?"

Kate joined her at the photo wall, and even from his post near the door, Jake could see where they stopped—at the photo of a tall, thin man with dark brows, a handlebar

mustache and a stone face. The one who bore a strong re-
semblance to himself.

"That's Jacob Tyler," his mother said, indicating the
picture with her chin. "An early settler and founder of the
J-Bar-T spread."

Kate stared at the picture a long time before turning back
to Faith. "The ranch is really old then, isn't it?"

He had told her that. Just hadn't told her whose name
was on the original deed.

"A hundred and ten this past summer," Faith replied.
"And it's been in the family the whole time. Never been
owned by anybody but a Tyler."

"Really?"

"And only two of the Tylers have been JTs," Faith said.
"Old Jacob there and my boy Jake."

But he's wasn't a JT anymore, Jake wanted to say.
Somehow silence seemed safer, though.

"Here's another picture of old Jacob," Faith said.

Kate followed Faith down the row of pictures to the one
of Jacob with a woman and several young children.

No, he hadn't remained faithful to Caitlin forever, Jake
silently told her, but if a descendant was supposed to return
in his place, then he couldn't have.

"This his family?" Kate asked.

"Wife Lizzy and sons Colin and Michael, and daughter
Kathleen," Faith said. "He married late. Guess he was all
fired up to stake his claim when he came out here in the early
1870s. Did well, too, as the story goes, but lost everything
'cept his land a bit later. Terrible drought one summer followed by the bitterest winter on record. Lotta settlers went
belly up that year."

"But he started over and did well?" Kate asked.

"Married the daughter of the wealthiest man around,
joined their lands for the biggest ranch around, but never
seemed happy, tales tell."

Kate stood staring at the picture for a long time. What did
she see in it? What was there to see but an unhappy-looking
man with an unhappy-looking wife and kids?

Hell, Jake should have told her back in Chicago that he had an ancestor by the name of Jacob Tyler. Should have got it out in the open, where they could all have a good laugh at the coincidence.

Right now, he had better things to do than to wait around for lightning to start another prairie fire.

"I'm going back to the ranch," he said. "I promised Bo I'd be back to help him."

"You need help, hire more hands," Faith said sharply.

"Mom, today's just one of those days. We got a bunch of calves to vaccinate and check out before the snows hit."

"I'd like to get back, too," Kate said. "I don't like to be away from Laura too long."

"Oh, all right," Faith exclaimed, ushering them out into the brisk air.

Jake squinted in the sunlight. He'd never liked the gloomy, dusty smell of the museum and now he liked it even less.

"So you never heard of Jacob Tyler," Kate snapped once he'd pulled out of his mother's driveway. "And I thought you were into honesty."

"I never lied to you," he said. "I had my name legally changed to MacNeill years ago, and as far as I'm concerned, that's what I am."

"But you are a Tyler. Your father was one and Jacob Tyler was your great-great-something-grandfather."

"I can't help what their names were. I had mine changed. And I want no part of them."

"You can't choose what you're a part of," she said.

"Sure you can."

He pulled out onto Main Street, and Kate stared at the museum as they passed, feeling a strange weariness in her soul. She had found old Jacob. She had tried to look into his eyes, to see into his soul and judge who he was, but the old picture had been blurry and his eyes had been in shadow. Or was it that they were Tyler eyes—dark and shuttered to the world all the time?

Jake was a Tyler. It was clear from the photo, from all the things Faith had said, from everything. So why had he lied? Why had he pretended not to have ever heard the name?

Granny had been right and so had Laura. What did it all mean, though?

"It doesn't mean anything, you know," he said, as if reading her mind. "This whole Caitlin and Jacob stuff. It's just a coincidence."

She shrugged her shoulders, cutting off any more conversation between them. They sailed across the vast, open prairie, carrying a heavy load of silence between them.

He'd named one daughter Kathleen. Was that his way of remembering Caitlin? Had he wished things had been different or had he put Chicago and all that it held out of his thoughts forever?

She thought of Caitlin passing the ring down to her daughters, so sure that he would return one day.

"We don't even know if it's the right Jacob Tyler," he said suddenly. "It's not exactly an uncommon name."

"It's the same one," she said, her anger deflating into weariness. "And you're right. It doesn't mean anything. It's just so weird."

"Yeah."

He sounded less defensive, too, and Kate grinned his way. Would it have mattered to her that he was a Tyler? Would she have not come if she'd known? It truly didn't mean anything.

"I guess the weirdness of it is why I didn't say anything," he admitted. "I don't want to be the puppet of some ancestor. Hey, if he screwed up, it's his fault. I have my own life to lead."

But had they screwed up or were they just the victims of bad luck? Kate didn't know what to think anymore.

"And from the Tyler men I've known," Jake said, "Caitlin might have been better off without him. Both my father and grandfather were cold, distant men. All they thought about was getting more money, owning more property. Old Jacob doesn't sound much different."

Neither did Jake, Kate thought, if you just put a negative twist on everything he did. "Maybe all you Tyler men learned from each other," she said.

"I didn't learn anything from my father or grandfather," he said. "They were never a part of my life. How could they teach me anything?"

"Maybe their absence taught you to reject relationships. Maybe watching them from a distance taught you to keep people at a distance."

He stared ahead. "Maybe it taught me not to promise what I can't deliver," he said, his voice edged with bitterness. "Or maybe I am like them and that seems a good reason not to have kids of my own."

Kate watched the ribbon of road unfurl before them, seeming to head endlessly into the immense sky. "Even knowing the bad about your family makes you luckier than a lot of kids," Kate said, suddenly thinking of Laura.

Laura knew nothing about Miguel, nothing of his family history. Miguel's family wasn't even aware of her. Now, for the first time since Laura was born, Kate saw how she had cheated them all.

"You know so much about your family tree," she said. "You know where you came from. It's all laid out in that museum, in what you called useless junk. Damn it, Jake. You're so well grounded. You know exactly where you fit in your world."

"Yeah." His resentment was so strong she could almost taste it. "I'm George Tyler's bastard son. I know it and everybody in this whole damned state knows it."

"Jake!" Kate felt like screaming at him. "I don't know what kind of problems your father had, and I'm sure he had many, but he did accept you as his son."

"This is a small town," Jake said. "Everybody knew he was my father. He had to admit it."

"He didn't have to. You said he was a rich and powerful man. He could have totally ignored you."

"He did," Jake replied quietly. "Except for putting his name on a little bitty piece of paper, that's exactly what he did."

Kate sighed. She should stay out of this. It was a demon Jake had been wrestling with for a long time and nothing she could say would change anything. She had enough problems of her own, the most serious of which was how to tell Laura the truth.

"Do you want to stop at the house?" Jake asked as he turned onto ranch property. "I'm going out to the calf roundup. Do you want me to let you off here?"

She shook her head. She needed to see Laura now—not to tell her, but just to see her. "Laura's out there, isn't she? I'd like to see how she's getting along."

"Okay."

He headed off toward the back section of his ranch. "One of the boys can bring you back when you're ready."

They bounced over open fields for several minutes before Kate saw the dust generated by cattle and the men working with them. As they drew closer, she got a better look.

"Those are calves?" she asked. "They look huge."

Jake laughed as he stopped the truck. "Were you expecting some cute, little, wobbly-legged creatures? You should've been around in early spring when they were born. These guys weigh anywhere from 400 to 600 pounds now."

"My God." She slowly let herself out of the pickup. She was glad to see that Laura was in the back of a truck, where she was relatively safe.

"What are you guys doing here?" the girl shouted.

"We came to help out," Jake replied.

"You're a little late for that."

Boy, that kid's mouth was getting big. "Laura," Kate said. "That's no way to talk to your host."

"You'd better get back," Laura said, her voice filled with self-importance. "Some calf could break away from the herd and run you guys down. And we're busy. Ain't got no time to play doctor with you."

Kate shook her head. The girl's tone of voice seemed especially grating today. "Laura—"

"Look out!"

"Heads up!"

Kate looked up in time to see a calf bearing down on her. Somewhere in the distance, she could hear Laura yelling something at her. Then all of a sudden, she was down off the truck and running toward her. "Get out of the way," she screamed.

But Kate couldn't move.

Until she realized that Laura was putting herself on a collision course with the calf. "Laura!" As the cry left her lips, Kate's feet moved. She had to—

The calf plowed into both of them. Kate felt a sharp shove in her side, feet sweeping out from under her, dust and grass flying in her face. There was a hard thud when she landed and a slight twinge in her wrist, all mixed up with shouting and stamping and snorting.

She opened her eyes to find Jake's worried face looking down at her. "You all right?" he asked, even as she was getting to her feet.

"Laura?" Kate asked as she looked around.

Bo was kneeling next to the girl. Her eyes were open and she was rubbing her head. Kate ran over to them.

"She took a good rap on the noggin," Bo said. "We best get her to home."

Laura looked up at Kate with annoyance. "Damn tenderfoot," she mumbled. "I told you to get back out of the way. I told you. You just don't ever listen."

Chapter Eleven

The doctor was taking forever.

Kate stopped at the foot of the stairs and looked up into the shadows for the umpteenth time, but there was no movement, no sound. She turned to continue her pacing.

"Oh, God," she groaned. "I was so stupid."

"It was an accident," Jake said.

He didn't understand. He didn't know that all Kate had been able to see on that hurried ride back to the house was Laura's white face. And with only a little blurring, Laura's face when she'd been born.

"I was so careless."

"Kate, she'll be fine," Jake said. He took hold of her arms, stopping her pacing. "She's a tough little kid. She'll just have a headache, that's all."

She pulled away from him. She didn't deserve his comfort. "I almost killed her once before and now I almost did it again." She closed her eyes and saw again Laura's white face against the brown sand.

A step on the stair caused her to spin around. The doctor was down. She hurried over.

"Your sister is fine," he said.

Kate breathed a sigh of relief. She felt Jake behind her and leaned back into his strength for just a moment.

"She has a mild concussion, so she needs to rest and take it easy. By the beginning of next week, she should be fine."

"Thank goodness."

"She looks a little wan right now, so I'm sure she'll sleep. But wake her in a couple of hours to make sure everything is all right."

Kate nodded.

"And remember, call me if anything comes up." He turned and nodded at Jake. "See you later, Jake."

"Yeah, Purdy," Jake murmured. "Thanks."

The doctor's footsteps echoed in the hallway, and Kate found the strength to stand up straight. She smiled weakly at Jake. His eyes were dark and mysterious, but that was just because it was getting dark and no one had turned on any lights in the room.

"You look like the doctor should've put you to bed too."

Kate could only shake her head. "I'm all right. I was just so worried."

"I know. You were talking all crazy." He turned and walked over to a liquor cabinet in the corner. "Want something to drink? Maybe a little sherry to calm your nerves?"

She shook her head again. Crazy? She could hardly recall what she'd said. All she could remember was the terrible fear and the awful realization that she'd failed Laura again. She looked over at Jake, but he was staring out the window at the lengthening shadows, a glass of water in his hand.

She took a step toward the stairs. "I think I'll just go up and sit with her for a while."

He turned, but his eyes remained in the shadows. "You sure that won't bother her?"

"I'll be careful." She got to the stairway.

"You think it would make Laura feel any better for her mother to be here?" Jake called out. "Want me to check which airport has the first flight in from Chicago, then find someone to fly her here?''

Kate shook her head. "I don't think that's necessary."

"Hey, it's no problem. And wouldn't her mother want to be here?''

All of a sudden time stood still. She was freezing, and Jake was her warmth. She was starving, and he was her food.

She loved him. Wholly. Completely. Without question.

She wasn't sure when it had happened, but there was no denying it was there. Her heart was his, just as every hope in her body was for his happiness. She wanted to see laughter and sunshine in his eyes, and more than anything else, love and acceptance there, too.

The words were waiting to be said. A voice inside her was shouting at her to tell him. Screaming that the lie was too huge and heavy to carry any longer. That love demanded trust, and she had to trust that he would understand. Love was worth any risk.

"Her mother *is* here," Kate said, her words echoing in the silence.

A silence that had dropped down from the heavens and killed every last bit of sound in the house. Jake was still standing in the shadows, only halfway across the room, but it seemed like miles.

"My mother is Laura's grandmother," Kate said. "I'm her mother."

Still Jake said nothing, and her mouth went dry with fear.

"I was a freshman in college. My father was dying, and Miguel was there for me. He was a student at a neighboring university. His family were wealthy landowners in Central America." Kate paused to take a deep breath. "That's why Laura, unlike anyone else in our family, has dark hair and that touch of olive in her complexion."

She came slightly away from the stairs, but kept her hand on the railing for support. "That period of my life was a total disaster. My father died of cancer. Miguel was killed in some revolution in his country. And I was in an automobile accident. That's where I almost killed Laura."

"Why?" Jake asked.

She knew what he was asking. "I wasn't in any shape to take care of anyone, even myself," Kate replied. "But my mother couldn't bear to lose another member of the family. So she just took over raising Laura."

"I would guess that Laura's not part of this facade?"

Kate paused, blindsided by the censure in his voice. It took her a moment to find her voice. "That's correct," she finally said. "Laura doesn't know."

"Why not?"

"Why not?" Kate shrugged. "That's just the way things worked out. I wasn't in any shape to take care of her. I had to put my life together. It took a while."

"Ten years?" he asked.

She blinked, feeling very uncomfortable. "No, not ten years."

"Then why hasn't she been told?"

Suddenly the weariness fell off Kate's shoulders, and as that happened, fury filled her heart. Why had she felt this need to confess? She didn't need his approval or forgiveness or anything. This had nothing to do with him. Or with her love for him.

"Why should we tell her?" she snapped. "What good would it serve?"

He looked away, but not quickly enough for Kate to miss the growing disgust on his face.

"When Laura jumped off that wagon and I thought the calf was running toward her, I tried to get in the way. Why do you think I did that?"

He didn't answer.

"It was love," Kate said. "That means protecting those you love from all harm. Or don't you agree?"

"I agree." The words came out terse through his tight lips. "But what were your lies protecting Laura from? How would the truth hurt?"

Kate sighed and looked away. "You don't understand."

"Damn right, I don't. You lie and in the end everyone suffers."

"The world isn't all that simple." She felt so tired, but there was no sympathy in his eyes. "It's complex."

"Yeah," Jake said. "And the longer you hide the truth, the more complex things become."

"We were trying to protect Laura." Another wave of anger filled Kate's heart. "And it worked. Damn it, it worked. She's a normal, happy little girl."

"Until she finds out."

"You just don't understand," she said.

"The hell I don't," he snapped. "I know what it's like when people hide things from you. People that you should be able to trust."

"Oh, you're full of it." She was sick and tired of his sanctimonious attitude. "No one hid anything from you. Your father admitted you were his son, right? He put his name on your birth certificate, right? And he paid for your education and a whole lot of other things, right?"

"Money isn't everything," he muttered through clenched teeth.

"I know," Kate said. "Money doesn't buy happiness. Well, call me a cynic if you want, but it does make a nice down payment."

"He threw money at a lot of things." Jake's voice was rising. "That was easy for him. He had a lot. But he never treated me like a son. He wouldn't even acknowledge my presence on the street. Bo was more of a father to me then he was."

Kate slumped against the wall, feeling drained. "So your father wasn't a man who could easily express his feelings. That doesn't make him bad."

"No," Jake said. "Just dishonest."

"And you're the great expert on honesty." Kate shook her head. "Except honesty isn't really the issue here. It's fear. You've built your whole life on the concept of honesty above all else because then you could condemn your father. You just can't admit you might have been wrong. That sometimes love might demand a compromise."

"That's crazy. Compromise was what my father did, and that was wrong."

"That's the real heart of the matter, isn't it?" she said. "You're terrified that you're like your father. Terrified that you're unable to really love, so you set up all sorts of barriers around your heart. Are they some kind of test—whoever knocks them all down and reaches your heart first wins your love?"

"Where'd all this crap about me come from?" Jake's voice was raw with barely leashed anger. "We were talking about Laura and the way you've been lying to her."

"We were talking about love and what it means."

"Well, it doesn't mean a damn thing to me. It's all a myth. It's either an excuse people use to justify their behavior or a reason you're getting hurt. You say you love Laura and that's why you're lying to her. My mother loved George Tyler and that's why she stood by him even when he would barely give her the time of day. Believe me, love is something I want no part of."

The room seemed filled with shadows now, hungry mouths ready to engulf them. Kate shivered. Unhappiness swirled around her, desperate to settle on its prey. She took one step up the stairway.

"You know, all your anger and self-righteousness has made you just like your father," she said in almost a whisper. "Unable to reach out to those who love you most."

She turned and fled up the stairs, thinking only of escaping from Jake's presence. But she'd gone only halfway up when she found two dark eyes staring at her.

"Laura!" she gasped, trying to find her voice. "You should be in bed."

"I hate you."

"The doctor said—"

But Laura had fled to her room. Kate followed, trembling still from the encounter with Jake, but unable to let her flee. She stopped just inside the door as Laura flung herself on the bed, then went over slowly.

"Honey," she said, reaching for Laura. "Take it easy, sweetheart."

But Laura slapped her hands away. "Don't touch me," she shouted. "You're not my mother. I don't want you to touch me."

"Laura, I'm so sorry."

"You lied to me. You and Mom..." Laura burst into tears. "Or whatever she is. The two of you lied to me."

"We just didn't tell you everything," Kate said.

"That's the same as lying."

"Please, honey," Kate implored. "It isn't. We were going to tell you. We were going to tell you everything."

"Oh, yeah." A heavy sneer hung in Laura's words. "When?"

When? When she was brave enough? When she had to? When? When? When?

"When it was right, honey."

"You're lying again."

"We didn't lie to you," Kate insisted. "You never asked and we never said anything."

"How can I ask about something when I don't even know there's anything to ask about?"

There was no answer to that, and Kate just sank back. "I'm sorry," she said. "We didn't mean to hurt you."

"It doesn't matter. I can't trust you guys anymore."

It was so hard to think straight, to know what to say. "Laura, we'll talk about it when we get home. Mom... Grandma and I will tell you everything."

"I'm not going home."

"Laura, please." Kate felt tears of panic well up in her eyes.

"I'm never going back to Chicago, never in my whole life."

"Chicago is your home."

"No, it's not. I'm staying here. I'm going to be a cowboy and I'm going to live with Bo. Bo would never lie to me."

"Laura, honey. Please." Kate moved forward, hungry to pull her to her heart, but the girl squirmed out of her grasp and ran down the hallway toward the stairs.

"You can't make me go back," Laura shouted over her shoulder. "If you try, I'll just run away and hide in the mountains with the Indians and the trappers."

Then she was gone, the hallway echoing with the patter of her bare feet on the stairs. Kate just stared ahead, listening to the ensuing silence. It was as empty as the years looming before her.

Jake stepped into the shadowy confines of the barn and paused a moment. The dimensions and layout were pretty much like the old barn, but the smell of fresh-cut wood still hung in the air. Sighing, he walked over to a stand of hay bales where two furry giants were reposing.

"Hey, guys," he said. "How's it going?"

Nickolai gave a halfhearted tail wag, while Boris just yawned.

Jake sat down on a solitary bale. "Good to be back home, huh? Nice to be able to run around without having to watch out for a zillion cars and trucks?"

Both dogs yawned.

It didn't look like they wanted to talk to him, but then he wasn't sure that anyone ever did. The ranch hands just looked to him for orders, and Bo had been on the grumpy side lately. And he sure as hell didn't have any friends in the community. Not with his standoffishness.

The only people he'd let close to him were the three women in his life—his mother, Kate and Laura. And how much did they care? His mother was always hassling him, constantly trying to improve his character. Laura was more Bo's friend, just as Jake had been as a youth. And now Kate thought he was a stiff-necked, sanctimonious SOB.

"Hell," he said to the now-sleeping dogs. "She's probably right."

He was just like his father, unable to care about anyone. He was good at fixing up the ranch, but fixing up his life was impossible. He didn't know the first thing about relationships. All he brought to them was the certainty that the other person would get hurt.

He closed his eyes and saw the ranch how it must have been a hundred years back, with old Jacob wandering the prairie. Had he been unable to love, too? Or had this Tyler trait developed with Jacob's loss of Caitlin?

Jake could hear the wind outside, a mournful cry of loneliness. No, he told it. This whole Caitlin-Jacob thing was over. Had been over since Jacob had left her to come out west. Love just didn't last as long as the hills. No matter how much Jacob had loved Caitlin or she had loved him, it was over.

"Laura?" Kate called. Both dogs popped up, and Boris gave a low woof as she stepped into the barn.

Jake got to his feet, a frown shadowing his eyes. "Laura? Isn't she in bed?"

Boris and Nickolai rushed over to welcome Kate, and she bent forward to gave each a hug, lingering longer than necessary with her head against Nickolai's furry back. She straightened up and turned to face Jake.

"She ran off."

"Ran off?"

"Just a few minutes ago. I looked through the house, then thought maybe she'd be out here."

"What happened?"

Kate wiped at her eyes. "She overheard us. She's upset."

"Damn."

All his earlier anger was gone, leaving only pain in its place. Laura was hurting and so was Kate, none of which he'd wanted to have happen. It showed how criminal it was for him to get involved—all he brought was pain.

"I've looked everywhere for her," Kate was saying, "She's not wearing any shoes and it's getting cool out."

"She's probably with Bo," Jake said. "I always..." What would she care what he'd done as a child? "Kids always run to him when they've got problems."

"You mean to his cabin?"

"Come on. I'll take you there."

But Jake had just reached her side when Bo's short square figure appeared in the door.

"Is Laura at your place?" Kate asked.

Bo shook his head. "Took her over to Mary Redwing. Woman's good at mendin' little critters."

"I'd like to see her," Kate murmured. Her hand had somehow found Jake's and she clutched at him.

"Mary gave her some sweetened tea," Bo said. "Now she's got her all bundled up in that big feather bed of hers."

"She's sleeping then?" Kate asked.

"Mary said she looks to be sawing a skidful a logs. May not be up 'til mornin'."

Kate nodded and then, as if realizing she was holding on to Jake, let go. She looked so small and alone herself—a little girl with nobody to lean on. If he were more of a man, Jake would step in and hold her, but he couldn't. It wasn't a space of a foot or so, it was a thousand miles. It was over mountainous terrain, a burning desert and a snake-infested swamp. His feet just wouldn't move.

The sound of Bo clearing his throat made Jake look up. His foreman was standing there, looking at the floor.

"Ah, ma'am." Bo cleared his throat again. "Laura's going to be needing to come back here for the summer. Girl's bought herself some livestock."

"Livestock?" Kate asked. "Where did she get the money?"

Bo cleared his throat again. "I'm not at liberty to discuss the particulars, ma'am, but she bought herself a colt."

"A baby horse?"

Jake knew what Bo was doing. Tears burned his eyes and he looked away. Cowboys rules were right firm about this— you could sing all the sad songs you wanted, but you couldn't show tears.

"It ain't born yet, ma'am," Bo said. "His momma'll probably drop him along toward the end of April."

It had been bitter cold that January more than twenty years ago. Jake had been coming up to his twelfth birthday, and the only thing he had leftover from Christmas was a heartful of bitterness. He had spent another holiday with just his mother, and things were generally going to hell. He'd been all packed up to run away.

"Mr. Werntz," Kate was saying. "Laura's just a little girl. She can't take on this kind of responsibility."

Then Bo had come by. Chatted about nothing and everything until Jake's mother had left to visit some folks. Once they were been alone, Bo had cut to the chase.

Told Jake he wanted to buy a colt, but he needed a business partner. Said his cash flow was a little thin. Jake hadn't known half of what the old foreman was talking about, but by the time his mother had come back, they'd had themselves a cowboy contract—a firm handshake and a solemn promise.

"She gave her word, ma'am."

Jake had had to contribute two dollars a month. And once the colt had been born, he'd had to care for it.

Bo had had long talks with him about responsibility and how a real cowboy didn't walk away from his. But by then, all the devils in hell couldn't have driven Jake away. He'd been a rancher. Owned himself a horse, the first one of his herd. And a rancher took care of his livestock. That's what a cowboy did.

"But…" Kate sputtered. "Aren't horses expensive to take care of? They are in Chicago."

"Ain't as costly out here, ma'am."

Jake watched as Kate just stared at Bo. Poor lady. She didn't know that once Bo shook on something, it was a done deal.

"But there will be some expenses," Bo said. "That's why Laura'll need to be out here this summer. She'll need to help with things."

"But she's a little girl."

"Mighty good ranch hand, though," Bo said. "Worth two fully growed men."

Kate looked at Jake, her lips working, but no sound came out.

"We'll take good care of her, ma'am."

Slumping, she turned back to Bo.

"And she surely does love the outdoors."

Kate slowly nodded, and Bo put his hat back on. Laura would be back here in the summer, no matter what Kate wanted. The kid would be back because it would help her heal, and Kate wouldn't be able to deny her.

"Best be goin'," he said. "Got things need doin'." He started toward the door, then stopped and turned. "Get yourself something to eat, Kate. Mary had her daughter set out a spread up at the house."

"I will," Kate said.

With a tip of his hat, Bo was gone.

Jake and Kate stood there in silence for a long, long time. It was a painful, oppressive kind of silence, with each feeling their own piece of hell.

"Well, I guess I'll drop by Mary's and see that Laura's okay," Kate said. "Though I know I'm not needed. Seems everybody around here's a better mother than me, anyway."

"Laura just needs time," he said.

Kate shrugged, adding a short, bitter laugh for emphasis. "Like maybe ten years? I mean, if I felt it was okay to wait that long, why shouldn't she?"

"Don't, Kate," he said. "You did what you thought best at the time."

"Yeah. Even if it was wrong."

He wished he had the magic words to make her stop hurting, but he'd never been blessed with a silver tongue. "Come on," he said. "I'll take you over to Mary's."

They walked from the barn without speaking. Their shoulders almost touched, their arms almost brushed. He wanted to take her hand and tell her that everything would be fine, but he had no right to. Who was he to make such predictions? When had he become the great expert on emotions and hurt?

Night was sweeping over the land as if it were racing for a finish line. He had exterior lights on the buildings, but his eyes couldn't keep from straying out to the open spaces beyond and the deep, dense darkness. Jacob had been lucky. When darkness covered the land, he'd been safe. The world would leave him alone. Jake had lights all over the place. Day or night, it didn't matter—the world was waiting and watching. He couldn't run or hide from the truth.

And the truth was that he brought only hurt to those he wanted most to find happiness.

Mary must have heard their feet on her porch, for she opened the door before they knocked, coming outside to join them. She left the door ajar.

"The child's just fine," she told Kate, coming to take her hands. "She's sleeping like a lamb. Come see for yourself."

She led Kate to the door, then pushed it open enough so that they could see across the room into the bedroom opposite. Laura was lying on her side, her hand in a fist on the pillow beside her as if she were ready to fight. But her face was relaxed, not angry.

Kate took a step back, and Mary pulled the door almost closed again.

"I'm really sorry to put you to such bother," Kate said. "We could take her back to the big house . . ."

Mary shook her head. "Let her sleep. Dreams will wash away some of her hurt and anger, and she will start to heal." Her eyes narrowed and her lips grew tight. "And you must do the same. The child is not the only one in pain."

Kate just shrugged.

Mary flashed Jake a look he couldn't read, then took Kate's hand again, drawing her over to a worn wooden bench. The two women sat as Jake turned to stare off into the night.

"There is an old Indian story," Mary said softly. "About Cano, a great white goose. When he was just a gosling, he wandered from his nest. The river called to him, and Cano got caught in the current and was swept far, far downstream. He was found by an old goose who no longer had young. She took care of him, but he always hurt inside. Finally, when he was big and strong enough, he flew north, searching until he found his home. And there he found healing. To this day, birds go south to find food, but they always fly back north to their homes in the spring."

Jake leaned wearily against the porch railing. What was Mary trying to do?

"Laura will heal best at her home," Mary said, as if she'd read his mind.

"But she loves it here," Kate argued. "To take her now seems so—"

"Her fears will not be put to rest here. This is her refuge, a place she can run to to heal. But not the place where she can defeat her fears."

The silence lasted almost forever. Jake scarcely dared to breath as he waited. He wanted Kate to say no, she wasn't leaving. That this could be home, too. He wanted her to believe that the argument they'd had today was silly and over.

But even as he waited and wanted, he knew it was wrong. Too many Tyler men had made too many good women unhappy. Jacob had done Elizabeth wrong. George had done Faith wrong. Jake wasn't turning his life into a bad cowboy song by doing Kate wrong.

He straightened, and his feet shuffling on the wooden flooring seemed to waken Kate. She got to her feet and rested her hand briefly on Mary's shoulder.

"You're right," she said. "We'll all be stronger at home."

She smiled briefly at Jake, then brushed past him as she hurried on up to the big house. Jake couldn't for the life of him move. His feet seemed to be sinking in quicksand. For all his brave thoughts, he didn't want her to leave.

Once she'd gone inside and the echo of the screen door swinging shut had died away, he turned to Mary.

"Where'd that story come from?" he asked. "I never heard of Cano the goose."

"I made it up." Mary got to her feet and gave him a quick glance as she walked to the door. "They needed to go home. The time was not right."

"For what?" He hated it when she spoke in riddles.

She stopped in the doorway and turned to face him. Her eyes were in shadow. All he could see was the glow of the room behind her, looking warm and inviting and homelike, yet blocked to his entrance by her body.

"For you," she answered. "She trusted you with her most precious secret, but you weren't ready. You must find the strength to bring her back."

Bring her back? Why let her leave, if he was supposed to bring her back? "I think the locoweed got you, too," he muttered and left the porch.

The shadows swallowed him up immediately, but the darkness brought him no peace. He couldn't bring Kate back. He wouldn't. That would be his gift to her—freedom from the pain Tyler men brought with them.

"How's the little girl?" a ranch hand—Kate thought his name was Ronnie—asked. "She okay?"

Kate stopped walking, but kept her hand on the door to the hallway. "Just a bump on the head," she said, trying hard not to let her voice break. From Laura's rejection or Jake's anger? It was too hard to try to sort it all out.

"Glad to hear it. She's a good little kid."

Kate just nodded, but he didn't move.

"You have your supper yet?"

The thought of food made the world dance around her, but she managed a weak smile. "I'm not too hungry right now. I've got a few things to do and then maybe..."

Luckily, his mother must have trained him not to press food on unwilling ladies, for he nodded and went on to the kitchen. Kate fled into the hallway and up the stairs. Maybe it was best that they leave. She needed a good cry and she wasn't sure one was available here.

Laura's room was empty, a silent reproach. Kate raced by and slipped into her own room, shutting the door and leaning against it as if she could keep all the demons chasing her from entering. After a moment or two, her breathing slowed to almost normal and she walked through the darkness to the window seat.

The ranch spread out below her. Blotches of light lay here and there, showing patches of normality, but her eyes sought the darkness. She gazed out at the prairie, or at least where she knew it was. Its vast reaches taunted her. She knew nothing about it, yet she'd ventured into its wilds full of certainty and confidence.

Like she'd ventured into this whole thing with Laura.

Like she'd ventured into loving Jake.

And like Custer, she'd been caught unaware. She'd thought love would be enough to make Laura understand. To make Jake come alive. What a fool she was.

A knock sounded at the door and she spun around as it opened. Jake stood silhouetted there, light streaming in around him but leaving his face in shadow. If only she'd recognized early on that that's how he lived his life.

"Kate?" he said.

She turned on the light next to the bed. "I'm here."

Light made the whole thing seem ordinary. Just two people talking. And if she kept her eyes away from the bed, she wouldn't have to remember the other things they'd once done.

"I made some calls," he said, and glancing at a paper in his hand. "I can get you and Laura on a flight to Chicago around noon tomorrow."

My, that was quick. She hadn't even said for sure they were going. "I see." She felt behind her for the window seat and sank back down.

"I just thought..." He cleared his throat roughly, then went on. "I thought from what you said at Mary's that you were anxious to get Laura home."

"Oh, I am," she said quickly. "I'm just surprised that you checked out the schedules already. I hadn't quite gotten that far in my thinking."

He looked past her at the night. "I thought it was probably best if you went soon."

His words hit her with the force of a wrecking ball, knocking the breath from her. Any hope that his anger was temporary or that anything was building between them fled abruptly. Nothing like putting it bluntly. But she'd be mature about it all.

They'd had their little fling and it was over. Winter was coming and it was time to fly south. Or actually, southeast.

She'd had her little try at melting the ice around his heart and had been frostbitten herself. It was time to find some warmth. At least at home she could cry whenever she wanted to.

Jake was ready to be rid of them. Maybe he was afraid they'd sue if Laura was seriously hurt. Maybe he was just tired of them hanging around. Most likely, he'd seen the love in her eyes and wanted no part of it.

That hurt more than anything, but Kate hadn't lost her father and Miguel without learning something. Hiding her pain was one thing she was very good at.

She got to her feet, looked Jake straight in the face and smiled. "Where's the airport we'd be flying from?"

Chapter Twelve

"I want you to call me if anything goes wrong," Laura told Bo. "It don't matter if it's, like, midnight or really early in the morning, you know? You gotta call. Okay?"

She was clutching the mare's face to her own. From the sound of her voice, Kate was sure she was near to tears, if not already crying.

"She'll be fine," Bo assured Laura. "She's already done this a few times. She's got a heap of experience in the momma business."

"I got money saved," Laura insisted. "I can get on a plane and be out here real quick."

"She'll be fine," Bo repeated, patting the mare on her side. "Cross my heart and hope to die."

"But stuff happens."

Laura had pulled her face away from the mare, and there was no doubt that she was crying. Her face was dirty from being rubbed in the horse's hair, and tears had cut little rivers in the dirt. Kate would have cried herself, except her tear ducts were running on empty.

"You know it does, Bo. You told me so. Remember?"

A grimace dashed across Bo's face for a flicker of a moment. "Yeah, I know stuff happens. That's why I'm going to keep an eye on Momma here. Watch over her extra careful. Make sure everything goes down just fine."

Laura sniffled.

"Hey, Buckaroo." Bo's voice suddenly turned gentle. "Folks can't always do exactly what they want. You got your momma and grandma to take care of."

Kate's heart fluttered for several beats. News spread across the ranch like a prairie fire through dry grass. She hadn't come to terms with publicly admitting that Laura was her daughter, yet it seemed that everyone on the ranch already knew. Were they also discussing Jake's rejection of her? It was time to go back to Chicago. Time to retreat and put her life in order.

"We should be going, honey," she said. "I want to drop by Mrs. MacNeill's before we go to the airport."

Kate thought that her tone was chock-full of gentleness and understanding, but all she got for her pains was a glare from Laura.

"Hey, little buckaroo," Bo said. "A good cowpoke always listens to their momma."

"Okay," Laura murmured.

Laura and Bo hugged hard. Kate stared at them, wrestling with the pain in her heart, then turned quickly on her heel and strode toward the Jeep. She felt rather than saw Laura approach. She was afraid that if she looked at the girl, the dam would burst, so she stared straight ahead. Laura climbed in. Kate put the vehicle in gear.

"Goodbye, Pardner," Laura shouted out to Bo. He just waved.

A strained silence rode with them as they bounced down the track toward the main house. Kate was thankful for the effort required to keep the vehicle on the trail. She wasn't up to thinking about anything more complex.

As they neared the house, she saw Jake standing on the porch, along with her and Laura's suitcases. They had packed right after breakfast, before they had gone out to visit the pregnant mare.

Even with the weight of her sorrows, Kate's heart still did a little flip at the sight of him. He was a Western man through and through. Slim and hard, yet relaxed as he leaned against the porch post—a battered cowboy hat on his head, a short sheepskin jacket with the collar turned up, faded jeans and scuffed boots on his lean frame.

She let the image of him burn into her memory as she pulled the Jeep to a stop in front of the steps. By the time she'd turned the ignition off and climbed out, Jake had carried their bags down to the back of the vehicle.

"Anxious to get rid of us, huh?" she asked.

Her bright words met his silence and tumbled to earth like colored beads thrown against a towering cliff. His face looked even more closed.

"I'm not pushing anybody out," he said. "You're welcome to stay as long as you like."

"I'm sorry." Kate bent down and grabbed a bag, throwing it into the back of the Jeep. "I was just trying to put a little humor into the situation."

From the look on his face, Kate could see that humor was about as acceptable as hoof-and-mouth disease. She wiped her hands on her jeans, wishing she could wipe the pain from her heart as easily.

"Well..." She paused to stare into his eyes, then extended her hand. "It's been an interesting experience." There was so much she wanted to say, and so much that she wouldn't. She'd opened her heart to him, shared all the shadows hiding there, but it hadn't been enough for him. So it was time to pack up the tent and move on.

His hand inched out to meet hers. "Thanks for bringing my dogs home."

"Always glad to help out."

They shook hands quickly and with the affection of business associates who did not trust each other. Then, without another word to Kate, Jake strode to where Laura stood.

"Glad you could help us out," he said. "I mean, with the dogs, the cattle and everything."

"Don't go working Daisy too hard," Laura warned.

"Ain't gonna happen," Jake said, shaking his head. "That mare's on maternity leave."

Laura nodded again. "Bo says it's gonna be a hard winter. You got enough hay in?"

"Yup."

"Good," Laura replied.

They stood for a long moment, then Jake stuck his hand out again. "See you in the summer, Buckaroo."

Laura took his hand. "I'm gonna try and come out over the Christmas holidays."

"Whatever works," he said as they shook hands.

Kate just stared. Bo had looked like a throwback to the strong, silent men of the past, yet he'd had no trouble hugging a child. Jake looked like a man of today, yet the only thing he'd allowed himself to do with Laura was shake her hand. For a moment Kate's vision blurred. Maybe he was never going to be able to show caring.

"Come on, Laura. We need to be going."

They climbed back into the Jeep and left. Kate's heart felt ready to break, a real physical pain stronger than she'd ever felt before. It was over. She wasn't sure why or how or when, but she knew it was. Just as quickly as she'd discovered her love for Jake, he'd rejected it. Rejected her.

She found herself swallowing hard as she raced down the lane toward the road. Laura knelt on the seat, facing backwards, obviously trying to remember every single detail of the ranch that she'd taken over as her own. Kate knew it wasn't safe for her to sit like that, but she wasn't up to speaking. She slowed down instead.

Once they were on the blacktop road to town, Laura turned around and slumped in her seat. She put her seat belt on without being told. Kate no longer felt tense, just tired and washed out.

"Somebody's gonna have to come out from the ranch and pick up the Jeep," Laura said.

"Bo said it would work out fine. One of the hands is visiting his mother in Wyoming and he's flying in tomorrow night. He'll drive it back to the ranch."

They came to the edge of town, and Kate turned toward her daughter. "I promised Mrs. MacNeill we'd stop by and say goodbye."

Laura just shrugged.

Even though she'd only been there once, it was easy to find the little cottage in the small town. Kate's eyes drank in the peaceful serenity of the area. In some ways, what with everyone knowing the circumstances of his birth, it had probably been hard for Jake growing up here. But in other ways...

She sighed. In other ways, it would be so nice to spend your days in a place where everyone knew everyone else and looked out for one another. She pulled into the drive. Faith MacNeill was standing at the door as they walked up.

"Hello, ladies," she said as she came out to hug Kate, then Laura.

"Hello, Faith," Kate said.

"Hello, ma'am," Laura said.

"You can call me Faith, honey." Mrs. MacNeill gave Laura an extra hug. "Although, if you want to pretend I'm your grandma, that would be just fine and dandy."

"I got a grandma back in Chicago," Laura said. "And I promised Mary Redwing she could be my grandma, too. I don't think I can have more than two grandmas."

"Oh, you can have as many as you want, honey." Faith mussed Laura's hair. "Actually, you should always have a few extra. You never know when one of 'em will just plumb wear out."

"Okay." Laura nodded solemnly. "You can be my grandma."

Faith put an arm around each of them and led them into the house. "I hear you both took some bumps last night."

Laura nodded and bent her head down, fingers working in her hair. "Mine's right here," she said. "Doesn't hurt much, though."

Faith dutifully looked where Laura was indicating. "Good idea to have your own doc check it out, though. Don't want no cracks forming to let your good sense leak out."

Laura looked up at her, her eyes betraying her uncertainty as to whether Faith was pulling her leg or not. Kate wanted to laugh, but it would have taken too great an effort.

"Think you could do me a favor?" Faith asked, still looking at Laura. "I was just about to have me a cup of coffee, but the cats are looking to be fed. Could you hand out some vittles to them?"

"Sure." Laura's voice was filled with almost her normal enthusiasm.

"Just open that there can of food and divvy it up between the three bowls. They'll come running."

As Laura got started, Faith poured two cups of coffee. After handing one to Kate, she led her into the living room. Three cats rushed by, hearing their own dinner bell.

"So what about the bump you took?" Faith asked as they sat down.

Kate just shrugged and sipped at her coffee. "I'm okay. The calf knocked Laura down harder."

"I wasn't talking about no calf and you know it." Faith gave her a look that rivaled Granny Nan's for putting people in their place. "I was talking about that fool son of mine."

Kate's coffee needed staring at—long, hard staring. "Hey, we weren't looking for anything long-term. Laura and I came out for a vacation and now it's time to go."

"You love him."

Kate wanted to look away, wanted to look anywhere but into Faith's eyes, yet she found she had no will of her own. She just shrugged. "A summer romance. It'll pass."

"Summer's over."

"It'll still pass."

Faith put her cup down, looking as if she'd like nothing better than to knock Kate and Jake's heads together until some sense came into them. "You're the best thing that ever happened to my son. The first woman I've ever met who could break through that concrete wall he's built around himself. There was something between you two...."

Faith's voice drifted off and they both let the silence reign for a time. Laura's voice as she talked to the cats came in from the kitchen. She was telling them about her colt.

Kate got to her feet and walked over to the front window to stare outside. Winter was on its way. The leaves were off the trees and the bare branches shivered in the wind. Was she leaving because it was best for Laura or because she couldn't stay around Jake any longer? Mary had given her the opening and she had jumped at it, but why?

"Jake had his chance," Kate said slowly. "Maybe he prefers living by himself."

"Maybe he doesn't have the guts to try something else. He's a Tyler through and through."

Silence came back and seized control, holding them in its grip. It wasn't a comfortable silence, filled with peace and contentment, but one of restlessness and tension. The wind whistled through the bare trees outside. A floorboard creaked toward the back of the house. Faith's old hound woofed quietly in her sleep. Kate felt a sadness descend on her as she thought of leaving, as she thought of the plane that would take her away from this vast, open land forever.

She shook her head and turned around. "Could we go back to the museum? I think there's time before Laura and I have to leave."

If Faith thought it a strange request, she gave no sign. "Sure. I've still got the key." She got to her feet. "Laura, hon, are the cats done? Your mom wants to go to the museum."

Laura appeared in the doorway, her face reflecting a mixture of annoyance at the reminder of Kate's status and curiosity. "Museum?"

"It's just a little bitty place, but it's all Cold Spring has."

They drove there in a matter of minutes. Faith left Laura no time to start pouting again, though, for she spent the whole drive pointing out spots of interest. Jenny Tate's house, where a whole flock of birds once came down the

chimney. The house where Jack Hollaran got knocked out
when his wife accidently hit him with a frozen rabbit. And
the place where Gene Kuski's house stood before it blew up
when he was installing indoor plumbing.

The stories stopped abruptly when Kate pulled up in front
of the old building.

"Neato," Laura said. "It's an old saloon."

Faith repeated the story about how the bar had been the
center of the community, but Kate tuned the words out as
she stepped into the street. She was here to end something
that had started generations ago. Maybe it was silly, and she
wasn't certain she believed any of it, but at the same time,
it seemed heartless to let it drag on forever.

Faith unlocked the door and went in first, turning on the
lights. Laura followed, making excited noises as she took in
the room. Kate just went inside and walked over to the display of the Tyler family.

To Jacob's picture.

Once again, the piercing eyes sent a shiver down her back.
It was as if Jake were standing there, staring at her. Faith
had said that all the Tyler men carried a dark strain of Irish
depression. Did that mean Jacob had never known happiness? That Jake never would?

"It's over," she whispered to the photo. "It was never
meant to be."

She fingered the ring in her pocket for a moment, then
pulled it out and stared down at it. There was no sense in
carrying it back to Chicago. Jacob needed to stop waiting
for the call. Caitlin needed to stop watching for his return.
Kate herself needed to be free of the ring and its lure. She
wouldn't use it to call him back, assuming that she ever had.
It was just that somehow it all felt so possible now, as if
she'd been caught in a spell.

"How come Jake's got a mustache?" Laura asked. "And
he's all dressed up, like some old-fashioned cowboy."

Kate let the spell go. She turned to Laura, who'd come up
next to her. "That's not Jake."

"That's an ancestor of Jake's," Faith told Laura. "His
name is Jacob. Jacob Tyler."

Laura gasped and drew her hands to her mouth. "Jacob Tyler? JT? The magic ring. It's his!"

"Magic ring?" Faith asked.

"Laura, please," Kate murmured. She had wanted to end this quietly.

"It's got to be," Laura said.

"What magic ring?" Faith asked again.

"It rained real hard in Chicago, you know?" Laura began. "And when we were cleaning up, we found a bunch of old stuff that we were keeping for Granny Nan. She had stuff from a woman called Kate, only it's pronounced a different kinda way. She's a great-great something to us."

"She's one of your ancestors," Faith said.

"Yeah," Laura replied. "And she had this magic ring that my Granny Nan was keeping."

"What's magic about it?" Faith asked.

"Granny Nan says it's supposed to set right what didn't get made right when it was supposed to."

Faith's brow wrinkled as questions danced in her eyes. What bothered Kate was that there wasn't the faintest touch of disbelief in them.

Kate felt a weariness, an inevitability about things, and handed the ring to Faith. "Her name was Caitlin Donahue and she was my great-great-grandmother," she said. "She and Jacob Tyler were in love, but they lost everything in the Chicago Five. Caitlin married a middle-aged butcher in order to take care of her family. Jacob came out west, but before he left, he promised to return if Caitlin ever needed him. He gave her the ring as his pledge."

Faith turned the ring over in her hand, staring at it, then staring at the picture. "And did he return?" she asked after a long moment.

"No." Kate found herself looking at the picture also. At the unhappiness in his eyes. "Caitlin always believed he would, though. The ring was to be passed down to the daughters in the family."

"And Kate's the first one."

"The first one?" Faith asked.

"All the rest were sons," Laura said. "And then we found it and Jake came."

Faith's long, low whistle said she was falling for the story just as Laura had. This was getting out of hand. Kate was sorry she'd come here, sorry she'd felt the urge to say good-bye to Jacob.

"And what was supposed to happen once Jacob came back?" Faith asked.

Kate just shrugged. It was time to go, time she escaped from this crazy fairy tale she'd fallen into. The mustiness of the room was getting to her. She was feeling as old and tired as the people in the pictures before her.

"Kate's supposed to give him back his angel," Laura said.

"What?" Kate frowned at the girl.

"Granny told me," Laura said. "Jacob gave Caitlin his guardian angel to watch over her. You know." The girl's voice grew impatient. "Granny always said the stars are angels with lanterns watching over us. Well, Jacob gave his to Caitlin and she has to give it back. Granny said it was something about trust."

"I never heard that." Kate remembered a little uneasily the compulsion she'd had to trust Jake yesterday with the truth about Laura. The unreasoning conviction that she couldn't keep secrets from him had seemed to come out of nowhere.

Laura's eyes turned eager. She clutched at Kate's hand. "Maybe that's it then," she said. "You've got to go back and give Jake his angel."

Kate shook her head. "Laura, I'm not Caitlin and Jake's not Jacob."

"But—"

Faith put her hand on Laura's shoulder. "I think Kate did trust him with something pretty special yesterday, honey. I think it just didn't work."

Laura obviously didn't understand. She looked from one woman to the other, then sighed.

Kate closed Faith's fingers around the ring. "Why don't you keep this for the museum? Jacob deserves to have it back."

Faith stared at the ring lying in her hand.

"But he doesn't want it," Laura said. "I just know it."

Kate turned away from the picture, from those eyes that would always haunt her. "It's time we left for the airport."

"Don't go dumping your spleen on me," Bo snapped. "Ain't my fault those pretty little ladies went back to Chicaw-go."

"Look who the hell is calling me grumpy," Jake shouted right back. "Sort of like the pot calling the kettle black."

"At least I'm honest enough to admit I'm gonna miss the kid."

"I'm going to miss the kid, too," Jake protested. Hell, he was gonna miss a hell of a lot more than the kid. Kate had somehow become part of his life, part of his very soul, and it seemed impossible to imagine living without her. But he sure wasn't admitting that to Bo.

Surrounded by hay bales, the two of them glared at each other. Jake could feel the bile bubbling up from his stomach. They were going to have themselves a knock-down, drag-out fight. Boris and Nickolai whined in nervousness, but his heart beat in eager anticipation as he waited for Bo's retort.

"If you're gonna miss them so all-fired much, then why don't you hightail your butt out to that airport and bring them back on home?" Bo asked quietly.

Jake felt like a horse had kicked him in the stomach. Bo wasn't playing fair at all. A knock-down, drag-out called for kicking, punching, scratching and gouging. Gentle words and mild tones had no place in a brawl like that.

"They're not cattle I can drag around where I please."

"You could ask her," Bo replied. "Ask her nice."

"Chicago's her home. She loves that big, crowded old city."

They stared at each other for several lifetimes, both knowing that Chicago wasn't the issue at all. Bo finally spoke. "There's a leak in the water tank in B section. I'd best check it out."

Unmoving, Jake stood there, watching Bo walk toward the door.

"You best find yourself a nice cave for the winter," the foreman said. "Grumpy as you're gettin', ain't nobody gonna want to live with you."

Jake turned away, listening to the creak of the door hinges. A whine drew his attention and he looked down at his dogs, sitting there and looking up at him with pleading eyes.

"Oh, stop giving me those damn moon eyes," he snapped.

The dogs whined again.

"Go with him if you want." Jack waved at the door. "If you guys don't want to stay with me, then fine. Just get the hell out of here."

Not needing a second invitation, the big dogs were gone in a flash.

"Damn bums." Jake picked up his toolbox and went over to the stall he'd been putting a latch on. "Give them a pretty face or a chance to chase jackrabbits and they're gone."

The chill that Bo and the dogs let into the barn lingered after their departure, slipping up the sleeves of his jacket and crawling down his bare skin. Forecasters were indicating that the coming winter was going to be a cold one.

Jake was glad. He liked winter. He liked the harshness it brought to the landscape and how it separated the weak from the strong. Winter suited his dark moods. And it didn't take fancy forecasting techniques to see that his mood was going to be pretty damn dark this year.

Why in the hell had he ever gone to Chicago? He had a comfortable life here. Sure, there were some things missing, but he'd come to terms with that void a long time ago. He had his land and he didn't need anything else. The only thing his little sojourn with Kate had given him was a realization of just what he was missing.

Whenever one of his moods hit him, Jake would just saddle up his favorite horse and ride off into the foothills. And it didn't matter what the season. Before long, the wide open spaces would set his soul at peace. He would become one with his land, like his Indian ancestors. But now, whenever he rode off, Kate's spirit would go with him. The spirit of a woman who was suited to the concrete canyons of Chicago instead of the plains of Montana. A woman of bright, sparkling eyes. A woman who would only be hurt by staying.

The door swung open behind him and the light step twisted Jake's stomach into a tight little ball, but he stayed kneeling in the stall opening.

"In one of your moods, are you?"

Jake didn't bother turning around. He made a mark with his pencil where the latch should go. "Hi, Mom. Nice to see you, too."

The light footsteps shuffled through the straw on the floor, and she dropped down to sit nearby on a bale of hay. "You could just go after her and get her back, you know."

"I've already had that discussion with Bo," he said with a sigh. "We ain't allowed to own people anymore. Last I heard, Lincoln freed all the slaves."

"Gonna be difficult, aren't you?"

"No." Being reasonable was hard, especially when dealing with unreasonable people. He marked the places the screws should go. "I'm not being difficult. I'm just being reasonable."

His mother snorted. "A Tyler man wouldn't know reasonable if it bit him on the ass."

Words danced around on the tip of his tongue, but Jake kept his mouth shut and started the screw holes with an awl. There was no talking to his mother when she was in one of her moods. It was like getting caught out on the prairie in a summer storm. You just had to find shelter and wait it out. He put one screw in, then another.

"You want anything, Mom?" As soon as he said the words, he knew he should have kept his mouth shut longer.

"No, I don't want anything much," Faith replied. "Just a little respect, a kind word, maybe even a smile."

Jake clenched his teeth for a moment. "Hellsfire, you hardly ever come out here."

"How many times do you invite me?"

"You're my mother, for crying out loud. You don't need an invitation. You can come out whenever you damn well please."

"And when I do, you get all grumpy with me."

"I'm always grumpy," he snapped.

"I noticed," she replied.

His shoulders slumped. Bo was right. He should just go out and find himself that cave up in the mountains and stay there until spring. Hell, why come down then? He should just stay there the rest of his life.

"There's something you should know," his mother said. "Your father's wife died when you were about two years old." Softness had come to roost in his mother's face. "And he asked me to marry him."

This was news to Jake. It surprised him, slowed him for the moment. "Why didn't you?" he asked.

Faith stood up. "Because he wasn't a man who knew how to be happy. If I married him, I would have spent my life trying to please him and I would only have brought myself misery."

"Mom, I'm sor—"

"You know, you are so like him."

Jake's weariness increased. "I know. Unable to love."

"No, scared to death to show it. Your father knew how to love, he just couldn't let anyone see it. Why the hell didn't you let Kate know you loved her?"

"Who says I do?"

She just shook her head. "I was wrong. You're worse than your father. You can't even admit what you feel." His mother took his hand and dropped something in it. "Here."

He stared at a ring she'd given him. "What the hell is this?"

"It's a ring, dear."

The sarcasm in his mother's voice was on the heavy side, but he decided to let it pass. "Thank you, Mom."

"It's got your initials in it."

Rolling the ring around, Jake looked on the inside of the ring. The inscription was worn with age, but it was still easy to make out the letters JT. He wanted to tell his mother that his initials were JM, but he wasn't up to that argument, either.

"Where did it come from?" he asked.

"Laura said they found it in their basement."

Jacob Tyler's ring. Great. What was he supposed to do with it?

"Well, I better be heading for home." His mother bent over and kissed him on the cheek. "Girl my age has to be careful how much fun she has in one day. My heart might not be able to take the strain."

"Mom, I—"

"You visit me next time. We'll sing and dance and tell jokes."

There was no use talking to her. Not when she was in one of her moods. "Bye, Mom."

She gave him a wave, then turned and quickly strode out of the barn. Jake looked at the ring and shook his head again, then dropped it in his pocket. Didn't matter who had the ring. There was nothing to the old story.

Not one damn thing.

Chapter Thirteen

"Isn't it awfully early to be calling one of your friends, honey?" Kate had just come into the kitchen and found Laura hanging up the phone.

Laura gave Kate one of her dark glares. Damn. Was this how life was going to be for them now that the family's little secret was out in the open? Boy, that was a hell of a trade. Get rid of the blues that came around her kid's birthday in exchange for a constant, year-round barrage of venom.

"Laura," Kate said softly as she filled the coffeepot with water. "We're going to have to live together, so we might as well treat each other civilly."

"We don't have to live with each other."

The mixture of hope and darkness that filled her daughter's face was like scraping open an old wound on Kate's heart. They'd been home barely a week, yet it seemed as if they'd been having this discussion for years. And for a good part of the past seven days Laura had been sleeping and attending school. Kate wondered if she'd last until the kid was eighteen and away at college.

"You were talking to Bo again."

"I've got money," Laura said, her voice petulant and defiant. "I can pay for my telephone calls."

"I'm not worried about the money, but I don't think you should be bothering Bo all the time."

"He said I could call any time I want."

Words. Angry words. Gentle words. Solicitous words. Words of every shape and kind whirled in Kate's mind, but none came out. She poured the water into the coffeemaker.

It wouldn't do to get in a battle over Bo. To make it look as if she were trying to drive a wedge between Laura and the grizzled old foreman. Right now, Bo was the one who'd given Laura her first colt. Kate was the one who'd taken the kid out of Montana. The woman who'd sprung all kinds of little surprises on the child. No, there was no way she'd want to put Laura in a position of chosing between Bo and herself. Kate knew that the odds were totally stacked against her.

"I'm not saying you shouldn't call," Kate said. "You just have to remember that he's got work to do out there and can't always talk to you. And I wouldn't want to see you neglecting your friends here at home."

"The kids around here are a bunch of dummies." Laura threw herself into a kitchen chair, laying her head down on her hands on the table. "What would happen to me if you marry Jake?"

Where had this come from? "I'm not going to marry Jake," Kate said. The words whipped at her heart, bringing a stinging pain.

"What about Lance?"

"Lance?" Kate suddenly saw there was more to it than a simple question. She joined Laura at the table. "Well, I'm definitely not marrying him."

"That's good."

"And if I should ever marry, what you would do—where you would live—would be up to you."

"That's no answer." The tone was surly.

"Yes, it is. Letting you know the truth about your birth doesn't have to change anything. You can still call Grandma 'Mom' if you want, and still live with her if I should move someplace else, though I can't foresee that happening."

"If you married Jake, could I live on the ranch with you?"

"Laura." Was she deaf? Hadn't she seen how Jake had treated Kate when they were leaving? The pain bit at her, stealing the thin mask of contentment she'd erected since coming back, but she just sighed and stood up. "It's not going to happen, but if it did, yes, you could live with us."

"What about Grandma?" Laura pressed.

Kate felt almost at the end of her rope, but stopped fighting. "Mom could live with us, too, if she wanted."

"And Granny Nan?"

"Whatever they want."

"Cool." Laura jumped to her feet, almost sounding like her old self. She grabbed a cookie from the jar, then started out the door.

"Laura?" Kate felt bound to call her back. "It's not going to happen, you know. Jake and I are through."

Laura just shrugged, her eyes reflecting her disbelief. "Bo says he misses you."

Kate didn't want to hear it, didn't want her heart to jump with hope when there was none. "Bo's being polite."

"He says Jake is a big grump."

"He likes being grumpy."

"He needs his angel back."

"I'll mail it to him."

Laura gave her a look and turned away. "I gotta go to school."

Kate was left alone with a steaming pot of coffee and her thoughts. Not a great combination. She poured herself a cup and walked into the living room. The furniture was covered with canvas drop cloths, ready for the painters who were due to finish the cleanup of the apartment that day.

Kate sat on the edge of an end table and stared out the front window. She supposed she should be glad that Laura was actually talking to her, though what would happen when this hoped-for reunion with Jake didn't take place?

"Are you okay, dear?"

Kate started. She hadn't heard her mother come into the living room.

"I'm sorry," her mother said. "I didn't mean to scare you."

"Oh, it's not your fault, Mom. I was just...thinking."

"Sometimes a person has to do that, but don't make it the main focus of your life."

Kate laughed and went over to hug her. "Coffee's made," she said. "And Laura's getting dressed for school."

"I know." Her mother went over to rummage in her purse. "I've got an early meeting at the library, so I said I'd drop her off." She pulled out her car keys as Laura came down the hall, jacket on and school books in her hand. "You sure you don't mind hanging around to let the painters in?"

"No, I'm fine," Kate said. "You all have a great day."

"We will, dear," her mother assured her as she ushered Laura toward the door.

Laura poked her head around the doorway. "If Jake calls, tell him hi from me." She was gone before Kate had a chance to warn her it wasn't coming true.

Why was life so complex? The only way Laura seemed to accept her was to pretend she and Jake would get together again. Should Kate play along with the fantasy to keep things on an even keel or should she keep trying to push reality?

No answers were coming even after a second cup of coffee and a shower. The painters came and got started on the living room, but no wisdom followed them in, either. Maybe the real problem was that she wished Laura was right, that Jake would call her and that the misery of the last few days would turn out to be a temporary phenomenon.

She wanted to believe that Jake missed her, that he was as miserable without her as she was without him. That whatever had caused him to turn away from her would bring him back.

Except that none of that would happen. Jake was just like his father.

Kate was relieved when a knock sounded on the door and it turned out to be Granny Nan. She was tired of her own company.

"You look like you need another vacation," the old woman said as she came in.

"I do not," Kate argued. "I need to get back to work."

"Huh." Granny went into the kitchen and poured herself a cup of coffee, then sat down. "How's Laura doing?"

Kate shrugged and sat down herself. "Okay. Maybe a little better."

"Heard from your cowboy yet?"

"I'm not going to." Didn't anyone understand that it was over?

Granny made a face and sipped at her coffee. "You looked just like Caitlin when you said that," she said. "A younger one, of course. She must have been almost eighty when Patrick and I married."

"What was she like?" Kate asked.

"Tired. Regretful."

That wasn't the answer Kate expected. "Of what?"

Granny didn't answer for a long moment, but looked up into Kate's eyes. "You believe in the ring?"

Kate looked away, seeking her own refuge. "I don't know," she said. "Sort of. It seems like too great a coincidence and yet . . ."

"I think she loved her Jacob until she died," Granny said. "She ever talk about him?"

"Only once, I think, and then it wasn't directly. Your dad was about two and she was talking about the stars being angels with lanterns to watch over us. That someone had once given her his angel to watch over her and she always wished she could give it back."

Kate leaned back in her chair. "That was what Laura said I was supposed to do."

Granny sipped at her coffee, then pushed the cup away. "She was the one that pushed Patrick and me to get married. We were going to wait. You know, get better jobs, save up some money. She said love didn't come but once and you were a fool to take chances with it. That the angels couldn't protect you from everything, least of all your own regrets, so you should grab love while it was there and never let it go."

Granny's meaning wasn't lost on Kate. "It's not always that simple. Sometimes—"

"Actually, I think it is that simple," Granny said. "I think Caitlin made it complicated, too, and found out later that love was the only thing that counted. I think that's why she held on to the ring and the hope that she'd get a second chance."

"But she didn't."

"No, and one lifetime spent in regrets seems enough, don't you think?"

Sue was on the phone when Kate walked into the office, so they exchanged silent waves and quick smiles, while Kate sat down in one of the guest chairs.

It felt funny sitting on this side of the desk, but then a lot of things about the office felt funny to Kate since she'd come back. She just couldn't seem to concentrate, to put the effort and hours into the job that she used to. It annoyed her. She felt as if she had turned into a weepy, clingy female who could do nothing but think about a man.

Well, that wasn't quite true, for Laura's problem had about equal billing with Jake in her mind. It was just that Kate's Katering was getting about no time at all.

Kate had just come back from visiting two luncheons that Sue had organized. There had been a few minor glitches to be ironed out, but Kate hadn't been too concerned about them. Neither, though, had she felt that sweet blush of pride when everyone sang her praises. There just seemed to be so much more to life than work, yet that was all she was left with.

Sue wrapped up her phone conversation, obviously with her sister.

"How's Dani?" Kate asked as she hung up.

"Fine," Sue replied, then glanced around at the desk. "I should probably let you sit here, Boss."

"Don't worry about it," Kate said. "It looks like it fits you just fine."

"Things seem to be going well."

"Maybe we need to talk about that." There were a lot of things they should talk about. Like where did Kate fit into the firm now that she was back?

"Kelly had her first counseling session today," Sue said.

Kelly was the little Korean girl Sue's sister and brother-in-law had adopted. "But she's only six years old," Kate said. "Is something wrong?"

"No, she's fine," Sue assured her. "Dani and Chris just want to make sure they're on top of problems that are going to come up. She has to come to terms with being an Oriental in a Caucasian world."

"Has she been having problems in school?"

"No," Sue replied. "The counselor said that kind of stuff comes in junior high, when kids are so scared about fitting in themselves that they band together and attack anyone who looks different."

Kate tried to imagine what her junior-high years had been like, but she couldn't remember much of anything. She thought of Laura and her confident, braggadocio attitude. It was hard to imagine her having those kinds of identity problems, but now that she thought about it, Kate was worried.

"And then, when girls get to their late teens, the whole adoption thing throws them."

"Why?" Kate asked.

"I don't know." Sue shrugged. "They start worrying about who they are and why they're the way they are. They start wondering about their roots. I guess girls like to be solidly grounded in a personal sort of way."

When she'd first come into the office, Kate had been concerned about her place in the catering business, but at the moment she couldn't care less. She was even more worried about Laura than ever.

There had been some trauma in Kate's life, but now she could see how solidly grounded she'd always been. And it wasn't just knowing who her mother and father were. She knew where her reddish hair and blue eyes came from, but she could also see now she'd absorbed so many things as she grew up. How she was good at math just like Aunt Hilda; how her talent for singing came from Cousin Lou on her father's side, and her temper came from Granny Nan. All her talents, weaknesses and idiosyncracies were all explained. All had a cause, a source, a root.

"Boys seem to miss that late-high-school trauma," Sue was saying. "According to the counselor, they don't have many problems until their first child is born. Then they fall apart completely."

Kate blinked as she stared at Sue, hearing the words but not really comprehending. Laura wasn't adopted and, although she had some falsehoods to contend with, knew the family she lived with. But that was only half of her family tree.

"Enough about my family, though," Sue said. "You seem preoccupied lately. You still got that cowboy on your mind?"

Kate shook her head. "Who? Jake? No, not at all."

It was obvious from Sue's expression that she wasn't buying it.

"Really," Kate went on. "That trip out to Montana was the best thing I could have done. I got to know a lot of cowboys."

"Oh, yeah?" Sue's grin filled her face.

"Get your mind out of the gutter," Kate scolded. "I got to know them as people."

"Whatever," Sue replied with a shrug.

"Anyway, they're like a town dog that's never belonged to anybody." She tried to sound carefree and careless, but didn't know if she even came close. "They're fun to play with and they like it when you feed them. And sometimes when it's wet or cold, they'd like you to take them in. But don't ever try to put a leash on them. They'll just get crazy."

Sue's dark eyes sparkled as if she didn't believe a word Kate said, but she appeared to let it go. "So, when do you want your chair back?"

Kate sighed and looked away. She couldn't do anything about the ache in her heart from losing Jake, but there were other things that had to be dealt with. "I really need a favor."

"Sure," Sue replied. "Anything."

"Can you keep on running the show for a little while longer? I have a few things I need to get caught up on."

"Sure, I'd be happy to."

Instead of going upstairs to the apartment, Kate went down to the basement and into the storage room. After rummaging around, she found the box of her high school and college stuff. She took out a large manila envelope of newspaper clippings and pictures from her freshman year in college. Some dealt with honors she'd received in school, but a lot were about Miguel.

She pulled out a photo of him, his Spanish features smiling out at her. For years Kate had feared that reliving those times would bring back painful memories, but now she just smiled fondly. It was as if she were looking at somebody else's memories, someone else's life. It seemed so long ago.

"Kate?" Laura called.

For just a moment, Kate felt a spurt of panic, then she realized maybe this was best. She had nothing to hide.

"In here, Laura."

The girl stepped in and glanced at the items in Kate's hand. "Whatcha doing?"

"I thought you should know about your father."

The same look of defiance came over Laura's face, but she didn't leave. In fact, she came over closer. "Is that him?" She nodded at the photo Kate had taken out.

"Yeah. He was five years older than me." Kate held the picture up. "You have his eyes."

Laura took the photo and stared at it a long, silent moment. A lump rose in Kate's throat, but she swallowed it quickly.

"What was he like?" Laura asked, her voice small and quiet.

"Funny. Passionate about the things he liked. Determined to make a difference."

Laura carefully put the photo down and looked at the other things Kate had. "Are these all of him?"

"Mostly."

Together they went through the items. Kate and Miguel at a picnic. The two of them at a bar. Kate glanced quickly at Laura, but apparently the girl wasn't thinking about her being underage. There were other pictures of Miguel with his friends from the university. One of the last pictures was obviously taken at his home. It was of Miguel dressed in a vest, with leather chaps on his legs and a large sombrero on his head. A horse was behind him.

Laura took that picture from Kate's hand and stared at it a long moment. Finally she looked up. "I guess you've always liked cowboys, huh?"

The dogs stopped and turned back to look at Jake. One of them whined.

"I know it's cold," Jake snapped. "But I didn't say you had to come out here with me."

They snuffled in reply, sending small jets of steamlike vapor into the air. After waiting a moment for him to come closer, they took off, crisscrossing the prairie as they coursed for game.

There was a full moon shining brightly down on the land, giving off so much light it was almost as if it were daytime. Jake could see the dogs running up ahead, he could see the frigid west wind bending the tall grass and he could see the fingerlike shadows cast by the leafless trees.

It was cold tonight, which probably meant winter was coming early to the high country. Weather forecasters were talking about snow toward the end of the week or the beginning of the next. The quiet time was coming. Time for all God's critters to hunker down someplace and wait for the new life of spring.

There were any number of fireplaces and stoves in his rambling old place, and wood enough to last from now to then. So Jake figured he should be warm enough. Physically, at least.

He knew all the firewood in the world wouldn't be enough to warm him clear through to the center of his heart. It would take a special lady to do that. A super special lady with reddish hair, sparkling eyes and a smile big enough to light up the skies of Montana. But he knew that wasn't going to happen. Not in his lifetime.

Jake stopped at the fork in the road and whistled. The dogs had run on toward the creek, where their walks usually took them. Down where the prairie grass was full of rabbits, possum, quail and all kinds of other critters. But that wasn't his destination tonight. Tonight he was taking the high road. On up to where a passel of Tylers had their final home.

When the dogs reached him, they hung back, letting Jake lead the way. He didn't think it bothered old Boris and Nickolai to walk in a cemetery at night—actually, the wee hours of the morning. It wasn't all that dark, anyhow.

"Ain't no reason for you fellers to be tense," he told the dogs. "Halloween's come and gone. So all these souls will be quiet for another year."

Of course, seeing as most of those reposing here were Tylers, that wasn't necessarily true. Tylers were always brooding about something. It wouldn't have surprised Jake to find out that Tyler ghosts roamed the J-Bar-T at any time of the day or night, all year round.

Old Jacob Tyler had come up on this knob of a hill and had buried his first wife up against a small stand of hickory. It was a pretty little place, and on a clear day, a body could see from one end of the spread to the other. Jacob's children had planted him here when his own time had come.

Jake went over to a big log lying on the ground and sat down. The dogs sat down facing him. Sighing, he rubbed his face. He'd like to blame his present condition on too much wine at dinner or dipping into his mother's bourbon after dinner, but he had no such excuses. Unless it was the fact that he hadn't hardly slept in the past week.

"Nice view up here, huh, guys?"

His companions chose not to respond.

"You guys want to be buried up here?"

Both dogs growled low in their throats.

"Hey, ease up," Jake said. "I ain't pushing anything. Just talking about when the time comes. Always a good idea to think ahead, you know."

Apparently mollified, the dogs took the time to look around.

"Don't matter where I'm planted," Jake said. "You fellers can put me wherever it's convenient."

The dogs lay down, heads up, and looked out over the prairie. Watching their breath hang on the air reminded Jake how cold it was. He turned up his sheepskin collar and scrunched down into his coat. Weren't no need to bring his dogs up here to talk. He could talk to them anywhere. There were others who he had to put things right with.

"So," Jake said loudly, turning to face the lined up tombstones. "What are you folks planning on for the holidays?"

There was no reply, probably indicating that whatever he had in mind was okay with them. Jake shook his head. Lordy, but he was getting weird. Must be old age creeping up on him.

Actually, he knew it had nothing to do with age. Bo was older than him by a good many years and folks didn't catch him wandering around cemeteries talking to the residents. No, it wasn't age. It was that dag-gone trip to Chicago had done it. Nothing had been right for him ever since his visit to the big city by the lake. Coming home hadn't helped him all that much, either. He was still acting stranger than a loon on corn whiskey.

"Sort of strange being up here and talking to dead people," he told the dogs.

They looked at him for a moment before going back to keeping an eye on the prairie's night stage.

"Oh, hell." Jake shut his eyes tight and held his hands over his face. "I got to get this over and done with."

He dropped his hands and looked to his right. "We need to talk, George." Jake shook his head. "I know you're my father, but I ain't never called you Dad when you were living, so calling you that now don't seem to fit all that well."

The wind whistled through the trees—moaning, as if George had been pulled from a sound sleep. Jake felt a little guilty about that, but then George had the rest of eternity to sleep.

"I been bad-mouthing you, George."

There was a sharp squeal off to his left, causing Jake and the dogs to stare out that way for a long moment. After awhile Nickolai snorted. Boris checked out his partner's ear and then both dogs relaxed. It was just the eternal drama of tooth and claw being played out on the prairie. Jake took a deep breath and returned to his conversation.

"And I know that ain't right, seeing as how you ain't here to defend yourself. So I apologize."

He waited, but George didn't reply. Jake was a little disappointed, but not surprised. George had been a stiff-necked man in life. No reason to believe he'd be any different in death.

"I appreciate all that you left, especially the land, and I promise to care for it to the best of my ability."

Jake rubbed his face with his hands. His moodiness was starting to wear off, making the cold and the wind feel all that much sharper.

"I thought you didn't want to marry Mom. She says she was the one who turned you down." He shook his head. "Looks like neither of us is lucky with women. We find a special one and we screw up. Turn 'em against us."

This was the first time he'd admitted to himself that he cared about Kate. The admission brought an extra pain to his heart.

"Probably for the best," Jake said. "Us Tylers are an arrogant, stiff-necked kind of a breed. I don't think we'd wear all that well on a gentle lady."

For a moment, he clenched his teeth, held hard and waited for the pain to pass. Waited for the image of laughing eyes to fade away into the spooky prairie scene before him.

"Kate ain't coming back, you know."

A huge lump rose up and lodged in his throat. Such a sadness welled up within him that he was fit to bust. Jake looked at the dogs and saw that they had turned away. Grateful for their consideration of cowboy sensibilities, he let some tears flow. One from each eye. It wasn't much, but it did ease the pain.

It was best for Kate that she wasn't coming back. Tyler men weren't easy to live with. And sure as God made green apples, the world didn't need another Tyler male.

"Ah, phooey." Jake stood up. "Time to head back to the house, guys. Another two to three hours and we have to be up and about. This is a working ranch, you know."

The dogs stood up and shook themselves vigorously.

"Oh, George." Jake looked off toward his father's grave. "I'm changing my name back to Tyler. No sense in hiding what I am. Maybe you could have a talk with Mom and tell her she can quit fussin' at me now."

He nodded toward the gate that would take them back to the prairie. "Okay, guys. Head 'em out."

His hands were cold, and Jake put them in his pocket as he carefully picked his way along the path, but he stopped when he felt something in his jacket pocket. He pulled it out and looked at it in the moonlight.

"Old Jacob's ring." He turned it over, letting the moonbeams flash off it. "Probably should just leave it with Jacob. I sure ain't got no use for it."

Jake looked around, trying to remember where Jacob was buried, but he wasn't sure and didn't really want to go stumbling around in the dark looking. Hell, he'd leave the damn ring on his grave sometime when it was light.

Jake took one last look at it. Dang thing could use a little cleaning. It didn't sparkle all that much anymore. He breathed on it and rubbed the ring on his jacket. That didn't really help any. Probably needed Mary Redwing and some of her silver polish to get it in shape.

He wished his life was as easy to shape up. Just put on a little polish, rub it up some and everything would be hunky-dory. He'd have the guts to take a chance. Kate would be all smiles. Bo would stop grumping at him and Boris and Nickolai would choose his company over anyone else's.

Jake put the ring back in his pocket.

He took one last look around the graveyard and pondered on the fact that he would be the last Tyler to be buried here. That lump rose in his throat again.

"Ah, just as well," he told the dogs. "World's well to be rid of us anyway."

He walked down through the prairie, his fingers idly rubbing the ring. His heart idly making wishes that no one would ever hear.

Chapter Fourteen

There really was no use going over it again. She'd bared her soul to Jake and he'd rejected her. There was nothing else she could have done, nothing to regret. Kate punched her pillow into submission and tried sleeping on her left side. Granny was wrong. There was absolutely no connection between Caitlin and Jacob and her and Jake.

None. Not one little bit. Not even a speck.

Her bed seemed to be filled with lumps, or was it just her mind working overtime? Kate threw her pillow onto the floor and lay flat on her stomach like she used to when she was a kid. That lasted about two seconds. She hadn't had a chest when she was a kid. She tried lying on her back, staring at the shadows dancing across the ceiling from the branches outside her window.

Opening up and sharing secrets was a good policy—there shouldn't be secrets between two people who really cared about each other. But it wasn't everything. Well, at least she hadn't told him she loved him. Nobody knew that for sure but her.

Whoa. The world stood still.

Just what was a deep, dark secret anyway? Something no one knew. Mom knew Laura was Kate's daughter. And so did Granny Nan and Aunt Hilda and Cousin Lou and . . .

Kate slowly sat up. Who knew that she loved Jake? His mother suspected and so, probably, did her own mother. But had Kate actually admitted it to anyone?

No. It was her deepest, darkest secret.

She fell back on the bed like a rag doll too limp to sit up. So what? Would it really have made a difference if she'd told Jake she loved him? He wasn't about to care if she did.

She grabbed her pillow back and smoothed it out at the head of her bed. No, not telling him was smart. It kept one last little shred of dignity to hold on to.

Even the angels can't protect you from your regrets. Kate heard Granny's voice saying the words, but saw Caitlin's eyes in the darkness. She just rolled over. She was not into regrets. She was going to sleep.

Kate.

Kate sat up straight in bed, her heart racing as she glanced around the room. It was dark, but silent. Nothing was different. Nothing was out of place. The house was still.

Slowly her heart returned to normal and she lay back down. It must have been a dream. She hadn't thought she was asleep—she'd never fallen asleep that fast before—but what else could it be? She closed her eyes and let her breath out slowly, then pulled the covers up over her shoulders. Winter might not be officially here yet, but the nights were sure cold.

Please come. I need you.

Kate sat up again—flew up, rather. It hadn't been a dream. She hadn't been asleep yet. But still there was no one here, no further sounds from the hallway.

She slipped out of bed, her feet seeking her slippers, but not finding them quickly, she sped into the hall in her bare feet. The faint glow from the night-light in the bathroom was the only light visible. She peered into the bathroom. It was empty.

She quietly pushed open the door to her mother's room and heard her rhythmic breathing as she slept. Laura's room was the same, except that she could see the girl's form sprawled across the bed in the light pouring in through the open curtains. Kate pulled the door closed and leaned against the wall for a long moment.

Maybe it had been a dream. Maybe—

Kate. Kate. Kate.

She turned slowly toward the sound, the voice, the breath carried on the winds. It wasn't coming from her mother's or Laura's room, but from the northwest corner of the apartment, from the direction of the living room. She tiptoed down the hall, but that room, too, was silent and empty. Even the street below was deserted.

"Kate?"

Kate spun, relief washing over at the sight of her mother standing in the hallway. "There you are."

Her mother frowned at her. "What's wrong? Why are you up?"

Kate frowned back. "I heard you calling and—"

"I wasn't calling you. Not until just now."

Laura appeared behind Kate's mother, looking sleepy-eyed and crumpled. "What's everybody doing?"

"I don't know," Kate's mother said.

"Did you call me?" Kate asked Laura. "I heard someone call my name and . . ."

She closed her eyes and smelled the scent of pine needles, heard the sound of the river rushing over the stones in its banks. She felt the wind blowing freely across the miles and miles of prairie. Her eyes flew open. Laura and her mother were staring at her. Even through the dim light in the room she could feel their concern.

"Are you all right?" her mother asked. "Maybe it was just a dream."

But Kate shook her head. A strange certainty was growing in her heart, giving her stength, giving her hope.

"No, it wasn't a dream," she said. Her feet began moving back toward her bedroom. "I have to go."

"Where?" Laura asked.

"Montana."

"What?"

But Kate left them in the hallway as she hurried into her room. The words said, the decision made, she wasn't going to waste a second. She grabbed her suitcase from the closet and tossed it onto her bed.

"What are you doing?" her mother asked from the doorway.

"I'm packing, Mom."

Laura slipped into the room, jumping onto Kate's bed next to the suitcase. "She wants to know if Jake's still hot to trot."

"Laura." Kate frowned at the girl as she grabbed up a handful of underwear from her drawer. "A true relationship is made up of many elements. You have to match psychologically, spiritually and emotionally, as well as physically."

"She wants to see if Jake is still hot to trot," her mother said, joining Laura on the bed.

"It's not that simple."

"Are you giving him back his angel?" Laura asked.

Kate stopped for a moment and folded the sweater she'd taken from the closet. Maybe that's why the Tyler men had such trouble showing emotion—they had no angel to stand beside them, to give them courage. But she didn't need an extra one anymore and neither did Caitlin.

"Yes," Kate said. "I am."

Her mother got up and took the sweater from Kate's hands. "Are you sure you're all right?" she asked. "You've been under a strain lately. Maybe you should wait until morning—"

But Kate just hugged her mother tight. "I've already waited too long," she said. "Caitlin waited too long."

Her mother stared at her as if she'd taken leave of her senses, but Laura got to her feet. "Your new jeans are in the laundry room. Want me to get them?"

Suddenly, packing became a family affair—everyone grabbing things and sorting them out and tossing other things aside. Laura got Kate's jeans, then her toothbrush, toothpaste and shampoo, while Kate's mother called the airlines and got her a seat on a flight that left at eight in the morning.

Then she was ready, all packed and dressed. There was nothing more to do but answer Jake's call and tell him she loved him. Kate's mother and Laura walked with her to the door.

"Holy cow," Laura said, and stopped. "You forgot something."

"What?" Kate asked.

"A rope," Laura said. "Bo says if you want to make a cowboy do something, you gotta hog-tie him first."

"Having trouble sleeping?" Bo asked as he walked into the kitchen, his cowboy boots beating a dull stomp on the plank floor.

Jake looked up from the cup of coffee he was pouring for himself. "Since when are my sleeping habits any of your business? You got nothing better to do at night than sneak around and peek in my window?"

"That's one of the first signs of old age for a man," Bo said. "Can't sleep so good anymore."

"Go to hell."

"You find yourself needin' to go to the bathroom in the middle of the night?"

"I just happen to like getting an early start on the day. That okay by you?"

"You don't have to explain yourself to me." Bo ambled over to help himself to breakfast. "But near as I can remember, this 'early start' business came on 'bout last week. Seems a little sleep wouldn't matter one way or the other. Seein' the dumps you been in lately, it might help."

"When did you become my baby-sitter?"

"When did you started needin' one?"

Jake glared at him, trying to hold onto his temper as Bo filled his plate with pancakes and bacon and fresh fruit and—

Jake had to look away. Sleep wasn't the only thing he hadn't had much of lately. Food didn't have any appeal, either.

"So you going into town to get the salt blocks today?" Bo asked.

"Yes. We need something else?"

Bo shrugged. Probably couldn't talk with all the pancakes he'd stuffed into his mouth. Jake sipped his coffee and found that he'd lost all taste for it, too. He pushed his cup away.

"Promised Mary I'd fix her chicken coop," Bo finally said. "Need to pick up some tar paper and roofing nails. I'll hitch a ride with you."

Jake tried not to grimace. He wasn't in the mood for company, unless it was Boris and Nickolai. "I'm leaving in five minutes," he said. "Just give me your list."

"I'll be ready," Bo said as he crammed another wad of pancakes into his mouth.

Jake got up from the table and went out to get his jacket. Hell, he'd been looking forward to a solitary ride with no one trying to make conversation. Ever since Kate and Laura left it seemed that there was always someone hanging around. He didn't need cheering up. He didn't want cheering up.

He went outside, to be met by a brisk westerly wind. It sent shivers right through him and brought a thin smile to his lips. The cold matched his mood.

Boris and Nickolai were hanging around the truck as if they knew he had a trip planned. "All right," he said as he opened the truck door. "Might as well make a party of it."

"Hey, you know the sheriff don't like them monsters in town," Bo called as he hurried over, buttoning his jacket as he came.

"They're less likely to start a fight than I am," Jake noted, climbing into the truck.

Bo got in the passenger side. "Don't blame me if folks tell you you ain't welcome."

"Never thought I was." Jake started the truck and pealed out of the yard. "Besides, I never said I wanted to be."

"Huh."

Bo's grunt was the only sound he made for several miles. Jake was almost starting to relax. Maybe the man had some sense after all and knew that he wanted to be left alone.

"Why don't you just break down and call her?"

Jake flashed a glare in Bo's direction. "Ain't got nothing to say to her."

"Kid said Kate really misses you."

"Kid doesn't know that what's for the best ain't always what's the easiest to swallow."

"Kid probably knows better than you," Bo said as they got close to town.

"Huh." It was Jake's turn to grunt. And Boris's turn to whine. "What's your problem?" Jake called over his shoulder.

"Car coming," Bo noted.

"I see it," Jake snapped. "You think I don't know how to drive anymore?"

Nickolai joined in the whining, so that it sounded like a concert in the back.

"Will you two cut it out?"

"Better slow down and pull over," Bo said. "Looks like the driver's practicing for the Indy 500. Probably some damn tourist."

Jake eased up on the gas even as the dogs increased their volume. The road was a mite narrow and a tourist in a big boat like that was liable to become edgy. He'd slow down as they passed and—

"What the—" Bo cried.

The car had spun on the road, not in a skid, but like the driver was turning. Except there was no road to turn onto. It pulled to a stop sideways on the road just ahead of them.

"Damn, stupid—" Jake slammed on the brakes and screeched to a halt about a foot from the other car. Just what he needed was a crazy driver causing accidents.

The dogs were on their feet, barking. Jake got hit in the back of the head with a wagging tail. It added to his irritation.

He flung open his door and threw himself out at the same time the driver of the other car got out. "What the hell do you think—"

Suddenly his tongue froze up on him and his feet took root in the blacktop. Boris and Nickolai raced past him, their bodies quivering with excitement. Kate?

She came up to him with a smile that lit up every dark corner of his heart. "You'll be okay now," she said. "I'm here."

She was a mirage, conjured up out the murky recesses of his mind. She wasn't here. In a moment, he'd be alone and miserable once more.

"Everything's under control now," the vision said again.

The dogs were dancing around her and she took a moment to pet them. He heard the truck door open behind him and heard Bo's heavy step on the road.

"Kate." Bo's cowboy drawl had changed from a growl to molasses and honey. "Good morning to ya."

They could all see her, too? Maybe she *was* here; maybe this wasn't some dream. But he didn't want her here. He'd let her go once. Where the hell was he supposed to find the strength to do it again?

"What are you doing here?" he demanded.

She brushed the hair back from her face and straightened up to look at him. The wind was brisk and chilly, but she acted as if it was a spring breeze, while it chilled him to the bone.

"You called me and I'm here."

"I didn't..." He stopped. He'd longed for her, seen her in the moonlight and heard her laughter dance on the wind. Was that calling for her?

"You've got the ring, don't you?"

He reached into his coat pocket and pulled it out, staring down at it as if he'd never seen it before. "I didn't." He thought of last night in the cemetery and the long walk back, of holding the ring and wishing he were someone else. Someone who could love. He looked up, forcing his heart to remain strong. "But even if I did, it doesn't mean anything."

"Sure, it does." Her smile was all sweet and gentle, it looked to be warm enough to melt the snowcaps off the rockies. "It means that there's something between us, something we can't deny."

He tried to look away, but his eyes fell on his stupid dogs, sitting before her in adoration. Even Boris looked like nothing more than a giant lapdog. He turned. The prairie, with all its harsh vastness, was safe to stare at. It hadn't suddenly turned tropical just because Kate was back.

"You're forgetting something," he pointed out. "I'm a Tyler, and Tyler men don't have relationships."

"That's a lot of crap," Bo said with a snort.

Jake turned toward him.

The older man raised his hands as if surrendering. "All right, I'll butt out," he said, looking over at Kate. "But if you need help hog-tying him, I'm your man."

Kate just smiled, and Jake could have sworn he heard the song of birds in the air. Happy, noisy, springlike singing. Mary Redwing must have slipped some of his mom's bourbon into his coffee.

"I don't think I'll need any help."

That's for damn sure. She wouldn't need any help because he was ending this thing here and now. Jake squared his shoulders and moved a step closer. "Look, I don't know why you're here, but nothing's changed. I'm not any different from my father. I'm stiff-necked and stubborn and—"

"Bullheaded and close-minded and willful," Kate finished for him.

"Right," he said slowly. Why was she smiling when she said all that?

"It would be so much better to do this at night," she said softly, taking slow steps forward. The dogs moved out of her way, but trailed at her side, adoring drudges. "When the stars are out and the moon is shining bright."

"Why?" He felt uneasy. She was acting like the locoweed had gotten her. He wasn't sure he should let her close to him, but to move away would seem like he was running, and cowboy rules said he couldn't do that.

"To explain this," she said as she stuck something to his jacket.

He looked down, a little cautiously, and saw a tiny angel sticker on his collar. He was sure it was the locoweed and took a step backward. Damn, if she wasn't making him break all the rules.

"What's this?" he asked.

"An angel," she said. "Your angel."

"Okay." Maybe one step backwards wasn't enough. Maybe he ought to make a dash for the truck, but would the dogs follow?

"You see, the stars are really angels with lanterns, there to watch over us," Kate said. "Way back when, Jacob gave Caitlin his angel to watch over her. I'm officially giving it back. Now you don't have to be afraid. You have your own angel watching over you."

"I'm never afraid," Jake grumbled, though he had a very clear recollection of something awfully close to fear filling his heart the day she'd left. The thought of never seeing her again had nagged at him, worried him some. Hell, it had sent shivers of pure terror into his soul.

"Who's Caitlin?" Bo called. "And who's Jacob? And how do they pass angels around?"

"Shut up," Jake grumbled. How had she known? A cowboy wasn't supposed to show the mess in his soul. Not ever. Had he broken that rule, too?

"Caitlin Mallory was my great-great-grandmother," Kate said. "And the first Jacob Tyler's true love."

Bo let out a laugh that echoed over the prairie and back. "No fooling? Hot damn, don't that beat all."

"As for passing angels around," Kate went on, though her eyes were on Jake, "I guess that's something you can do when you really and truly love someone with all your heart. Like Jacob loved Caitlin. Like I love you, Jake."

The last words were said in a whisper. Not one of shyness or hesitation, but of intensity, and they hit Jake with the force of an earthquake. He heard the love in her voice and saw it in her eyes. He felt it in the air around him, but knew only despair. God, he didn't want her to be hurt.

His damn eyes got watery and he turned to look away, seeking the peace of the mountains off in the distance. "It's no good, Kate," he said. His voice was as shaky as a newborn colt's legs. "I won't let you be hurt by me. And that's all that would happen. My father couldn't really love and I can't, either."

She was supposed to wait where she was, patiently and silently, until he regained his composure. Cowboy rules said so, but she wasn't a cowboy and so she came around to face him. Came around to where she could see that the water had extended beyond his eyes and onto his cheeks.

"If you can't love, why are crying when you're telling me to go away?" she asked. The dogs whined their agreement.

"I'm not," Jake snapped. "It's the sun."

"The sun's at your back," Bo called out. "Try the wind."

Jake desperately wanted to kick some old man's butt. Unfortunately, he had his hands full at the moment.

"You're not unable to love," Kate said softly. "You're afraid to show it, that's all. You're just so afraid of being rejected, as you feel you were by your father, that you don't want to take that first step."

"Maybe take any step," he said.

She shook her head. "But you did. You called me here last night. If you can do that, you can move on to other things."

She took a step closer. "You can put your arms around me." Her eyes looked up into his, telling him it was all right, they would be strong together.

He put his arms around her lightly, as if afraid their weight would hurt her.

"You can tell me you're glad to see me."

He shook his head, staring deep into her eyes, trying so hard to believe all the dreams and promises he saw there. Wanting to claim that happiness as his own and that future for his tomorrows.

"I don't want to hurt you," he told her, tightening his hold and pulling her closer into his arms. "God, I am so afraid I won't be able to make you happy."

"I have a part in that, too, you know," she said. "It's not totally up to you."

He was starting to believe it was all possible. The love in her voice assured him it was, the light in her eyes said there was no denying it. "Promise you'll kick my butt when I get moody?"

"I do."

"And box my ears when I get distant?"

"I will."

Her eyes just laughed at his worries, so he let the wind blow them all away. He was tired of fighting anyway.

"You two gonna spend all day making up?" Bo asked. "Some of us are a mite cold."

Kate laughed as Jake pulled her closer into his arms. "Not me," he said. He'd never feel cold or alone or left out again. "What about your business? And Laura?"

Kate just snuggled in tighter. "I'm thinking of starting a new one. Maybe a mail-order one." She lay her head against his chest as if she intended to stay for a while. "And as for Laura, it's her choice. She can come with me, stay in Chicago or spend time in both places. Although I think she's already decided that we're all coming out here, Mom and Granny Nan included."

"You should have lots of help keeping me in line then."

She looked up at him with so much love in her eyes that he knew it was all going to work out fine. "I think Laura's decided it's time Caitlin's family finally made the trek out west."

"I think I'm glad they never made it here until now."

He bent down slightly to meet her lips and the world faded away. There was no more prairie, no more chilling winds or loneliness. There was just Kate and all her love and warmth and openness. Every tomorrow would be an adventure because he would share it with her.

"This lovey-dovey stuff is getting boring," Bo called out. "The cows are waiting for their salt blocks."

Kate pulled away with a laugh. "Well, we sure can't keep those cows waiting."

"No, ma'am, we can't," Bo said. "The cows come first—cowboy's-wife rule number one."

* * * * * *

Get Ready to be Swept Away by
Silhouette's Spring Collection

Abduction
&
Seduction

These passion-filled stories explore both the dangerous
desires of men and the seductive powers of women.
Written by three of our most celebrated authors, they are
sure to capture your hearts.

Diana Palmer
Brings us a spin-off of her Long, Tall Texans series

Joan Johnston
Crafts a beguiling Western romance

Rebecca Brandewyne
New York Times bestselling author
makes a smashing contemporary debut

Available in March at your favorite retail outlet.

MARRIAGE ON DEMAND
(SE #939, February)
by Susan Mallery

Hometown Heartbreakers: Those heart-stoppin' hunks
are rugged, ready and able to steal your heart....

Austin Lucas was as delicious as forbidden sin—that's
what the Glenwood womenfolk were saying. And
Rebecca Chambers couldn't deny how sexy he looked
in worn, tight jeans. But when their impulsive
encounter obliged them to get married, could their
passion lead to everlasting love?

Find out in *MARRIAGE ON DEMAND,* the next story
in Susan Mallery's *Hometown Heartbreakers* series,
coming to you in February...only from
Silhouette Special Edition.

HH-2

A ROSE AND A WEDDING VOW (SE #944)
by Andrea Edwards

Matt Michaelson returned home to face Liz—his brother's widow...a woman he'd never forgotten. Could falling in love with *this* Michaelson man heal the wounds of Liz's lonely past?

A ROSE AND A WEDDING VOW, SE #944 (3/95), is the next story in this stirring trilogy by Andrea Edwards. THIS TIME, FOREVER—sometimes a love is so strong, nothing can stand in its way, not even time. Look for the last installment, A SECRET AND A BRIDAL PLEDGE, in May 1995.

THE BLACKTHORN BROTHERHOOD

by Diana Whitney

Three men bound by a childhood secret are freed through family, friendship...and love.

Watch for the first book in Diana's Whitney's compelling new miniseries:

THE ADVENTURER
Special Edition #934, January 1995

Devon Monroe had finally come home, home to a haunting memory that made him want to keep running. Home to a woman who made him want to stand still and stare into her eyes. For there was something about Jessica Newcomb that made him forget about his own past and wonder long and hard about hers....

Look for THE AVENGER coming in the fall of 1995.